D1324227

Conan in chains . .

Conan's awakening was abrupt and crystal
clear. He possessed full knowledge of the
battle in the mountains, and he had a good
idea of where he was. He lay on a velvet
couch, his limbs loaded with chains even he
could not break. The figure seated on a silver,
thronelike chair before him seemed unreal –
with a suggestion of more than human
knowledge. 'What the devil did you do to me?'
demanded Conan. 'I blasted your
consciousness,' answered Xaltotum. 'How,
you would not understand. Call it black
magic, if you will.' Conan felt a chill along
his spine. . . .

Cover painting by Frank Frazetta . . . with
grateful acknowledgement to Roy Krenkel,
adviser.

Conan the Conqueror

ROBERT E. HOWARD

Edited by L. Sprague de Camp

SPHERE BOOKS LIMITED
30-32 Gray's Inn Road, London WC1X 8JL

First published in Great Britain by Sphere Books Ltd 1974
Copyright © L. Sprague de Camp 1967
Reprinted 1975, 1976 (twice), 1981

This novel was originally published as *The Hour of the Dragon* in *Weird Tales* for December 1935, and January, February, March and April 1936; copyright 1935, 1936 by Popular Fiction Publishing Co. It was reprinted as *Conan the Conqueror*, with an introduction by John D. Clark, N.Y., Gnome Press, 1950; Ace Books, Inc., 1953; T. V. Boardman, London, 1954.

TRADE
MARK

This book is sold subject to the condition that
it shall not, by way of trade or otherwise, be lent,
re-sold, hired out or otherwise circulated without
the publisher's prior consent in any form of
binding or cover other than that in which it is
published and without a similar condition
including this condition being imposed on the
subsequent purchaser

Set in Intertype Plantin

Printed and bound in Great Britain by
©ollins, Glasgow

Pages 6 and 7: A map of the world of Conan in the Hyborian Age, based upon notes and sketches by Robert E. Howard and upon previous maps by P. Schuyler Miller, John D. Clark, David Kyle, and L. Sprague de Camp, with a map of Europe and adjacent regions superimposed for reference.

INTRODUCTION

CONAN THE CIMMERIAN is the hero of over two dozen stories by Robert Ervin Howard (1906–36). Howard was born and lived most of his short life in Cross Plains, Texas. There he turned out a huge volume of fiction for the pulp magazines: sport, detective, Western, and Oriental adventure stories. But the yarns for which he is most renowned are his heroic fantasies, especially the Conan tales.

Heroic fantasy is a type of story of the supernatural, laid in an imaginary world – either this planet as it is once supposed to have been, or as it will be long hence, or some other world or dimension – where magic works and all men are mighty, all women beautiful, all problems simple, and all life adventurous. The genre was developed by William Morris in the late nineteenth century and by Lord Dunsany and Eric R. Eddison in the early twentieth. Writing in the early 1930s, Howard was one of its strongest formative forces.

Eighteen Conan stories were published during Howard's lifetime; several others, from complete manuscripts to mere fragments, have been found among his papers since 1950. It has been my fortune to edit these last for publication and to complete some that were incomplete or in the form of an outline only. Lancer Books plans to bring out the entire Conan saga in eight paperback volumes, of which this will be the seventh.

Of all Howard's Conan stories, the present one is the only book-length novel. It is one of the last that he wrote before his lamented suicide and forms a fitting climax to the series. It is worthy to stand beside such comparable works of heroic fantasy as E. R. Eddison's *The Worm Ouroboros*, Fletcher Pratt's *The Well of the Unicorn*, and J. R. R. Tolkien's *The Fellowship of the Ring* series. While it may be inferior to some of these in literary grace or philosophical profundity, it yields to none in action, color, excitement, and headlong drive.

Although he had his faults as a writer, Howard was a natural storyteller. In reading the Conan stories, the reader gets the illusion that he is listening to the mighty adventurer himself, sitting before a fire and reeling off tales of his exploits. In fiction, the difference between a writer who is a natural storyteller and one who is not is like the difference between a boat that will float and one that will not. If the writer has the quality, we can forgive many other faults; if not, no other virtues can make up for this lack, any more than gleaming paint and shiny brass fittings on a boat can make up for the fact that it cannot float.

The present novel was originally published as a serial in *Weird Tales* – a magazine that carried, mixed with a lot of ephemeral trash, many stories of notably high literary quality. The present Conan story appeared under the title 'The Hour of the Dragon'. When it was reprinted as a book, the name was changed to *Conan the Conqueror*. I have kept the latter title because, while 'The Hour of the Dragon' is intriguing, it has practically nothing to do with the narrative. I have made a few very small editorial changes in the story to eliminate inconsistencies in the original version.

Conan lived, loved, and fought in Howard's imaginary Hyborian Age, about twelve thousand years ago, between the sinking of Atlantis and the beginnings of recorded history. A gigantic barbarian adventurer from the backward northern land of Cimmeria, Conan arrived as a youth in the kingdom of Zamora (see map) and for several years made a precarious living there and in neighboring lands as a thief. Then he served as a mercenary soldier, first in the oriental realm of Turan and then in the Hyborian kingdoms.

Forced to flee from Argos, Conan became a pirate along the coasts of Kush, in partnership with a Shemitish she-pirate, Bêlit, and with a crew of black corsairs. After Bêlit's death, he returned to the trade of mercenary in Shem and the adjacent Hyborian kingdoms. Subsequently he adventured among the nomadic outlaws of the eastern steppes, the pirates of the Sea of Viyalet, and the hill tribes of the Himelian Mountains on the borders of Iranistan and Vendhya.

After another stretch of soldiering in Koth and Argos, Conan went back to the sea, first as a pirate of the Baracha Isles, then as captain of a ship of the Zingaran buccaneers. When other buccaneers sank his ship, he returned to adventuring ashore in the black countries. He worked his way north and became a scout on the western frontier of Aquilonia, fighting the savage Picts. After rising to command in the Aquilonian army and defeating a Pictish invasion, Conan was lured back to Tarantia, the capital, and imprisoned by the jealous King Numedides. Escaping, he was chosen to lead a revolution against the worthless king. Conan slew Numedides on his own throne and became the ruler of the mightiest Hyborian kingdom.

Conan soon found that being king was no bed of houris. A cabal of discontented nobles almost succeeded in assassinating him. By a ruse, the kings of Koth and Ophir trapped and imprisoned him, in order to have a free hand in the conquest of Aquilonia. With the help of a fellow prisoner – a wizard – Conan escaped in time to turn the tables on the invaders. And the next adventure of Conan is the one chronicled in this present work.

L. Sprague de Camp

For nearly two years after the events of The Scarlet Citadel, *Aquilonia flourishes under Conan's firm but tolerant rule. The lawless, hard-bitten adventurer of former years has, through force of circumstance, gradually matured into an able and responsible statesman. But a plot is brewing in the neighboring kingdom of Nemedia, and the plotters plan to bring down the king of Aquilonia by means of the sinister sorcery of an elder day. At this time, Conan is about forty-six years old, showing few signs of age save the countless scars that crisscross his mighty frame and a somewhat more cautious, deliberate approach to wine, women, and bloodshed than was the case in his uproarious youth. Although he keeps a harem of luscious concubines, he has never taken an official wife – a queen –, and hence has no legitimate son to inherit the throne. His secret enemies mean to take full advantage of this fact.*

THE LONG TAPERS flickered, sending the black shadows wavering along the walls, and the velvet tapestries rippled. Yet there was no wind in the chamber. Four men stood about the ebony table on which lay the green sarcophagus that gleamed like carven jade. In the upraised right hand of each man, a curious black candle burned with a weird greenish light. Outside was night and a lost wind moaning among the black trees.

Inside the chamber was tense silence, and the wavering of the shadows, while four pairs of eyes, burning with intensity, were fixed on the long green case across which cryptic hieroglyphics writhed, as if lent life and movement by the unsteady light. The man at the foot of the sarcophagus leaned over it and moved his candle as if he were writing with a pen, inscribing a mystic symbol in the air. Then he set down the candle in its black gold stick at the foot of the case, and, mumbling some formula unintelligible to his companions, he thrust a broad white hand into his fur-trimmed robe. When he brought it forth again it was as if he cupped in his palm a ball of living fire.

The other three drew in their breath sharply, and the dark, powerful man who stood at the head of the sarcophagus whispered: 'The Heart of Ahriman!' The other lifted a quick hand for silence. Somewhere a dog began howling dolefully, and a stealthy step padded outside the barred and bolted door. But none looked aside from the mummy case over which the man in the ermine-trimmed robe was now moving the great flaming jewel, while he muttered an incantation that was old when Atlantis sank. The glare of the gem dazzled their eyes, so that they could not be sure of what they saw; but with a splintering crash, the carven lid of the sarcophagus burst outward as if from some irresistible pressure applied from within, and the four men, bending eagerly forward, saw the occupant – a huddled, withered, wizened shape, with dried brown limbs like dead wood showing through moldering bandages.

'Bring that thing *back*?' muttered the small dark man who stood on the right, with a short, sardonic laugh. 'It is ready to crumble at a touch. We are fools—'

'Shhh!' It was an urgent hiss of command from the large man who held the jewel. Perspiration stood upon his broad white forehead and his eyes dilated. He leaned forward and, without touching the thing with his hand, laid on the breast of the mummy the blazing jewel. Then he drew back and watched with fierce intensity, his lips moving in soundless invocation.

It was as if a globe of living fire flickered and burned on the dead, withered bosom. And breath sucked in, hissing, through the clenched teeth of the watchers. For, as they watched, an awful transmutation became apparent. The withered shape in the sarcophagus was expanding, was growing, lengthening. The bandages burst and fell into brown dust. The shriveled limbs swelled, straightened. Their dusky hue began to fade.

'By Mitra!' whispered the tall, yellow-haired man on the left. 'He was *not* a Stygian. That part at least was true.'

Again a trembling finger warned for silence. The hound outside was no longer howling. He whimpered, as with an evil dream; and then that sound, too, died away in silence, in which the yellow-haired man plainly heard the straining of the heavy door, as if something outside pushed powerfully upon it. He half turned, his hand at his sword, but the man in the ermine robe hissed an urgent warning: 'Stay! Do not break the chain! And on your life do not go to the door!'

13

The yellow-haired man shrugged and turned back, and then he stopped short, staring. In the jade sarcophagus lay a living man: a tall, lusty man, naked, white of skin, and dark of hair and beard. He lay motionless, his eyes wide open, and blank and unknowing as a newborn babe's. On his breast the great jewel smoldered and sparkled.

The man in ermine reeled as if from some let-down of extreme tension.

'Ishtar!' he gasped. 'It is Xaltotun! – *and he lives!* Valerius! Tarascus! Almaric! Do you see? Do you see? You doubted me – but I have not failed! We have been close to the open gates of Hell this night, and the shapes of darkness have gathered close about us – aye, they followed *him* to the very door – but we have brought the great magician back to life.'

'And damned our souls to purgatories everlasting, I doubt not,' muttered the small, dark man, Tarascus.

The yellow-haired man, Valerius, laughed harshly.

'What purgatory can be worse than life itself? So we are all damned together from birth. Besides, who would not sell his miserable soul for a throne?'

'There is no intelligence in his stare, Orastes,' said the large man.

'He has long been dead,' answered Orastes. 'He is as one newly awakened. His mind is empty after the long sleep – nay, he was *dead*, not sleeping. We brought his spirit back over the voids and gulfs of night and oblivion. I will speak to him.'

He bent over the foot of the sarcophagus, and fixing his gaze on the wide dark eyes of the man within, he said, slowly: 'Awake, Xaltotun!'

The lips of the man moved mechanically. 'Xaltotun!' he repeated in a groping whisper.

'*You* are Xaltotun!' exclaimed Orastes, like a hypnotist driving home his suggestions. 'You are Xaltotun of Python, in Acheron.'

A dim flame flickered in the dark eyes.

'I was Xaltotun,' he whispered. 'I am dead.'

'You *are* Xaltotun!' cried Orastes. 'You are not dead! You live!'

'I am Xaltotun,' came the eerie whisper. 'But I am dead. In my house in Khemi, in Stygia, there I died.'

'And the priests who poisoned you mummified your body with their dark arts, keeping all your organs intact!' ex-

14

claimed Orastes. 'But now you live again! The Heart of Ahriman has restored your life, drawn your spirit back from space and eternity.'

'The Heart of Ahriman!' The flame of remembrance grew stronger. 'The barbarians stole it from me!'

'He remembers,' muttered Orastes. 'Lift him from the case.'

The others obeyed hesitantly, as if reluctant to touch the man they had re-created, and they seemed not easier in their minds when they felt firm muscular flesh, vibrant with blood and life, beneath their fingers. But they lifted him upon the table, and Orastes clothed him in a curious dark velvet robe, splashed with gold stars and crescent moons, and fastened a cloth-of-gold fillet about his temples, confining the black wavy locks that fell to his shoulders. He let them do as they would, saying nothing, not even when they set him in a carven throne-like chair with a high ebony back and wide silver arms, and feet like golden claws. He sat there motionless, and slowly intelligence grew in his dark eyes and made them deep and strange and luminous. It was as if long-sunken witchlights floated slowly up through midnight pools of darkness.

Orastes cast a furtive glance at his companions, who stood staring in morbid fascination at their strange guest. Their iron nerves had withstood an ordeal that might have driven weaker men mad. He knew it was with no weaklings that he conspired, but men whose courage was as profound as their lawless ambitions and capacity for evil. He turned his attention to the figure in the ebon-black chair. And this one spoke at last.

'I remember,' he said in a strong, resonant voice, speaking Nemedian with a curious, archaic accent. 'I am Xaltotun, who was high priest of Set in Python, which was in Acheron. The Heart of Ahriman — I dreamed I had found it again — where is it?'

Orastes placed it in his hand, and he drew breath deeply as he gazed into the depths of the terrible jewel burning in his grasp.

'They stole it from me, long ago,' he said. 'The red heart of the night it is, strong to save or to damn. It came from afar, and from long ago. While I held it, none could stand before me. But it was stolen from me, and Acheron fell, and I fled an exile into dark Stygia. Much I remember, but much

15

I have forgotten. I have been in a far land, across misty voids and gulfs and unlit oceans. What is the year?'

Orastes answered him. 'It is the waning of the Year of the Lion, three thousand years after the fall of Acheron.'

'Three thousand years!' murmured the other. 'So long? Who are you?'

'I am Orastes, once a priest of Mitra. This man is Amalric, baron of Tor, in Nemedia; this other is Tarascus, younger brother of the king of Nemedia; and this tall man is Valerius, rightful heir of the throne of Aquilonia.'

'Why have you given me life?' demanded Xaltotun. 'What do you require of me?'

The man was now fully alive and awake, his keen eyes reflecting the working of an unclouded brain. There was no hesitation or uncertainty in his manner. He came directly to the point, as one who knows that no man gives something for nothing. Orastes met him with equal candor.

'We have opened the doors of Hell this night to free your soul and return it to your body because we need your aid. We wish to place Tarascus on the throne of Nemedia, and to win for Valerius the crown of Aquilonia. With your necromancy you can aid us.'

Xaltotun's mind was devious and full of unexpected slants.

'You must be deep in the arts yourself, Orastes, to have been able to restore my life. How is it that a priest of Mitra knows of the Heart of Ahriman, and the incantations of Skelos?'

'I am no longer a priest of Mitra,' answered Orastes. 'I was cast forth from my order because of my delving in black magic. But for Amalric there I might have been burned as a magician.

'But that left me free to pursue my studies. I journeyed in Zamora, in Vendhya, in Stygia, and among the haunted jungles of Khitai. I read the iron-bound books of Skelos, and talked with unseen creatures in deep wells, and faceless shapes in black reeking jungles. I obtained a glimpse of your sarcophagus in the demon-haunted crypts below the black, giant-walled temple of Set in the hinterlands of Stygia, and I learned of the arts that would bring back life to your shriveled corpse. From moldering manuscripts I learned of the Heart of Ahriman. Then for a year I sought its hiding-place, and at last I found it.'

'Then why trouble to bring me back to life?' demanded

16

Xaltotun, with his piercing gaze fixed on the priest. 'Why did you not employ the Heart to further your own power?'

'Because no man today knows the secrets of the Heart,' answered Orastes. 'Not even in legends live the arts by which to loose its full powers. I knew it could restore life; of its deeper secrets I am ignorant. I merely used it to bring you back to life. It is the use of your knowledge we seek. As for the Heart, you alone know its awful secrets.'

Xaltotun shook his head, staring broodingly into the flaming depths.

'My necromantic knowledge is greater than the sum of all the knowledge of other men,' he said; 'yet I do not know the full power of the jewel. I did not invoke it in the old days; I guarded it lest it be used against me. At last it was stolen, and in the hands of a feathered shaman of the barbarians it defeated all my mighty sorcery. Then it vanished, and I was poisoned by the jealous priests of Stygia before I could learn where it was hidden.'

'It was hidden in a cavern below the temple of Mitra, in Tarantia,' said Orastes. 'By devious ways I discovered this, after I had located your remains in Set's subterranean temple in Stygia.

'Zamorian thieves, partly protected by spells I learned from sources better left unmentioned, stole your mummy-case from under the very talons of those which guarded it in the dark, and by camel-caravan and galley and ox-wagon it came at last to this city.

'Those same thieves – or rather those of them who still lived after their frightful quest – stole the Heart of Ahriman from its haunted cavern below the temple of Mitra, and all the skill of men and the spells of sorcerers nearly failed. One man of them lived long enough to reach me and give the jewel into my hands, before he died slavering and gibbering of what he had seen in that accursed crypt. The thieves of Zamora are the most faithful of men to their trust. Even with my conjurements, none but they could have stolen the Heart from where it has lain in demon-guarded darkness since the fall of Acheron, three thousand years ago.'

Xaltotun lifted his lionlike head and stared far off into space, as if plumbing the lost centuries.

'Three thousand years!' he muttered. "Set! Tell me what has chanced in the world.'

'The barbarians who overthrew Acheron set up new kingdoms,' quoth Orastes. 'Where the empire had stretched now rose realms called Aquilonia, and Nemedia, and Argos, from the tribes that founded them. The older kingdoms of Ophir, Corinthia, and western Koth, which had been subject to the kings of Acheron, regained their independence with the fall of the empire.'

'And what of the people of Acheron?' demanded Xaltotun. 'When I fled into Stygia, Python was in ruins, and all the great, purple-towered cities of Acheron fouled with blood and trampled by the sandals of the barbarians.'

'In the hills small groups of folk still boast descent from Acheron,' answered Orastes. 'For the rest, the tide of my barbarian ancestors rolled over them and wiped them out. They – my ancestors – had suffered much from the kings of Acheron.'

A grim and terrible smile curled the Pythonian's lips.

'Aye! Many a barbarian, both man and woman, died screaming on the altar under this hand. I have seen their heads piled to make a pyramid in the great square of Python when the kings returned from the west with their spoils and naked captives.'

'Aye. And when the day of reckoning came, the sword was not spared. So Acheron ceased to be, and purple-towered Python became a memory of forgotten days. But the younger kingdoms rose on the imperial ruins and waxed great. And now we have brought you back to aid us to rule these kingdoms, which, if less strange and wonderful than Acheron of old, are yet rich and powerful, well worth fighting for. Look!' Orastes unrolled before the stranger a map drawn cunningly on vellum.

Xaltotun regarded it and then shook his head, baffled.

'The very outlines of the land are changed. It is like some familiar thing seen in a dream, fantastically distorted.'

'Howbeit,' answered Orastes, tracing with his forefinger, 'here is Belverus, the capital of Nemedia, in which we now are. Here run the boundaries of the land of Nemedia. To the south and southeast are Ophir and Corinthia, to the east Brythunia, to the west Aquilonia.'

'It is the map of a world I do not know,' said Xaltotun softly, but Orastes did not miss the lurid fire of hate that flickered in his dark eyes.

'It is a map you shall help us change,' answered Orastes. 'It is our desire first to set Tarascus on the throne of Nemedia. We wish to accomplish this without strife, and in such a way that no suspicion will rest on Tarascus. We do not wish the land to be torn by civil wars, but to reserve all our power for the conquest of Aquilonia.

'Should King Nimed and his sons die naturally, in a plague, for instance, Tarascus would mount the throne as the next heir, peacefully and unopposed.'

Xaltotun nodded, without replying, anc Orastes continued.

'The other task will be more difficult .We cannot set Valerius on the Aquilonian throne without a war, ana that kingdom is a formidable foe. Its people are a hardy, warlike race, toughened by continual wars with the Picts, Zingarians, and Cimmerians. For five hundred years Aquilonia and Nemedia have intermittently waged war, and the ultimate advantage has always lain with the Aquilonians.

'Their present king is the most renowned warrior among the western nations. He is an outlander, an adventurer who seized the crown by force during a time of civil strife, strangling King Numedides with his own hands, upon the very throne. His name is Conan, and no man can stand before him in battle.

'Valerius is now the rightful heir of the throne. He had been driven into exile by his royal kinsman, Numedides, and has been away from his native realm for years; but he is of the blood of the old dynasty, and many of the barons would secretly hail the overthrow of Conan, who is a nobody without royal or even noble blood. But the common people are loyal to him, and the nobility of the outlying provinces. Yet if his forces were overthrown in the battle that must first take place, and Conan himself slain, I think it would not be difficult to put Valerius on the throne. Indeed, with Conan slain, the only center of the government would be gone. He is not part of a dynasty, but only a lone adventurer.'

'I wish that I might see this king,' mused Xaltotun, glancing toward a silvery mirror which formed one of the panels of the wall. This mirror cast no reflection, but Xaltotun's expression showed that he understood its purpose, and Orastes nodded with the pride a good craftsman takes in the recognition of his accomplishments by a master of his craft.

'I will try to show him to you,' he said. And seating himself before the mirror, he gazed hynotically into its depths, where presently a dim shadow began to take shape.

It was uncanny, but those watching knew it was no more than the reflected image of Orastes' thought, embodied in that mirror as a wizard's thoughts are embodied in a magic crystal. It floated hazily, then leaped into startling clarity – a tall man, mightily shouldered and deep of chest, with a massive corded neck and heavily muscled limbs. He was clad in silk and velvet, with the royal lions of Aquilonia worked in gold upon his rich jupon, and the crown of Aquilonia shone on his square-cut black mane; but the great sword at his side seemed more natural to him than the regal accouterments. His brow was low and broad, his eyes a volcanic blue that smoldered as if with some inner fire. His dark, scarred, almost sinister face was that of a fighting man, and his velvet garments could not conceal the hard, dangerous lines of his limbs.

'That man is no Hyborian!' exclaimed Xaltotun.

'No; he is a Cimmerian, one of those wild tribesmen who dwell in the gray hills of the north.'

'I fought his ancestors of old,' muttered Xaltotun. 'Not even the kings of Acheron could conquer them.'

'They still remain a terror to the nations of the south,' answered Orastes. 'He is a true son of that savage race and has proved himself, thus far, unconquerable.'

Xaltotun did not reply; he sat staring at the pool of living fire that shimmered in his hand. Outside, the hound howled again, long and shudderingly.

2 – A BLACK WIND BLOWS

THE YEAR OF THE DRAGON had birth in war and pestilence and unrest. The black plague stalked through the streets of Belverus, striking down the merchant in his stall, the serf in his kennel, the knight at his banquet board. Before it the arts of the leeches were helpless. Men said it had been sent from Hell as punishment for the sins of pride and lust. It was swift and deadly as the stroke of an adder. The victim's body turned purple and then black, and within a few minutes he sank down dying, and the stench of his own putrefaction was in his nostrils even before death wrenched his soul from his rotting body. A hot, roaring wind blew incessantly from the south, and the crops withered in the fields, the cattle sank and died in their tracks.

Men cried out on Mitra, and muttered against the king;

for somehow, throughout the kingdom, the word was whispered that the king was secretly addicted to loathsome practices and foul debauches in the seclusion of his nighted palace. And then in that palace death stalked grinning on feet about which swirled the monstrous vapors of the plague. In one night the king died with his three sons, and the drums that thundered their dirge drowned the grim and ominous bells that rang from the carts that lumbered through the streets gathering up the rotting dead.

That night, just before dawn, the hot wind that had blown for weeks ceased to rustle evilly through the silken window curtains. Out of the north rose a great wind that roared among the towers, and there was cataclysmic thunder, and blinding sheets of lightning, and driving rain. But the dawn shone clean and green and clear; the scorched ground veiled itself in grass, the thirsty crops sprang up anew, and the plague was gone – its miasma swept clean out of the land by the mighty wind.

Men said the gods were satisfied because the evil king and his spawn were slain, and when his young brother Tarascus was crowned in the great coronation hall, the populace cheered until the towers rocked, acclaiming the monarch on whom the gods smiled.

Such a wave of enthusiasm and rejoicing as swept the land is frequently the signal for a war of conquest. So no one was surprised when it was announced that King Tarascus had declared the truce made by the late king with their western neighbors void, and was gathering his hosts to invade Aquilonia. His reason was candid; his motive, loudly proclaimed, gilded his actions with something of the glamor of a crusade. He espoused the cause of Valerius, "rightful heir to the throne"; he came, he proclaimed, not as an enemy of Aquilonia, but as a friend, to free the people from the tyranny of a usurper and a foreigner.

If there were cynical smiles in certain quarters, and whispers concerning the king's good friend Amalric, whose vast personal wealth seemed to be flowing into the rather depleted royal treasury, they were unheeded in the general wave of fervor and zeal of Tarascus's popularity. If any shrewd individuals suspected that Amalric was the real ruler of Nemedia, behind the scenes, they were careful not to voice such heresy. And the war went forward with enthusiasm.

The king and his allies moved westward at the head of fifty thousand men – knights in shining armor with their pennons streaming above their helmets, pikemen in steel caps and brigandines, crossbowmen in leather jerkins. They crossed the border, took a frontier castle and burned three mountain villages, and then, in the valley of the Valkia, ten miles west of the boundary line, they met the hosts of Conan, king of Aquilonia – forty-five thousand knights, archers, and men-at-arms, the flower of Aquilonian strength and chivalry. Only the knights of Poitain, under Prospero, had not yet arrived, for they had far to ride up from the southwestern corner of the kingdom. Tarascus had struck without warning. His invasion had come on the heels of his proclamation, without formal declaration of war.

The two hosts confronted each other across a wide, shallow valley, with rugged cliffs, and a shallow stream winding through masses of reeds and willows down the middle of the vale. The camp-followers of both hosts came down to this stream for water, and shouted insults and hurled stones across at one another. The last glints of the sun shone on the golden banner of Nemedia with the scarlet dragon, unfurled in the breeze above the pavilion of King Tarascus on an eminence near the eastern cliffs. But the shadow of the western cliffs fell like a vast purple pall across the tents and the army of Aquilonia, and upon the black banner with its golden lion that floated above King Conan's pavilion.

All night the fires flared the length of the valley, and the wind brought the call of trumpets, the clangor of arms, and the sharp challenges of the sentries who paced their horses along either edge of the willow-ground stream.

It was in the darkness before dawn that King Conan stirred on his couch, which was no more than a pile of silks and furs thrown on a dais, and awakened. He started up, crying out sharply and clutching at his sword. Pallantides, his commander, rushing in at the cry, saw his king sitting upright, his hand on his hilt, and perspiration dripping from his strangely pale face.

'Your Majesty!' exclaimed Pallantides. 'Is aught amiss?'

'What of the camp?' demanded Conan. 'Are the guards out?'

'Five hundred horsemen patrol the stream, Your Majesty,' answered the general. 'The Nemedians have not offered to move against us in the night. They wait for dawn, even as we.'

'By Crom,' muttered Conan. 'I awoke with a feeling that doom was creeping on me in the night.'

He stared up at the great golden lamp which shed a soft glow over the velvet hangings of the great tent. They were alone; not even a slave or a page slept on the carpeted floor; but Conan's eyes blazed as they were wont to blaze in the teeth of great peril, and the sword quivered in his hand. Pallantides watched him uneasily. Conan seemed to be listening.

'Listen!' hissed the king. 'Did you hear it? A furtive step!'

'Seven knights guard your tent, Your Majesty,' said Pallantides. 'None could approach it unchallenged.'

'Not outside,' growled Conan. 'It seemed to sound *inside* the tent.'

Pallantides cast a swift, startled look around. The velvet hangings merged with shadows in the corners, but if there had been anyone in the pavilion besides themselves, the general would have seen him. Again he shook his head.

'There is no one here, sire. You sleep in the midst of your host.'

'I have seen death strike a king in the midst of thousands,' muttered Conan. 'Something that walks on invisible feet and is not seen—'

'Perhaps you were dreaming, Your Majesty,' said Pallantides, somewhat perturbed.

'So I was,' grunted Conan. 'A devilish strange dream it was, too. I trod again all the long, weary roads I traveled on my way to the kingship.'

He fell silent, and Pallantides stared at him unspeaking. The king was an enigma to the general, as to most of his civilized subjects. Pallantides knew that Conan had walked many strange roads in his wild, eventful life, and had been many things before a twist of Fate set him on the throne of Aquilonia.

'I saw again the battlefield whereon I was born,' said Conan, resting his chin moodily on a massive fist. 'I saw myself in a pantherskin loin-clout, throwing my spear at the mountain beasts. I was a mercenary swordsman again, a hetman of the *kosaki* who dwell along the Zaporoska River, a corsair looting the coasts of Kush, a pirate of the Barachan Isles, a chief of the Himelian hillmen. All these things I've been, and of all these things I dreamed; all the shapes that

23

have been *I* passed like an endless procession, and their feet beat out a dirge in the sounding dust.

'But throughout my dream moved strange, veiled figures and ghostly shadows, and a far-away voice mocked me. And toward the last I seemed to see myself lying on this dais in my tent, and a shape bent over me, robed and hooded. I lay unable to move, and then the hood fell away and a moldering skull grinned down at me. Then it was that I awoke.'

'This is an evil dream, Your Majesty,' said Pallantides, suppressing a shudder. 'But no more.'

Conan shook his head, more in doubt than in denial. He came of a barbaric race, and the superstitions and instincts of his heritage lurked close beneath the surface of his consciousness.

'I've dreamed many evil dreams,' he said, 'and most of them were meaningless. But by Crom, this was not like most dreams! I wish this battle were fought and won, for I've had a grisly premonition ever since King Nimed died in the black plague. Why did it cease when he died?'

'Men say he sinned—'

'Men are fools, as always,' grunted Conan. 'If the plague struck all who sinned, then by Crom, there wouldn't be enough left to count the living! Why should the gods – who the priests tell me are just – slay five hundred peasants and merchants and nobles before they slew the king, if the whole pestilence were aimed at him? Were the gods smiting blindly, like swordsmen in a fog? By Mitra, if I aimed my strokes no straighter, Aquilonia would have had a new king long ago.

'No! The Black Plague's no common pestilence. It lurks in Stygian tombs, and is called forth into being only by wizards. I was a swordsman in Prince Almuric's army that invaded Stygia, and of his thirty thousand, fifteen thousand perished by Stygian arrows, and the rest by the black plague that rolled on us like a wind out of the south. I was the only man who lived.'

'Yet only five hundred died in Nemedia,' argued Pallantides.

'Whoever called it into being knew how to cut it short at will,' answered Conan. 'So I know there was something planned and diabolical about it. Someone called it forth, someone banished it when the work was completed – when Tarascus was safe on the throne and being hailed as the deliverer of the people from the wrath of the gods. By Crom,

I sense a black, subtle brain behind all this. What of this stranger who men say gives counsel to Tarascus?'

'He wears a veil,' answered Pallantides; 'they say he is a foreigner; a stranger from Stygia.'

'A stranger from Stygia!' repeated Conan, scowling. 'A stranger from Hell, more like! – Ha! What is that?'

'The trumpets of the Nemedians!' exclaimed Pallantides. 'And hark, how our own blare upon their heels! Dawn is breaking, and the captains are marshaling the hosts for the onset! Mitra be with them, for many will not see the sun go down behind the crags.'

'Send my squires to me!' exclaimed Conan, rising with alacrity and casting off his velvet night-garment; he seemed to have forgotten his forebodings at the prospect of action. 'Go to the captains and see that all is in readiness. I will be with you as soon as I don my armor.'

Many of Conan's ways were inexplicable to the civilized people he ruled, and one of them was his insistence on sleeping alone in his chamber or tent. Pallantides hastened from the pavilion, clanking in the armor he had donned at midnight after a few hours' sleep. He cast a swift glance over the camp, which was beginning to swarm with activity, mail clinking and men moving about dimly in the uncertain light, among the long lines of tents. Stars still glimmered palely in the western sky, but long pink streamers stretched along the eastern horizon, and against them the dragon banner of Nemedia flung out its billowing silken folds.

Pallantides turned toward a smaller tent near by, where slept the royal squires. These were tumbling out already, roused by the trumpets. And as Pallantides called to them to hasten, he was frozen speechless by a deep fierce shout and the impact of a heavy blow inside the king's tent, followed by the heart-stopping crash of a falling body. There sounded a low laugh that turned the general's blood to ice.

Echoing the cry, Pallantides wheeled and rushed back into the pavilion. He cried out again as he saw Conan's powerful frame stretched out on the carpet. The king's great two-handed sword lay near his hand, and a shattered tent-pole seemed to show where his stroke had fallen. Pallantides' sword was out, and he glared about the tent, but nothing met his gaze. Save for the king and himself it was empty, as it had been when he left it.

'Your Majesty!' Pallantides threw himself on his knee beside the fallen giant.

Conan's eyes were open; they blazed up at him with full intelligence and recognition. His lips writhed, but no sound came forth. He seemed unable to move.

Voices sounded without. Pallantides rose swiftly and stepped to the door. The royal squires and one of the knights who guarded the tent stood there.

'We heard a sound within,' said the knight apologetically. 'Is all well with the king?'

Pallantides regarded him searchingly.

'None has entered or left the pavilion this night?'

'None save yourself, my lord,' answered the knight, and Pallantides could not doubt his honesty.

'The king stumbled and dropped his sword,' said Pallantides briefly. 'Return to your post.'

As the knight turned away, the general covertly motioned to the five royal squires, and when they had followed him in, he drew the flap closely. They turned pale at sight of the king stretched upon the carpet, but Pallantides' quick gesture checked their exclamations.

The general bent over him again, and again Conan made an effort to speak. The veins in his temples and the cords in his neck swelled with his efforts, and he lifted his head clear of the ground. Voice came at last, mumbling and half intelligible.

'*The thing – the thing in the corner!*'

Pallantides lifted his head and looked fearfully about him. He saw the pale faces of the squires in the lamplight, the velvet shadows that lurked along the walls of the pavilion. That was all.

'There is nothing here, Your Majesty,' he said.

'It was there, in the corner,' muttered the king, tossing his lion-maned head from side to side in his efforts to rise. 'A man – at least he looked like a man – wrapped in rags like a mummy's bandages, with a moldering cloak drawn about him, and a hood. All I could see was his eyes, as he crouched there in the shadows. I thought he was a shadow himself, until I saw his eyes. They were like black jewels.

'I made at him and swung my sword, but I missed him clean – how, Crom knows – and splintered that pole instead. He caught my wrist as I staggered off balance, and his fingers burned like hot iron. All the strength went out of me, and the floor rose and struck me like a club. Then he was gone, and I was down, and – curse him! – I can't move! I'm paralyzed!'

Pallantides lifted the giant's hand, and his flesh crawled. On the king's wrist showed the blue marks of long, lean fingers. What hand could grip so hard as to leave its print on that thick wrist? Pallantides remembered that low laugh he had heard as he rushed into the tent, and cold perspiration beaded his skin. It had not been Conan who laughed.

'This is a thing diabolical!' whispered a trembling squire. 'Men say the children of darkness war for Tarascus!'

'Be silent!' ordered Pallantides sternly.

Outside, the dawn was dimming the stars. A light wind sprang up from the peaks, and brought the fanfare of a thousand trumpets. At the sound a convulsive shudder ran through the king's mighty form. Again the veins in his temples knotted as he strove to break the invisible shackles which crushed him down.

'Put my harness on me and tie me into my saddle,' he whispered. 'I'll lead the charge yet!'

Pallantides shook his head, and a squire plucked his skirt.

'My lord, we are lost if the host learns the king has been smitten! Only he could have led us to victory this day.'

'Help me lift him on the dais,' answered the general.

They obeyed, and laid the helpless giant on the furs, and spread a silken cloak over him. Pallantides turned to the five squires and searched their pale faces long before he spoke.

'Our lips must be sealed for ever as to what happens in this tent,' he said at last. 'The kingdom of Aquilonia depends upon it. One of you go and fetch me the officer Valannus, who is a captain of the Pellian spearmen.'

The squire indicated bowed and hastened from the tent, and Pallantides stood staring down at the stricken king, while outside trumpets blared, drums thundered, and the roar of the multitudes rose in the growing dawn. Presently the squire returned with the officer Pallantides had named – a tall man, broad and powerful, built much like the king. Like him, also he had thick black hair. But his eyes were gray and he did not resemble Conan in his features.

'The king is stricken by a strange malady,' said Pal-

27

lantides briefly. 'A great honor is yours; you are to wear his armor and ride at the head of the host today. None must know that it is not the king who rides.'

'It is an honor for which a man might gladly give up his life,' stammered the captain, overcome by the suggestion. 'Mitra grant that I do not fail of this mighty trust!'

And while the fallen king stared with burning eyes that reflected the bitter rage and humiliation that ate his heart, the squires stripped Valannus of mail shirt, burganet and leg-pieces, and clad him in Conan's armor of black plate-mail, with the vizored salade, and the dark plumes nodding over the wivern crest. Over all they put the silken surcoat with the royal lion worked in gold upon the breast, and they girt him with a broad gold-buckled belt which supported a jewel-hilted broadsword in a cloth-of-gold scabbard. While they worked, trumpets clamored outside, arms clanged, and across the river rose a deep-throated roar as squadron after squadron swung into place.

Full-armed, Valannus dropped to his knee and bent his plumes before the figure that lay on the dais.

'Lord King, Mitra grant that I do not dishonor the harness I wear this day!'

'Bring me Tarascus's head and I'll make you a baron!' In the stress of his anguish Conan's veneer of civilization had fallen from him. His eyes flamed, he ground his teeth in fury and blood-lust, as barbaric as any tribesmen in the Cimmerian hills.

3 – THE CLIFFS REEL

THE AQUILONIAN HOST was drawn up, long serried lines of pikemen and horsemen in gleaming steel, when a giant figure in black armor emerged from the royal pavilion, and as he swung up into the saddle of the black stallion held by four squires, a roar that shook the mountains went up from the host. They shook their blades and thundered forth their acclaim of their warrior king – knights in gold-chased armor, pikemen in mail coats and basinets, archers in their leather jerkins, with their longbows in their left hands.

The host on the opposite side of the valley was in motion, trotting down the long gentle slope toward the river; their steel shone through the mists of the morning that swirled about their horses' feet.

The Aquilonian host moved leisurely to meet them. The measured trump of the armored horses made the ground tremble. Banners flung out long silken folds in the morning wind; lances swayed like a bristling forest, dipped and sank, their pennons fluttering about them.

Ten men-at-arms, grim, taciturn veterans who could hold their tongues, guarded the royal pavilion. One squire stood in the tent, peering out through a slit in the doorway. But for the handful in the secret, no one else in the vast host knew that it was not Conan who rode on the great stallion at the head of the army.

The Aquilonian host had assumed the customary formation: the strongest part was the center, composed entirely of heavily armed knights; the wings were made up of smaller bodies of horsemen, mounted men-at-arms, mostly, supported by pikemen and archers. The latter were Bossonians from the western marches, strongly built men of medium stature, in leathern jackets and iron headpieces.

The Nemedian army came on in similar formation, and the two hosts moved toward the river, the wings in advance of the centers. In the center of the Aquilonian host the great lion banner streamed its billowing black folds over the steel-clad figure on the black stallion.

But on his dais in the royal pavillion Conan groaned in anguish of spirit, and cursed with strange heathen oaths.

'The hosts move together,' quoth the squire, watching from the door. 'Hear the trumpets peal! Ha! The rising sun strikes fire from lance-heads and helmets until I am dazzled. It turns the river crimson – aye, it will be truly crimson before this day is done!

'The foe have reached the river. Now arrows fly between the hosts like stinging clouds that hide the sun. Ha! Well loosed, bowmen! The Bossonians have the better of it! Hark to them shout!'

Faintly in the ears of the king, above the din of trumpets and clanging steel, came the deep fierce shout of the Bossonians as they drew and loosed in perfect unison.

'Their archers seek to hold ours in play while their knights ride into the river,' said the squire. 'The banks are not steep; they slope to the water's edge. The knights come on, they crash through the willows. By Mitra, the clothyard shafts find every crevice of their harness! Horses and men go down, struggling and thrashing in the water. It is not deep, nor is the current swift, but men are drowning there, dragged under by their armor, and trampled by the frantic horses. Now the knights of Aquilonia advance. They ride into the water and engage the knights of Nemedia. The water swirls about their horses' bellies and the clang of sword against sword is deafening.'

'Crom!' burst in agony from Conan's lips. Life was coursing sluggishly back into his veins, but still he could not lift his mighty frame from the dias.

'The wings close in,' said the squire. 'Pikemen and swordsmen fight hand to hand in the stream, and behind them the bowmen ply their shafts.

'By Mitra, the Nemedian arbalesters are sorely harried, and the Bossonians arch their arrows to drop amid the rear ranks. Their center gains not a foot, and their wings are pushed back up from the stream again.'

'Crom, Ymir, and Mitra!' raged Conan. 'Gods and devils, could I but reach the men fighting, if but to die at the first blow!'

Outside through the long hot day the battle stormed and thundered. The valley shook to charge and counter-charge, to the whistling of shafts, and the crash of rending shields and splintering lances. But the hosts of Aquilonia held fast. Once they were forced back from the bank, but a counter-charge, with the black banner flowing over the black stallion, regained the lost ground. And like an iron rampart they held the right bank of the stream, and at last the squire gave Conan the news that the Nemedians were falling back from the river.

'Their wings are in confusion!' he cried. 'Their knights reel back from the sword-play. But what is this? Your banner is in motion – the center sweeps into the stream! By Mitra, Valannus is leading the host across the river!'

'Fool!' groaned Conan. 'It may be a trick. He should hold his position; by dawn Prospero will be here with the Poitanian levies.'

'The knights ride into a hail of arrows!' cried the squire. 'But they do not falter! They sweep on – they have crossed! They charge up the slope! Pallantides has hurled the wings across the river to their support! It is all he can do. The lion banner dips and staggers above the mêlée.

'The knights of Nemedia make a stand. They are broken! They fall back! Their left wing is in full flight, and our pikemen cut them down as they run! I see Valannus, riding and smiting like a madman. He is carried beyond himself by the fighting-lust. Men no longer look to Pallantides. They follow Valannus, deeming him Conan, as he rides with closed visor.

'But look! There is method in his madness! He swings wide of the Nemedian front, with five thousand knights, the pick of the army. The main host of the Nemedians is in confusion – and look! Their flank is protected by the cliffs, but there is a defile left unguarded! It is like a great cleft in the wall that opens again behind the Nemedian lines. By Mitra, Valannus sees and seizes the opportunity! He has driven their wing before him, and he leads his knights toward that defile. They swing wide of the main battle; they cut through a line of spearmen, they charge into the defile!'

'An ambush!' cried Conan, striving to struggle upright.

No!' shouted the squire exultantly. 'The whole Nemedian host is in full sight! They have forgotten the defile! They never expected to be pushed back that far. Oh, fool, fool, Tarascus, to make such a blunder! Ah, I see lances and pennons pouring from the farther mouth of the defile, beyond the Nemedian lines. They will smite those ranks from the rear and crumple them. *Mitra, what is this?*'

He staggered as the walls of the tent swayed drunkenly. Afar over the thunder of the fight rose a deep bellowing roar, indescribably ominous.

'The cliffs reel!' shrieked the squire. 'Ah, gods, what is this? The river foams out of its channel, and the peaks are crumbling! The ground shakes and horses and riders in armor are overthrown! The cliffs! The cliffs are falling!'

With his words came a grinding rumble and a thunderous concussion, and the ground trembled. Over the roar of the battle sounded screams of mad terror.

'The cliffs have crumbled!' cried the livid squire. 'They have thundered down into the defile and crushed every living creature in it! I saw the lion banner wave an instant amid the dust and falling stones, and then it vanished! Ha, the Nemedians shout with triumph! Well may

31

they shout, for the fall of the cliffs has wiped out five thousand of our bravest knights – hark!'

To Conan's ears came a vast torrent of sound, rising and rising in frenzy: '*The king is dead! The king is dead! Flee! Flee! The king is dead!*'

'Liars!' panted Conan. 'Dogs! Knaves! Cowards! Oh, Crom, if I could but stand – but crawl to the river with my sword in my teeth! How, boy, do they flee?'

'Aye!' sobbed the squire. 'They spur for the river; they are broken, hurled on like spume before a storm. I see Pallantides striving to stem the torrent – he is down, and the horses trample him! They rush into the river, knights, bowmen, pikemen, all mixed and mingled in one mad torrent of destruction. The Nemedians are on their heels, cutting them down like corn.'

'But they will make a stand on this side of the river!' cried the king. With an effort that brought the sweat dripping from his temples, he heaved himself up on his elbows.

'Nay!' cried the squire. 'They cannot! They are broken! Routed! Oh gods, that I should live to see this day!'

Then he remembered his duty and shouted to the men-at-arms who stood stolidly watching the flight of their comrades. 'Get a horse, swiftly, and help me lift the king upon it. We dare not bide here.'

But before they could do his bidding, the first drift of the storm was upon them. Knights and spearmen and archers fled among the tents, stumbling over ropes and baggage, and mingled with them were Nemedian riders, who smote right and left at all alien figures. Tent-ropes were cut, fire sprang up in a hundred places, and the plundering had already begun. The grim guardsmen about Conan's tent died where they stood, smiting and thrusting, and over their mangled corpses beat the hoofs of the conquerors.

But the squire had drawn the flap close, and in the confused madness of the slaughter none realized that the pavilion held an occupant. So the flight and the pursuit swept past, and roared away up the valley, and the squire looked out presently to see a cluster of men approaching the royal tent with evident purpose.

'Here comes the king of Nemedia with four companions and his squire,' quoth he. 'He will accept your surrender, my fair lord—'

'Surrender the devil's heart!' gritted the king.

He had forced himself up into a sitting posture. He swung his legs painfully off the dais, and staggered upright, reeling drunkenly. The squire ran to assist him, but Conan pushed him away.

'Give me that bow!' he gritted, indicating a longbow and quiver that hung from a tent-pole.

'But Your Majesty!' cried the squire in great pertubation. 'The battle is lost! It were the part of majesty to yield with dignity becoming one of royal blood!'

'I have no royal blood,' ground Conan. 'I am a barbarian and the son of a blacksmith.'

Wrenching away the bow and an arrow he staggered toward the opening of the pavilion. So formidable was his appearance, naked but for short leather breeks and sleeveless shirt, open to reveal his great, hairy chest, with his huge limbs and his blue eyes blazing under his tangled black mane, that the squire shrank back, more afraid of his king than of the whole Nemedian host.

Reeling on wide-braced legs Conan drunkenly tore the door-flap open and staggered out under the canopy. The king of Nemedia and his companions had dismounted, and they halted short, staring in wonder at the apparition confronting them.

'Here I am, you jackals!' roared the Cimmerian. 'I am the king! Death to you, dog-brothers!'

He jerked the arrow to its head and loosed, and the shaft feathered itself in the breast of the knight who stood beside Tarascus. Conan hurled the bow at the king of Nemedia.

'Curse my shaky hand! Come in and take me if you dare!'

Reeling backward on unsteady legs, he fell with his shoulders against a tent-pole, and propped upright, he lifted his great sword with both hands.

'By Mitra, it *is* the king!' swore Tarascus. He cast a swift look about him, and laughed. 'That other was a jackal in his harness! In, dogs, and take his head!'

The three soldiers – men-at-arms wearing the emblem of the royal guards – rushed at the king, and one felled the squire with the blow of a mace. The other two fared less well. As the first rushed in, lifting his sword, Conan met him with a sweeping stroke that severed mail-links like cloth, and sheared the Nemedian's arm and shoulder

33

clean from his body. His corpse, pitching backward, fell across his companion's legs. The man stumbled, and before he could recover, the great sword was through him.

Conan wrenched out his steel with a racking gasp, and staggered back against the tent-pole. His great limbs trembled, his chest heaved, and sweat poured down his face and neck. But his eyes flamed with exultant savagery and he panted: 'Why do you stand afar off, dog of Belverus? I can't reach you; come in and die!'

Tarascus hesitated, glanced at the remaining man-at-arms, and his squire, a gaunt, saturnine man in black mail, and took a step forward. He was far inferior in size and strength to the giant Cimmerian, but he was in full armor, and was famed in all the western nations as a swordsman. But his squire caught his arm.

'Nay, your Majesty, do not throw away your life. I will summon archers to shoot this barbarian, as we shoot lions.'

Neither of them had noticed that a chariot had approached while the fight was going on, and now came to a halt before them. But Conan saw, looking over their shoulders, and a queer chill sensation crawled along his spine. There was something vaguely unnatural about the appearance of the black horses that drew the vehicle, but it was the occupant of the chariot that arrested the king's attention.

He was a tall man, superbly built, clad in a long unadorned silk robe. He wore a Shemitish head-dress, and its lower folds hid his features, except for the dark, magnetic eyes. The hands that grasped the reins, pulling the rearing horses back on their haunches, were white but strong. Conan glared at the stranger, all his primitive instincts roused. He sensed an aura of menace and power that exuded from this veiled figure, a menace as definite as the windless waving of tall grass that marks the path of the serpent.

'Hail, Xaltotun!' exclaimed Tarascus. 'Here is the king of Aquilonia! He did not die in the landslide as we thought.'

'I know,' answered the other, without bothering to say how he knew. 'What is your present intention?'

'I will summon the archers to slay him,' answered the Nemedian. 'As long as he lives he will be dangerous to us.'

'Yet even a dog has uses,' answered Xaltotun. 'Take him alive.'

Conan laughed raspingly. 'Come in and try!' he challenged. 'But for my treacherous legs I'd hew you out of that chariot like a woodman hewing a tree. But you'll never take me alive, damn you!'

'He speaks the truth, I fear,' said Tarascus. 'The man is a barbarian, with the senseless ferocity of a wounded tiger. Let me summon the archers.'

'Watch me and learn wisdom,' advised Xaltotun.

His hand dipped into his robe and came out with something shining – a glistening sphere. This he threw suddenly at Conan. The Cimmerian contemptuously struck it aside with his sword – at the instant of contact there was a sharp explosion, a flare of white, blinding flame, and Conan pitched senseless to the ground.

'He is dead?' Tarascus's tone was more assertion than inquiry.

'No. He is but senseless. He will recover his senses in a few hours. Bid your men bind his arms and legs and lift him into my chariot.'

With a gesture Tarascus did so, and they heaved the senseless king into the chariot, grunting with their burden. Xaltotun threw a velvet cloak over his body, completely covering him from any who might peer in. He gathered the reins in his hands.

'I'm for Belverus,' he said. 'Tell Amalric that I will be with him if he needs me. But with Conan out of the way, and his army broken, lance and sword should suffice for the rest of the conquest. Prospero cannot be bringing more than ten thousand men to the field, and will doubtless fall back to Tarantia when he hears the news of the battle. Say nothing to Amalric or Valerius or anyone about our capture. Let them think Conan died in the fall of the cliffs.'

He looked at the man-at-arms for a long space, until the guardsman moved restlessly, nervous under the scrutiny.

'What is that about your waist?' Xaltotun demanded.

'Why, my girdle, may it please you, my lord!' stuttered the amazed guardsman.

'You lie!' Xaltotun's laugh was merciless as a sword-edge. 'It is a poisonous serpent! What a fool you are, to wear a reptile about your waist!'

With distended eyes the man looked down; and to his utter horror he saw the buckle of his girdle rear up at him. It *was* a snake's head! He saw the evil eyes and the dripping fangs,

35

heard the hiss and felt the loathsome contact of the thing about his body. He screamed hideously and struck at it with his naked hand, felt its fangs flesh themselves in that hand – and then he stiffened and fell heavily. Tarascus looked down at him without expression. He saw only the leathern girdle and the buckle, the pointed tongue of which was stuck in the guardsman's palm. Xaltotun turned his hypnotic gaze on Tarascus' squire, and the man turned ashen and began to tremble; but the king interposed: 'Nay, we can trust him.'

The sorcerer tautened the reins and swung the horses around.

'See that this piece of work remains secret. If I am needed, let Altaro, Orastes' servant, summon me as I have taught him. I will be in your palace at Belverus.'

Tarascus lifted his hand in salutation, but his expression was not pleasant to see as he looked after the departing mesmerist.

'Why should he spare the Cimmerian?' whispered the frightened squire.

'That I am wondering myself,' grunted Tarascus.

Behind the rumbling chariot, the dull roar of battle and pursuit faded in the distance; the setting sun rimmed the cliffs with scarlet flame, and the chariot moved into the vast blue shadows floating up out of the east.

4 – 'FROM WHAT HELL HAVE YOU CRAWLED?'

OF THAT LONG RIDE in the chariot of Xaltotun, Conan knew nothing. He lay like a dead man while the bronze wheels clashed over the stones of mountain roads and swished through the deep grass of fertile valleys, and finally, dropping down from the rugged heights, rumbled rhythmically along the broad white road that winds through the rich meadowlands to the walls of Belverus.

Just before dawn, some faint reviving of life touched him. He heard a mumble of voices, the groan of ponderous hinges. Through a slit in the cloak that covered him he saw faintly in the lurid glare of torches, the great black arch of a gateway, and the bearded faces of men-at-arms, the torches striking fire from their spearheads and helmets.

'How went the battle, my fair lord?' spoke an eager voice, in the Nemedian tongue.

'Well indeed,' was the curt reply. 'The king of Aquilonia lies slain and his host is broken.'

A babble of excited voices rose, drowned the next instant by the whirling wheels of the chariot on the flags. Sparks flashed from under the revolving rims as Xaltotun lashed his steeds through the arch. But Conan heard one of the guardsmen mutter: 'From beyond the border to Belverus between sunset and dawn! And the horses scarcely sweating! By Mitra, they—' Then silence drank the voices, and there was only the clatter of hoofs and wheels along the shadowy street.

What he had heard registered itself on Conan's brain but suggested nothing to him. He was like a mindless automaton that hears and sees, but does not understand. Sights and sounds flowed meaninglessly about him. He lapsed again into a deep lethargy, and was only dimly aware when the chariot halted in a deep, high-walled court, and he was lifted from it by many hands and borne up a winding stone stair, and down a long dim corridor. Whispers, stealthy footsteps, unrelated sounds surged or rustled about him, irrelevant and far away.

Yet his ultimate awakening was abrupt and crystal-clear. He possessed full knowledge of the battle in the mountains and its consequences, and he had a good idea of where he was.

He lay on a velvet couch, clad as he was the day before, but with his limbs loaded with chains not even he could break. The room in which he lay was furnished with somber magnificence, the walls covered with black velvet tapestries, the floor with heavy purple carpets. There was no sign of door or window, and one curiously carven gold lamp, swinging from the fretted ceiling, shed a lurid light over all.

In that light the figure seated in a silver, thronelike chair before him seemed unreal and fantastic, with an illusiveness of outline that was heightened by a filmy silken robe. But the features were distinct – unnaturally so in that uncertain light. It was almost as if a weird nimbus played about the man's head, casting the bearded face into bold relief, so that it was the only definite and distinct reality in that mystic, ghostly chamber.

It was a magnificent face, with strongly chiseled features of classical beauty. There was, indeed, something disquieting about the calm tranquillity of its aspect, a suggestion of more than human knowledge, of a profound certitude beyond human assurance. Also an uneasy sensation of familiarity twitched at the back of Conan's consciousness. He had never seen this man's face before, he well knew; yet those features reminded him of something or someone. It was like encountering in the flesh some dream-image that had haunted one in nightmares.

'Who are you?' demanded the king belligerently, struggling to a sitting position in spite of his chains.

'Men call me Xaltotun,' was the reply, in a strong, golden voice.

'What place is this?' the Cimmerian next demanded.

'A chamber in the palace of King Tarascus, in Belverus.'

Conan was not surprised. Belverus, the capital, was at the same time the largest Nemedian city so near the border.

'And where's Tarascus?'

'With the army.'

'Well,' growled Conan, 'if you mean to murder me, why don't you do it and get it over with?'

'I did not save you from the king's archers to murder you in Belverus,' answered Xaltotun.

'What the devil did you do to me?' demanded Conan.

'I blasted your consciousness,' answered Xaltotun. 'How, you would not understand. Call it black magic, if you will.'

Conan had already reached that conclusion, and was mulling over something else.

'I think I understand why you spared my life,' he rumbled. 'Amalric wants to keep me as a check on Valerius, in case the impossible happens and he becomes king of Aquilonia. It's well known that the baron of Tor is behind this move to seat Valerius on my throne. And if I know Amalric, he doesn't intend that Valerius shall be anything more than a figurehead, as Tarascus is now.'

'Amalric knows nothing of your capture,' answered Xaltotun. 'Neither does Valerius. Both think you died at Valkia.'

Conan's eyes narrowed as he stared at the man in silence.

'I sensed a brain behind all this,' he muttered, 'but I thought it was Amalric's. Are Amalric, Tarascus and Valerius all but puppets dancing on your string? Who are you?'

'What does it matter? If I told you, you would not believe me. What if I told you I might set you back on the throne of Aquilonia?'

Conan's eyes burned on him like a wolf.

'What's your price?'

'Obedience to me.'

'Go to hell with your offer!' snarled Conan. 'I'm no figure-head. I won my crown with my sword. Besides, it's beyond your power to buy and sell the throne of Aquilonia at your will. The kingdom's not conquered; one battle doesn't decide a war.'

'You war against more than swords,' answered Xaltotun. 'Was it a mortal's sword that felled you in your tent before the fight? Nay, it was a child of the dark, a waif of outer space, whose fingers were afire with the frozen coldness of the black gulfs, which froze the blood in your veins and the marrow of your thews. Coldness so cold that it burned your flesh like white-hot iron!

'Was it chance that led the man who wore your harness to lead his knights into the defile? – chance that brought the cliffs crashing down upon them?'

Conan glared at him unspeaking, feeling a chill along his spine. Wizards and sorcerers abounded in his barbaric mythology, and any fool could tell that this was no common man. Conan sensed an inexplicable something about him that set him apart – an alien aura of Time and Space, a sense of tremendous and sinister antiquity. But his stubborn spirit refused to flinch.

'The fall of the cliffs was chance,' he muttered truculently. 'The charge into the defile was what any man would have done.'

'Not so. You would not have led a charge into it. You would have suspected a trap. You would never have crossed the river in the first place, until you were sure the Nemedian rout was real. Hypnotic suggestions would not have invaded your mind, even in the madness of battle, to make you mad, and rush blindly into the trap laid for you, as it did the lesser man who masqueraded as you.'

'Then if this was all planned,' Conan grunted skeptically, 'all a plot to trap my host, why did not the "child of darkness" kill me in my tent?'

'Because I wished to take you alive. It took no wizardry to predict that Pallantides would send another man out in your harness. I wanted you alive and unhurt. You may fit into my scheme of things. There is a vital power about you greater than the craft and cunning of my allies. You are a bad enemy, but might make a fine vassal.'

39

Conan spat savagely at the word, and Xaltotun, ignoring his fury, took a crystal globe from a near-by table and placed it before him. He did not support it in any way, nor place it on anything; but it hung motionless in mid-air, as solidly as if it rested on an iron pedestal. Conan snorted at this bit of necromancy, but he was nevertheless impressed.

'Would you know of what goes on in Aquilonia?' he asked.

Conan did not reply, but the sudden rigidity of his form betrayed his interest.

Xaltotun stared into the cloudy depths, and spoke: 'It is now the evening of the day after the battle of Valkia. Last night the main body of the army camped at Valkia, while squadrons of knights harried the fleeing Aquilonians. At dawn the host broke camp and pushed westward through the mountains. Prospero, with ten thousand Poitanians, was miles from the battlefield when he met the fleeing survivors in the early dawn. He had pushed on all night, hoping to reach the field before the battle joined. Unable to rally the remnants of the broken host, he fell back toward Tarantia. Riding hard, replacing his wearied horses with steeds from the countryside, he approaches Tarantia.

'I see his weary knights, their armor gray with dust, their pennons drooping as they push their tired horses through the plain. I see, also, the streets of Tarantia. The city is in turmoil. Somehow word has reached the people of the defeat and the death of King Conan. The mob is mad with fear, crying out that the king is dead, and there is none to lead them against the Nemedians. Giant shadows rush on Aquilonia from the east, and the sky is black with vultures.'

Conan cursed deeply.

'What are these but words? The raggedest beggar in the street might prophesy as much. If you say you saw all that in the glass ball, then you're a liar as well as a knave, of which last there's no doubt! Prospero will hold Tarantia, and the barons will rally to him. Count Trocero of Poitain commands the kingdom in my absence, and he'll drive these Nemedian dogs howling back to their kennels. What are fifty thousand Nemedians? Aquilonia will swallow them up. They'll never see Belverus again. It's not Aquilonia which was conquered at Valkia; it was only Conan.'

'Aquilonia is doomed,' answered Xaltotun, unmoved. 'Lance and ax and torch shall conquer her; or if they fail, powers from the dark of ages shall march against her. As the cliffs fell at Valkia, so shall walled cities and mountains fall, if the need arise, and rivers roar from their channels to drown whole provinces.

'Better if steel and bowstring prevail without further aid from the *arts*, for the constant use of mighty spells sometimes sets forces in motion that might rock the universe.'

'From what hell have you crawled, you nighted dog?' muttered Conan, staring at the man. The Cimmerian involuntarily shivered; he sensed something incredibly ancient, incredibly evil. . . .

Xaltotun lifted his head, as if listening to whispers across the void. He seemed to have forgotten his prisoner. Then he shook his head impatiently, and glanced impersonally at Conan.

'What? Why, if I told you, you would not believe me. But I am wearied of conversation with you; it is less fatiguing to destroy a walled city than it is to frame my thoughts in words a brainless barbarian can understand.'

'If my hands were free,' opined Conan, 'I'd soon make a brainless corpse out of you.'

'I do not doubt it, if I were fool enough to give you the opportunity,' answered Xaltotun, clapping his hands.

His manner had changed; there was impatience in his tone, and a certain nervousness in his manner, though Conan did not think this attitude was in any way connected with himself.

'Consider what I have told you, barbarian,' said Xaltotun. 'You will have plenty of leisure. I have not yet decided what I shall do with you. It depends on circumstances yet unborn. But let this be impressed upon you: that if I decide to use you in my game, it will be better to submit without resistance than to suffer my wrath.'

Conan spat a curse at him, just as hangings that masked a door swung apart and four giant Negroes entered. Each was clad only in a silken breech-clout supported by a girdle, from which hung a great key.

Xaltotun gestured impatiently toward the king and turned away, as if dismissing the matter entirely from his mind. His fingers twitched queerly. From a carven green jade box he took a handful of shimmering black dust, and placed it in a brazier which stood on a golden tripod at his elbow. The crystal globe, which he seemed to have forgotten, fell suddenly to the floor, as if the invisible support had been removed.

Then the blacks had lifted Conan – for so loaded with chains was he that he could not walk – and carried him from

41

the chamber. A glance back, before the heavy, gold-bound teak door was closed, showed him Xaltotun leaning back in his throne-like chair, his arms folded, while a thin wisp of smoke curled up from the brazier. Conan's scalp prickled. In Stygia, that ancient and evil kingdom that lay far to the south, he had seen such black dust before. It was the pollen of the black lotus, which creates death-like sleep and monstrous dreams; and he knew that only the grisly wizards of the Black Ring, which is the nadir of evil, voluntarily seek the scarlet nightmares of the black lotus, to revive their necromantic powers.

The Black Ring was a fable and a lie to most folk of the western world, but Conan knew of its ghastly reality, and its grim votaries who practice their abominable sorceries amid the black vaults of Stygia and the nighted domes of accursed Sabatea.

He glanced back at the cryptic, gold-bound door, shuddering at what it hid.

Whether it was day or night the king could not tell. The palace of King Tarascus seemed a shadowy, nighted place, that shunned natural illumination. The spirit of darkness and shadow hovered over it, and that spirit, Conan felt, was embodied in the stranger Xaltotun. The Negroes carried the king along a winding corridor so dimly lighted that they moved through it like black ghosts bearing a dead man, and down a stone stair that wound endlessly. A torch in the hand of one cast the great deformed shadows streaming along the wall; it was like the descent into Hell of a corpse borne by dusky demons.

At last they reached the foot of the stair, and then they traversed a long straight corridor, with a blank wall on one hand pierced by an occasional arched doorway with a stair leading up behind it, and on the other hand another wall showing heavy barred doors at regular intervals of a few feet.

Halting before one of these doors, one of the blacks produced the key that hung at his girdle, and turned it in the lock. Then, pushing open the grille, they entered with their captive. They were in a small dungeon with heavy stone walls, floor and ceiling, and in the opposite wall there was another grilled door. What lay beyond that door Conan could not tell, but he did not believe it was another corridor. The glimmering light of the torch, flickering through the bars, hinted at shadowy spaciousness and echoing depths.

In one corner of the dungeon, near the door through which they had entered, a cluster of rusty chains hung from a great iron ring set in the stone. In these chains a skeleton dangled. Conan glared at it with some curiosity, noticing the state of the bare bones, most of which were splintered and broken; the skull, which had fallen from the vertebrae, was crushed as if by some savage blow of tremendous force.

Stolidly one of the blacks, not the one who had opened the door, removed the chains from the ring, using his key on the massive lock, and dragged the mass of rusty metal and shattered bones over to one side. Then they fastened Conan's chains to that ring, and the third black turned *his* key in the lock of the farther door, grunting when he had assured himself that it was properly fastened.

Then they regarded Conan cryptically, slit-eyed ebony giants, the torch striking highlights from their glossy skin.

He who held the key to the nearer door was moved to remark, gutturally: 'This your palace now, white dog-king! None but master and we know. All palace sleep. We keep secret. You live and die here, maybe. Like him!' He contemptuously kicked the shattered skull and sent it clattering across the stone floor.

Conan did not deign to reply to the taunt, and the black, galled perhaps by his prisoner's silence, muttered a curse, stooped, and spat full in the king's face. It was an unfortunate move for the black. Conan was seated on the floor, the chains about his waist; ankles and wrists locked to the ring in the wall. He could neither rise, nor move more than a yard out from the wall. But there was considerable slack in the chains that shackled his wrists, and before the bullet-shaped head could be withdrawn out of reach, the king gathered this slack in his mighty hand and smote the black on the head. The man fell like a butchered ox, and his comrades stared to see him lying with his scalp laid open, and blood oozing from his nose and ears.

But they attempted no reprisal, nor did they accept Conan's urgent invitation to approach within reach of the bloody chain in his hand. Presently, grunting in their guttural speech, they lifted the senseless black and bore him out like a sack of wheat, arms and legs dangling. They used his key to lock the door behind them, but did not remove it from the gold chain that fastened it to his girdle. They took the torch with them, and as they moved up the corridor the darkness slunk behind them like an animate thing. Their soft padding footsteps died away, with the glimmer of their torch, and darkness and silence remained unchallenged.

5 – THE HAUNTER OF THE PITS

CONAN LAY STILL, enduring the weight of his chains and the despair of his position with the stoicism of the wilds that had bred him. He did not move, because the jangle of his chains, when he shifted his body, sounded startlingly loud in the darkness and stillness, and it was his instinct, born of a thousand wilderness-bred ancestors, not to betray his position in his helplessness. This did not result from a logical reasoning process; he did not lie quiet because he reasoned that the darkness hid lurking dangers that might discover him in his helplessness. Xaltotun had assured him that he was not to be harmed, and Conan believed that it was in the man's interest to preserve him, at least for the time being. But the instincts of the wild were there, that had caused him in his childhood to lie hidden and silent while wild beasts prowled about his covert.

Even his keen eyes could not pierce the solid darkness. Yet after a while, after a period of time he had no way of estimating, a faint glow became apparent, a sort of slanting gray beam, by which Conan could see, vaguely, the bars of the door at his elbow, and even make out the skeleton of the other grille. This puzzled him, until at last he realized the explanation. He was far below ground, in the pits below the palace; yet for some reason a shaft had been constructed from somewhere above. Outside, the moon had risen to a point where its light slanted dimly down the shaft. He reflected that in this manner he could tell the passing of the days and nights. Perhaps the sun, too, would shine down that shaft, though on the other hand it might be closed by day. Perhaps it was a subtle method of torture, allowing a prisoner but a glimpse of daylight or moonlight.

His gaze fell on the broken bones in the farther corner, glimmering dimly. He did not tax his brain with futile speculation as to who the wretch had been and for what reason he had been doomed, but he wondered at the shattered

44

condition of the bones. They had not been broken on a rack. Then, as he looked, another unsavory detail made itself evident. The shin-bones were split lengthwise, and there was but one explanation; they had been broken in that manner in order to obtain the marrow. Yet what creature but man breaks bones for their marrow? Perhaps those remnants were mute evidence of a horrible, cannibalistic feast, of some wretch driven to madness by starvation. Conan wondered if his own bones would be found at some future date, hanging in their rusty chains. He fought down the unreasoning panic of a trapped wolf.

The Cimmerian did not curse, scream, weep, or rave as a civilized man might have done. But the pain and turmoil in his bosom were none the less fierce. His great limbs quivered with the intensity of his emotions. Somewhere, far to the westward, the Nemedian host was slashing and burning its way through the heart of his kingdom. The small host of the Poitanians could not stand before them. Prospero might be able to hold Tarantia for weeks, or months; but eventually, if not relieved, he must surrender to greater numbers. Surely the barons would rally to him against the invaders. But in the meanwhile he, Conan, must lie helpless in a darkened cell, while others led his spears and fought for his kingdom. The king ground his powerful teeth in red rage.

Then he stiffened as outside the farther door he heard a stealthy step. Straining his eyes he made out a bent, indistinct figure outside the grille. There was a rasp of metal against metal, and he heard the clink of tumblers, as if a key had been turned in the lock. Then the figure moved silently out of his range of vision. Some guard, he supposed, trying the lock. After a while he heard the sound repeated faintly somewhere farther on, and that was followed by the soft opening of a door, and then a swift scurry of softly shod feet retreated in the distance. Then silence fell again.

Conan listened for what seemed a long time, but which could not have been, for the moon still shone down the hidden shaft, but he heard no further sound. He shifted his position at last, and his chains clanked. Then he heard another, lighter footfall – a soft step outside the nearer door, the door through which he had entered the cell. An instant later a slender figure was etched dimly in the gray light.

'King Conan!' a soft voice intoned urgently. 'Oh, my lord, are you there?'

'Where else?' he answered guardedly, twisting his head about to stare at the apparition.

It was a girl who stood grasping the bars with her slender fingers. The dim glow behind her outlined her supple figure through the wisp of silk twisted about her loins, and shone vaguely on jeweled breast-plates. Her dark eyes gleamed in the shadows, her white limbs glistened softly, like alabaster. Her hair was a mass of dark foam, at the burnished luster of which the dim light only hinted.

'The keys to your shackles and to the farther door!' she whispered, and a slim white hand came through the bars and dropped three objects with a clink to the flags beside him.

'What game is this?' he demanded. 'You speak in the Nemedian tongue, and I have no friends in Nemedia. What deviltry is your master up to now? Has he sent you here to mock me?'

'It is no mockery!' The girl was trembling violently. Her bracelets and breast-plates clinked against the bars she grasped. 'I swear by Mitra! I stole the keys from the black jailers. They are the keepers of the pits, and each bears a key which will open only one set of locks. I make them drunk. The one whose head you broke was carried away to a leech, and I could not get his key. But the others I stole. Oh, please do not loiter! Beyond these dungeons lie the pits which are the doors to hell.'

Somewhat impressed, Conan tried the keys dubiously, expecting to meet only failure and a burst of mocking laughter. But he was galvanized to discover that one, indeed, loosed him of his shackles, fitting not only the lock that held them to the ring, but the locks on his limbs as well. A few seconds later he stood upright, exulting fiercely in his comparative freedom. A quick stride carried him to the grille, and his fingers closed about a bar and the slender wrist that was pressed against it, imprisoning the owner, who lifted her face bravely to his fierce gaze.

'Who are you, girl?' he demanded. 'Why do you do this?'

'I am only Zenobia,' she murmured, with a catch of breathlessness, as if in fright; 'only a girl of the king's seraglio.'

'Unless this is some cursed trick,' muttered Conan, 'I cannot see why you bring me these keys.'

She bowed her dark head, and then lifted it and looked full into his suspicious eyes. Tears sparkled like jewels on her long dark lashes.

'I am only a girl of the king's seraglio,' she said, with a certain proud humility. 'He has never glanced at me, and probably never will. I am less than one of the dogs that gnaw the bones in the banquet hall.

'But I am no painted toy; I am of flesh and blood. I breathe, hate, fear, rejoice and love. And I have loved you, King Conan, ever since I saw you riding at the head of your knights along the streets of Belverus when you visited King Numa, years ago. My heart tugged at its strings to leap from my bosom and fall in the dust of the street under your horse's hoofs.'

Color flooded her countenance as she spoke, but her dark eyes did not waver. Conan did not at once reply; wild and passionate and untamed he was, yet any but the most brutish of men must be touched with a certain awe or wonder at the baring of a woman's naked soul.

She bent her head then, and pressed her red lips to the fingers that imprisoned her slim wrist. Then she flung up her head as if in sudden recollection of their position, and terror flared in her dark eyes.

'Haste!' she whispered urgently. 'It is past midnight. You must be gone.'

'But won't they skin you alive for stealing these keys?'

'They'll never know. If the black men remember in the morning who gave them the wine, they will not dare admit the keys were stolen from them while they were drunk. The key that I could not obtain is the one that unlocks this door. You must make your way to freedom through the pits. What awful perils lurk beyond that door I cannot even guess. But greater danger lurks for you if you remain in this cell.

'King Tarascus has returned—'

'What? Tarascus?'

'Aye! He has returned, in great secrecy, and not long ago he descended into the pits and then came out again, pale and shaking, like a man who has dared a great hazard. I heard him whisper to his squire, Arideus, that despite Xaltotun you should die.'

'What of Xaltotun?' murmured Conan.

He felt her shudder.

'Do not speak of him!' she whispered. 'Demons are often summoned by the sound of their names. The slaves say that

47

he lies in his chamber, behind a bolted door, dreaming the dreams of the black lotus. I believe that even Tarascus secretly fears him, or he would slay you openly. But he has been in the pits tonight, and what he did here, only Mitra knows.'

'I wonder if that could have been Tarascus who fumbled at my cell door awhile ago?' muttered Conan.

'Here is a dagger!' she whispered, pressing something through the bars. His eager fingers closed on an object familiar to their touch. 'Go quickly through yonder door, turn to the left and make your way along the cells until you come to a stone stair. On your life do not stray from the line of cells! Climb the stair and open the door at the top; one of the keys will fit it. If it be the will of Mitra, I will await you there.' Then she was gone, with a patter of light slippered feet.

Conan shrugged his shoulders, and turned toward the farther grille. This might be some diabolical trap planned by Tarascus, but plunging headlong into a snare was less abhorrent to Conan's temperament than sitting meekly to await his doom. He inspected the weapon the girl had given him, and smiled grimly. Whatever else she might be she was proven by that dagger to be a person of practical intelligence. It was no slender stiletto, selected because of a jeweled hilt or gold guard, fitted only for dainty murder in milady's boudoir; it was a forthright poniard, a warrior's weapon, broad-bladed, fifteen inches in length, tapering to a diamond-sharp point.

He grunted with satisfaction. The feel of the hilt cheered him and gave him a glow of confidence. Whatever webs of conspiracy were drawn about him, whatever trickery and treachery ensnared him, this knife was real. The great muscles of his right arm swelled in anticipation of murderous blows.

He tried the farther door, fumbling with the keys as he did so. It was not locked. Yet he remembered the black man locking it. That furtive, bent figure, then had been no jailer seeing that the bolts were in place. He had unlocked the door, instead. There was a sinister suggestion about that unlocked door. But Conan did not hesitate. He pushed open the grille and stepped from the dungeon into the outer darkness.

As he had thought, the door did not open into another corridor. The flagged floor stretched away under his feet, and the line of cells ran away to right and left behind him, but he could not make out the other limits of the place into which he had come. He could see neither the roof nor any other wall. The moonlight filtered into the vastness only through the grilles of the cells, and was almost lost in the darkness. Less keen eyes than his could scarcely have discerned the dim gray patches that floated before each cell door.

Turning to the left, he moved swiftly and noiselessly along the line of dungeons, his bare feet making no sound on the flags. He glanced briefly into each dungeon as he passed it. They were all empty, but locked. In some he caught the glimmer of naked white bones. These pits were a relic of a grimmer age, constructed long ago when Belverus was a fortress rather than a city. But evidently their more recent use had been more extensive than the world guessed.

Ahead of him, presently, he saw the dim outline of a stair sloping sharply upward, and knew it must be the stair he sought. Then he whirled suddenly, crouching in the deep shadows at his foot.

Somewhere behind him something was moving – something bulky and stealthy that padded on feet which were not human feet. He was looking down the long row of cells, before each one of which lay a square of dim gray light that was little more than a patch of less dense darkness. But he saw something moving along these squares. What it was he could not tell, but it was heavy and huge, and yet it moved with more than human ease and swiftness. He glimpsed it as it moved across the squares of gray, then lost it as it merged in the expanses of shadow between. It was uncanny, in its stealthy advance, appearing and disappearing like a blur of the vision.

He heard the bars rattle as it tried each door in turn. Now it had reached the cell he had so recently quitted, and the door swung open as it tugged. He saw a great bulky shape limned faintly and briefly in the gray doorway, and then the thing had vanished into the dungeon. Sweat beaded Conan's face and hands. Now he knew why Tarascus had come so subtly to his door, and later had fled so swiftly. The king had unlocked his door, and somewhere in these hellish pits had opened a cell or cage that held some grim monstrosity.

Now the thing was emerging from the cell and was again advancing up the corridor, its misshapen head close to the ground. It paid no more heed to the locked doors. It was smelling out his trail. He saw it more plainly now; the gray light limned a giant anthropomorphic body, but vaster of bulk and girth than any man. It went on two legs, though it stooped forward, and it was grayish and shaggy, its thick coat shot with silver. Its head was a grisly travesty of the human, its long arms hung nearly to the ground.

Conan knew it at last – understood the meaning of those crushed and broken bones in the dungeon, and recognized the haunter of the pits. It was a gray ape; one of the grisly man-eaters from the forests that wave on the mountainous eastern shores of the Sea of Vilayet. Half mythical and altogether horrible, these apes were the goblins of Hyborian legendry, and were in reality ogres of the natural world, cannibals and murderers of the nighted forests.

He knew it scented his presence, for it was coming swiftly now, rolling its barrel-like body rapidly along on its short, mighty, bowed legs. He cast a quick glance up the long stair, but knew that the thing would be on his back before he could mount to the distant door. He chose to meet it face to face.

Conan stepped out into the nearest square of moonlight, so as to have all the advantage of illumination that he could; for the beast, he knew, could see better than himself in the dark. Instantly the brute saw him; its great yellow tusks gleamed in the shadows, but it made no sound. Creatures of night and the silence, the gray apes of Vilayet were voiceless. But in its dim, hideous features, which were a bestial travesty of a human face, showed ghastly exultation.

Conan stood poised, watching the oncoming monster without a quiver. He knew he must stake his life on one thrust; there would be no chance for another; nor would there de time to strike and spring away. The first blow must kill, and kill instantly, if he hoped to survive that awful grapple. He swept his gaze over the short, squat throat, the hairy swag-belly, and the mighty breast, swelling in giant arches like twin shields. It must be the heart; better to risk the blade being deflected by the heavy ribs than to strike in where a stroke was not instantly fatal. With full realization of the odds, Conan matched his speed of eye and hand and his muscular power against the brute might and ferocity of the man-eater. He must meet the brute breast to breast, strike a death-blow, and then trust to the ruggedness of his frame to survive the instant of manhandling that was certain to be his.

As the ape came rolling in on him, swinging wide its terrible arms, he plunged in between them and struck with all his desperate power. He felt the blade sink to the hilt in the hairy breast, and instantly, releasing it, he ducked his head and bunched his whole body into one compact mass of knotted muscles, and as he did so he grasped the closing arms and drove his knee fiercely into the monster's belly, bracing himself against that crushing grapple.

For one dizzy instant he felt as if he were being dismembered in the grip of an earthquake; then suddenly he was free, sprawling on the floor, and the monster was gasping out its life beneath him, its red eyes turned upward, the hilt of the poniard quivering in its breast. His desperate stab had gone home.

Conan was panting as if after long conflict, trembling in every limb. Some of his joints felt as if they had been dislocated, and blood dripped from scratches on his skin where the monster's talons had ripped; his muscles and tendons had been savagely wrenched and twisted. If the beast had lived a second longer, it would surely have dismembered him. But the Cimmerian's mighty strength had resisted, for the fleeting instant it had endured, the dying convulsion of the ape that would have torn a lesser man limb from limb.

6 – THE THRUST OF A KNIFE

CONAN STOOPED and tore the knife from the monster's breast. Then he went swiftly up the stair. What other shapes of fear the darkness held he could not guess, but he had no desire to encounter any more. This touch-and-go sort of battling was too strenuous even for the giant Cimmerian. The moonlight was fading from the floor, the darkness closing in, and something like panic pursued him up the stair. He breathed a gusty sigh of relief when he reached the head, and felt the third key turn in the lock. He opened the door slightly, and craned his neck to peer through, half expecting an attack from some human or bestial enemy.

He looked into a bare stone corridor, dimly lighted, and a slender, supple figure stood before the door.

'Your Majesty!' It was a low, vibrant cry, half in relief and half in rear. The girl sprang to his side, then hesitated as if abashed.

'You bleed,' she said. 'You have been hurt!'

He brushed aside the implication with an impatient hand.

'Scratches that wouldn't hurt a baby. Your skewer came in handy, though. But for it, Tarascus's monkey would be cracking my shin-bones for the marrow right now. But what now?'

'Follow me,' she whispered. 'I will lead you outside the city wall. I have a horse concealed there.'

She turned to lead the way down the corridor, but he laid a heavy hand on her naked shoulder.

'Walk beside me,' he instructed her softly, passing his massive arm about her lithe waist. 'You've played me fair so far, and I'm inclined to believe in you; but I've lived this long only because I've trusted no one too far, man or woman. So! Now if you play me false you won't live to enjoy the jest.'

She did not flinch at sight of the reddened poniard or the contact of his hard muscles about her supple body.

'Cut me down without mercy if I play you false,' she answered. 'The very feel of your arm about me, even in menace, is as the fulfillment of a dream.'

The vaulted corridor ended at a door, which she opened. Outside lay another black man, a giant in turban and silk loin-cloth, with a curved sword lying on the flags near his hand. He did not move.

'I drugged his wine,' she whispered, swerving to avoid the recumbent figure. 'He is the last, and outer, guard of the pits. None ever escaped from them before, and none has ever wished to seek them; so only these black men guard them. Only these of all the servants knew it was King Conan that Xaltotun brought a prisoner in his chariot. I was watching, sleepless, from an upper casement that opened into the court, while the other girls slept; for I knew that a battle was being fought, or had been fought, in the west, and I feared for you. . . .

'I saw the blacks carry you up the stair, and I recognized you in the torchlight. I slipped into this wing of the palace tonight, in time to see them carry you to the pits. I had not dared come here before nightfall. You must have lain in drugged senselessness all day in Xaltotun's chamber.

'Oh, let us be wary! Strange things are afoot in the palace tonight. The slaves said that Xaltotun slept as he often sleeps, drugged by the lotus of Stygia, but Tarascus is in the palace. He entered secretly, through the postern, wrapped in his cloak which was dusty as with long travel, and attended only by his squire, the lean silent Arideus. I cannot understand, but I am afraid.'

52

They came out at the foot of a narrow, winding stair, and mounting it, passed through a narrow panel which she slid aside. When they had passed through, she slipped it back in place, and it became merely a portion of the ornate wall. They were in a more spacious corridor, carpeted and tapestried, over which hanging lamps shed a golden glow.

Conan listened intently, but he heard no sound throughout the palace. He did not know in what part of the palace he was, or in which direction lay the chamber of Xaltotun. The girl was trembling as she drew him along the corridor, to halt presently beside an alcove masked with satin tapestry. Drawing this aside, she motioned for him to step into the niche, and whispered: 'Wait here! Beyond that door at the end of the corridor we are likely to meet slaves or eunuchs at any time of the day or night. I will go and see if the way is clear, before we essay it.'

Instantly his hair-trigger suspicions were aroused.

'Are you leading me into a trap?'

Tears sprang into her dark eyes. She sank to her knees and seized his muscular hand.

'Oh, my king, do not mistrust me now!' Her voice shook with desperate urgency. 'If you doubt and hesitate, we are lost! Why should I bring you up out of the pits to betray you now?'

'All right,' he muttered. 'I'll trust you; though, by Crom, the habits of a lifetime are not easily put aside. Yet I wouldn't harm you now, if you brought all the swordsmen in Nemedia upon me. But for you, Tarascus's cursed ape would have come upon me in chains and unarmed. Do as you wish, girl.'

Kissing his hands, she sprang lithely up and ran down the corridor, to vanish through a heavy double door.

He glanced after her, wondering if he was a fool to trust her; then he shrugged his mighty shoulders and pulled the satin hangings together, masking his refuge. It was not strange that a passionate young beauty should be risking her life to aid him; such things had happened often enough in his life. Many women had looked on him with favor, in the days of his wanderings, and in the time of his kingship.

Yet he did not remain motionless in the alcove, waiting for her return. Following his instincts, he explored the niche for another exit, and presently found one – the opening of a narrow passage, masked by the tapestries, that ran to an ornately carved door, barely visible in the dim light that filtered in from the outer corridor. And as he stared into it, somewhere beyond that carven door he heard the sound of another door opening and shutting, and then a low mumble of voices. The familiar sound of one of those voices caused a sinister expression to cross his dark face. Without hesitation he glided down the passage, and crouched like a stalking panther beside the door. It was not locked, and manipulating it delicately, he pushed it open a crack, with a reckless disregard for possible consequences that only he could have explained or defended.

It was masked on the other side by tapestries, but through a thin slit in the velvet he looked into a chamber lit by a candle on an ebony table. There were two men in that chamber. One was a scarred, sinister-looking ruffian in leather breeks and ragged cloak; the other was Tarascus, king of Nemedia.

Tarascus seemed ill at ease. He was slightly pale, and he kept starting and glancing about him, as if expecting and fearing to hear some sound or footstep.

'Go swiftly and at once,' he was saying. '*He* is deep in drugged slumber, but I know not when he may awaken.'

'Strange to hear words of fear issuing from the lips of Tarascus,' rumbled the other in a harsh, deep voice.

The king frowned.

'I fear no common man, as you well know. But when I saw the cliffs fall at Valkia I knew that this devil we had resurrected was no charlatan. I fear his powers, because I do not know the full extent of them. But I know that somehow they are connected with this accursed thing which I have stolen from him. It brought him back to life; so it must be the source of his sorcery.

'He had it hidden well; but following my secret order a slave spied on him and saw him place it in a golden chest, and saw where he hid the chest. Even so, I would not have dared steal it had Xaltotun himself not been sunk in lotus slumber.

'I believe it is the secret of his power. With it, Orastes brought him back to life. With it he will make us all slaves, if we are not wary. So take it and cast it into the sea as I have bidden you. And be sure you are so far from land that neither tide nor storm can wash it up on the beach. You have been paid.'

'So I have,' grunted the ruffian. 'And I owe more than gold to you, king; I owe you a debt of gratitude. Even thieves can be grateful.'

'Whatever debt you may feel you owe me,' answered

Tarascus, 'will be paid when you have hurled this thing into the sea.'

'I'll ride to Zingara and take ship from Kordava,' promised the other. 'I dare not show my head in Argos, because of the matter of a murder or so—'

'I care not, so it is done. Here it is; a horse awaits you in the court. Go, and go swiftly!'

Something passed between them, something that flamed like living fire. Conan had only a brief glimpse of it; and then the ruffian pulled a slouch hat over his eyes, drew his cloak about his shoulder, and hurried from the chamber. And as the door closed behind him, Conan moved with the devastating fury of unchained blood-lust. He had held himself in check as long as he could. The sight of his enemy so near him set his wild blood seething and swept away all caution and restraint.

Tarascus was turning toward an inner door when Conan tore aside the hangings and leaped like a blood-mad panther into the room. Tarascus wheeled, but even before he could recognize his attacker, Conan's poniard ripped into him.

But the blow was not mortal, as Conan knew the instant he struck. His foot had caught in a fold of the curtains and tripped him as he leaped. The point fleshed itself in Tarascus's shoulder and plowed down along his ribs, and the king of Nemedia screamed.

The impact of the blow and Conan's lunging body hurled him back against the table and it toppled and the candle went out. They were both carried to the floor by the violence of Conan's rush, and the foot of the tapestry hampered them both in its folds. Conan was stabbing blindly in the dark, Tarascus screaming in a frenzy of panicky terror. As if fear lent him superhuman energy, Tarascus tore free and blundered away in the darkness, shrieking: 'Help! Guards! Arideus! Orastes! *Orastes!*'

Conan rose, kicking himself free of the tangling tapestries and the broken table, cursing with the bitterness of his blood-thirsty disappointment. He was confused, and ignorant of the plan of the palace. The yells of Tarascus were still resounding in the distance, and a wild outcry was bursting forth in answer. The Nemedian had escaped him in the darkness, and Conan did not know which way he had gone. The Cimmerian's rash stroke for vengeance had failed, and there remained only the task of saving his own hide if he could.

Swearing luridly, Conan ran back down the passage and

into the alcove, glaring out into the lighted corridor, just as Zenobia came running up it, her dark eyes dilated with terror.

'Oh, what has happened?' she cried. 'The palace is roused! I swear I have not betrayed you—'

'No, it was I who stirred up this hornets' nest,' he grunted. 'I tried to pay off a score. What's the shortest way out of this?'

She caught his wrist and ran fleetly down the corridor. But before they reached the heavy door at the other end, muffled shouts arose from behind it and the portals began to shake under an assault from the other side. Zenobia wrung her hands and whimpered.

'We are cut off! I locked that door as I returned through it. But they will burst it in a moment. The way to the postern gate lies through it.'

Conan wheeled. Up the corridor, though still out of sight, he heard a rising clamor that told him his foes were behind as well as before him.

'Quick! Into this door!' the girl cried desperately, running across the corridor and throwing open the door of a chamber.

Conan followed her through, and then threw the gold catch behind them. They stood in an ornately furnished chamber, empty but for themselves, and she drew him to a gold-barred window, through which he saw trees and shrubbery.

'You are strong,' she panted. 'If you can tear these bars away, you may yet escape. The garden is full of guards, but the shrubs are thick, and you may avoid them. The southern wall is also the outer wall of the city. Once over that, you have a chance to get away. A horse is hidden for you in a thicket beside the road that runs westward, a few hundred paces to the south of the fountain of Thrallos. You know where it is?'

'Aye! But what of you? I had meant to take you with me.'

A flood of joy lighted her beautiful face.

'Then my cup of happiness is brimming! But I will not hamper your escape. Burdened with me you would fail. Nay, do not fear for me. They will never suspect that I aided you willingly. Go! What you have just said will glorify my life throughout the long years.'

He caught her up in his iron arms, crushed her slim, vibrant figure to him and kissed her fiercely on eyes, cheeks, throat, and lips, until she lay panting in his embrace; gusty and tempestuous as a storm wind, even his love-making was violent.

'I'll go,' he muttered. 'But by Crom, I'll come for you some day!'

Wheeling, he gripped the gold bars and tore them from their sockets with one tremendous wrench; threw a leg over the sill and went down swiftly, clinging to the ornaments on the wall. He hit the ground running and melted like a shadow into the maze of towering rose-bushes and spreading trees. The one look he cast back over his shoulder showed him Zenobia leaning over the window-sill, her arms stretched after him in mute farewell and renunciation.

Guards were running through the garden, all converging toward the palace, where the clamor momentarily grew louder – tall men, in burnished cuirasses and crested helmets of polished bronze. The starlight struck glints from their gleaming armor, among the trees, betraying their every movement; but the sound of their coming ran far before them. To Conan, wilderness-bred, their rush through the shrubbery was like the blundering stampede of cattle. Some of them passed within a few feet of where he lay flat in a thick cluster of bushes, and never guessed his presence. With the palace as their goal, they were oblivious to all else about them. When they had gone shouting on, he rose and fled through the garden with no more noise than a panther would have made.

So quickly he came to the southern wall, and mounted the steps that led to the parapet. The wall was made to keep people out, not in. No sentry patrolling the battlements was in sight. Crouching by an embrasure he glanced back at the great palace rearing above the cypresses behind him. Lights blazed from every window, and he could see figures flitting back and forth across them like puppets on invisible strings. He grinned hardly, shook his fist in a gesture of farewell and menace, and let himself over the outer rim of the parapet.

A low tree, a few yards below the parapet, received Conan's weight, as he dropped noiselessly into the branches. An instant later he was racing through the shadows with the swinging hillman's stride that eats up long miles.

Gardens and pleasure villas surrounded the walls of Belverus. Drowsy slaves, sleeping by their watchmen's pikes, did not see the swift and furtive figure that scaled walls, crossed alleys made by the arching branches of trees, and threaded a noiseless way through orchards and vineyards. Watch-dogs woke and lifted their deep-booming clamor at a gliding shadow, half scented, half sensed, and then it was gone.

In a chamber of the palace, Tarascus writhed and cursed on a blood-spattered couch, under the deft, quick fingers of Orastes. The palace was thronged with wide-eyed, trembling servitors, but the chamber where the king lay was empty save for himself and the renegade priest.

'Are you sure he still sleeps?' Tarascus demanded again, setting his teeth against the bite of the herb juices with which Orastes was bandaging the long, ragged gash in his shoulder and ribs. 'Ishtar, Mitra, and Set! That burns like the molten pitch of Hell!'

'Which you would be experiencing even now, but for your good fortune,' remarked Orastes. 'Whoever wielded that knife struck to kill. Yes, I have told you that Xaltotun still sleeps. Why are you so urgent upon that point? What has he to do with this?'

'You know nothing of what has passed in the palace tonight?' Tarascus searched the priest's countenance with burning intensity.

'Nothing. As you know, I have been employed in translating manuscripts for Xaltotun, for some months now, transcribing esoteric volumes written in the younger languages into script he can read. He was well versed in all the tongues and scripts of his day, but he has not yet learned all the newer languages, and to save time he has me translate these works for him, to learn if any new knowledge has been discovered since his time. I did not know that he had returned last night until he sent for me and told me of the battle. Then I returned to my studies, nor did I know that you had returned until the clamor in the palace brought me out of my cell.'

'Then you do not know that Xaltotun brought the king of Aquilonia a captive to this palace?'

Orastes shook his head, without particular surprise.

'Xaltotun merely said that Conan would oppose us no more. I supposed that he had fallen, but did not ask the details.'

'Xaltotun saved his life when I would have slain him,' snarled Tarascus. 'I saw his purpose instantly. He would hold Conan captive to use as a club against us – against Amalric, against Valerius, and against myself. So long as Conan lives he is a threat, a unifying factor for Aquilonia,

58

that might be used to compel us into courses we would not otherwise follow. I mistrust this undead Pythonian. Of late I have begun to fear him.

'I followed him, some hours after he had departed eastward. I wished to learn what he intended doing with Conan. I found that he had imprisoned him in the pits. I intended to see that the barbarian died, in spite of Xaltotun. And I accomplished—'

A cautious knock sounded at the door.

'That's Arideus,' grunted Tarascus. 'Let him in.'

The saturnine squire entered, his eyes blazing with suppressed excitement.

'How, Arideus??' exclaimed Tarascus. 'Have you found the man who attacked me?'

'You did not see him, my lord?' asked Arideus, as one who would assure himself of a fact he already knows to exist. 'You did not recognize him?'

'No. It happened so quick, and the candle was out – all I could think of was that it was some devil loosed on me by Xaltotun's magic—'

'The Pythonian sleeps in his barred and bolted room. But I have been in the pits.' Arideus twitched his lean shoulders excitedly.

'Well, speak, man!' exclaimed Tarascus impatiently. 'What did you find there?'

'An empty dungeon,' whispered the squire. 'The corpse of the great ape!'

'*What?*' Tarascus started upright, and blood gushed from his opened wound.

'Aye! The man-eater is dead – stabbed through the heart – and Conan is gone!'

Tarascus was gray of face as he mechanically allowed Orastes to force him prostrate again and the priest renewed work upon his mangled flesh.

'Conan!' he repeated. 'Not a crushed corpse – escaped! Mitra! He is no man, but a devil himself! I thought Xaltotun was behind this wound. I see now. Gods and devils! It was Conan who stabbed me! Arideus!'

'Aye, Your Majesty!'

'Search every nook in the palace. He may be skulking through the dark corridors now like a hungry tiger. Let no niche escape your scrutiny, and beware. It is not a civilized man you hunt, but a blood-mad barbarian whose strength and ferocity are those of a wild beast. Scour the palace-grounds and the city. Throw a cordon about the walls. If you find he has escaped from the city, as he may well do, take a troop of horsemen and follow him. Once past the walls, it will be like hunting a wolf through the hills. But haste, and you may yet catch him.'

'This is a matter which requires more than ordinary human wits,' said Orastes. 'Perhaps we should seek Xaltotun's advice.'

'No!' exclaimed Tarascus violently. 'Let the troopers pursue Conan and slay him. Xaltotun can hold no grudge against us if we kill a prisoner to prevent his escape.'

'Well,' said Orastes, 'I am no Acheronian, but I am versed in some of the arts, and the control of certain spirits which have cloaked themselves in material substance. Perhaps I can aid you in this matter.'

The fountain of Thrallos stood in a clustered ring of oaks beside the road a mile from the walls of the city. Its musical tinkle reached Conan's ears through the silence of the starlight. He drank deep of its icy stream, and then hurried southward toward a small, dense thicket he saw there. Rounding it, he saw a great white horse tied among the bushes. Heaving a deep gutsy sigh he reached it with one stride – a mocking laugh brought him about, glaring.

A dully glinting, mail-clad figure moved out of the shadows into the starlight. This was no plumed and burnished palace guardsman. It was a tall man in morion and gray chain-mail – one of the Adventurers, a class of warriors peculiar to Nemedia; men who had not attained to the wealth and position of knighthood, or had fallen from that estate; hard-bitten fighters, dedicating their lives to war and adventure. They constituted a class of their own, sometimes commanding troops, but themselves accountable to no man but the king. Conan knew that he could have been discovered by no more dangerous a foeman.

A quick glance among the shadows convinced him that the man was alone, and he expanded his great chest slightly, digging his toes into the turf, as his thews coiled tensely.

'I was riding for Belverus on Amalric's business,' said the Adventurer, advancing warily. The starlight was a long sheen on the great two-handed sword he bore naked in his hand. 'A horse whinnied to mine from the thicket. I investigated and thought it strange a steed should be tethered here. I waited – and lo, I have caught a rare prize!'

The Adventurers lived by their swords.

'I know you,' muttered the Nemedian. 'You are Conan, king of Aquilonia. I thought I saw you die in the valley of the Valkia, but—'

Conan sprang as a dying tiger springs. Practiced fighter though the Adventurer was, he did not realize the desperate quickness that lurks in barbaric sinews. He was caught off guard, his heavy sword half lifted. Before he could either strike or parry, the king's poniard sheathed itself in his throat, above the gorget, slanting downward into his heart. With a choked gurgle he reeled and went down, and Conan ruthlessly tore his blade free as his victim fell. The white horse snorted violently and shied at the sight and scent of blood on the dagger.

Glaring down at his lifeless enemy, dripping poniard in hand, sweat glistening on his broad breast, Conan poised like a statue, listening intently. In the woods about there was no sound, save for the sleepy cheep of awakened birds. But in the city, a mile away, he heard the strident blare of a trumpet.

Hastily he bent over the fallen man. A few seconds' search convinced him that whatever message the man might have borne was intended to be conveyed by word of mouth. But he did not pause in his task. It was not many hours until dawn. A few minutes later the white horse was galloping westward along the white road, and the rider wore the gray mail of a Nemedian Adventurer.

7 – THE RENDING OF THE VEIL

CONAN KNEW his only chance of escape lay in speed. He did not even consider hiding somewhere near Belverus until the chase passed on; he was certain that the uncanny ally of Tarascus would be able to ferret him out. Besides, he was not one to skulk and hide; an open fight or an open chase, either suited his temperament better. He had a long start, he knew. He would lead them a grinding race for the border.

Zenobia had chosen well in selecting the white horse. His speed, toughness, and endurance were obvious. The girl knew weapons and horses, and, Conan reflected with some satisfaction, she knew men. He rode westward at a gait that ate up the miles.

It was a sleeping land through which he rode, past grove-sheltered villages and white-walled villas amid spacious fields and orchards that grew sparser as he fared westward. As the villages thinned, the land grew more rugged, and the keeps that frowned from eminences told of centuries of border war. But none rode down from those castles to challenge or halt him. The lords of the keeps were following the banner of Amalric; the pennons that were wont to wave over these towers were now floating over the Aquilonian plains.

When the last huddled village fell behind him, Conan left the road, which was beginning to bend toward the northwest, toward the distant passes. To keep to the road would mean to pass by border towers, still garrisoned with armed men who would not allow him to pass unquestioned. He knew there would be no patrols riding the border marches on either side, as in ordinary times; but there were those towers, and with dawn there would probably be cavalcades of returning soldiers with wounded men in oxcarts.

This road from Belverus was the only road that crossed the border for fifty miles from north to south. It followed a series of passes through the hills, and on either hand lay a wide expanse of wild, sparsely inhabited mountains. He maintained his due westerly direction, intending to cross the border deep in the wilds of the hills that lay to the south of the passes. It was a shorter route, more arduous, but safer for a hunted fugitive. One man on a horse could traverse country an army would find impassable.

But at dawn he had not reached the hills; they were a long, low, blue rampart stretching along the horizon ahead of him. Here there were neither farms nor villages, no white-walled villas looming among the clustering trees. The dawn wind stirred the tall stiff grass, and there was nothing but the long rolling swells of brown earth, covered with dry grass, and in the distance the gaunt walls of a stronghold on a low hill. Too many Aquilonian raiders had crossed the mountains in not too distant days for the countryside to be thickly settled as it was farther to the east.

Dawn ran like a prairie fire across the grasslands, and high overhead sounded a weird crying as a straggling wedge of wild geese winged swiftly southward. In a grassy swale, Conan halted and unsaddled his mount. Its sides were heaving, its coat plastered with sweat. He had pushed it unmercifully through the hours before dawn.

While it munched the brittle grass and rolled, he lay at

the crest of the low slope, staring eastward. Far away to the northward he could see the road he had left, streaming like a white ribbon over a distant rise. No black dots moved along that glistening ribbon. There was no sign about the castle in the distance to indicate that the keepers had noticed the lone wayfarer.

An hour later the land still stretched bare. The only sign of life was a glint of steel on the far-off battlements, a raven in the sky that wheeled backward and forth, dipping and rising as if seeking something. Conan saddled and rode westward at a more leisurely gait.

As he topped the farther crest of the slope, a raucous screaming burst out over his head, and looking up, he saw the raven flapping high above him, cawing incessantly. As he rode on, it followed him, maintaining its position and making the morning hideous with its strident cries, heedless of his efforts to drive it away.

This kept up for hours, until Conan's teeth were on edge, and he felt that he would give half his kingdom to be allowed to wring that black neck.

'Devils of Hell!' he roared in futile rage, shaking his mailed fist at the frantic bird. 'Why do you harry me with your squawking? Begone, you black spawn of perdition, and peck for wheat in the farmers' fields!'

He was ascending the first pitch of the hills, and he seemed to hear an echo of the bird's clamor far behind him. Turning in his saddle, he presently made out another black dot hanging in the blue. Beyond that again he caught the glint of the afternoon sun on steel. That could mean only one thing: armed men. And they were not riding along the beaten road, which was out of his sight beyond the horizon. They were following him.

His face grew grim and he shivered slightly as he stared at the raven that wheeled high above him.

'So it is more than the whim of a brainless beast?' he muttered. 'Those riders cannot see you, spawn of hell; but the other bird can see you, and they can see him. You follow me, he follows you, they follow him. Are you only a craftily trained feathered creature, or some devil in the form of a bird? Did Xaltotun set you on my trail? Are *you* Xaltotun?'

Only a strident screech answered him, a screech vibrating with harsh mockery.

Conan wasted no more breath on his dusky betrayer. Grimly he settled to the long grind of the hills. He dared not push the horse too hard; the rest he had allowed it had not been enough to freshen it. He was still far ahead of his pursuers, but they would cut down that lead steadily. It was almost a certainty that their horses were fresher than his, for they had undoubtedly changed mounts at that castle he had passed.

The going grew rougher, the scenery more rugged, steep grassy slopes pitching up to densely timbered mountainsides. Here, he knew, he might elude his hunters, but for that hellish bird that squalled incessantly above him. He could no longer see them in this broken country, but he was certain that they still followed him, guided unerringly by their feathered allies. That black shape became like a demoniac incubus, hounding him through measureless hells. The stones he hurled with a curse went wide or fell harmless, though in his youth he had felled hawks on the wing.

The horse was tiring fast. Conan recognized the grim finality of his position. He sensed an inexorable driving fate behind all this. He could not escape. He was as much a captive as he had been in the pits of Belverus. But he was no son of the Orient to yield passively to what seemed inevitable. If he could not escape, he would at least take some of his foes into eternity with him. He turned into a wide thicket of larches that masked a slope, looking for a place to turn at bay.

Then ahead of him there rang a strange, shrill scream, human yet weirdly timbred. An instant later he had pushed through a screen of branches, and saw the source of that eldritch cry. In a small glade below him four soldiers in Nemedian chain-mail were binding a noose about the neck of a gaunt old woman in peasant garb. A heap of fagots, bound with cord on the ground near by, showed what her occupation had been when surprised by these stragglers.

Conan felt fury swell his heart as he looked silently down and saw the ruffians dragging her toward a tree whose low-spreading branches were obviously intended to act as a gibbet. He had crossed the frontier an hour ago. He was standing on his own soil, watching the murder of one of his own subjects. The old woman was struggling with surprising strength and energy, and as he watched, she lifted her head and voiced again the strange, weird, far-carrying call he had heard before. It was echoed as if in mockery by the raven flapping above the trees. The soldiers laughed roughly, and one struck her in the mouth.

Conan swung from his weary steed and dropped down the

face of the rocks, landing with a clang of mail on the grass. The four men wheeled at the sound and drew their swords, gaping at the mailed giant who faced them, sword in hand.

Conan laughed harshly. His eyes were bleak as flint.

'Dogs!' he said without passion and without mercy. 'Do Nemedian jackals set themselves up as executioners and hang my subjects at will? First you must take the head of their king. Here I stand, awaiting your lordly pleasure!'

The soldiers stared at him uncertainly as he strode toward them.

'Who is this madman?' growled a bearded ruffian. 'He wears Nemedian mail, but speaks with an Aquilonian accent.'

'No matter,' quoth another. 'Cut him down, and then we'll hang the old hag.'

And so saying he ran at Conan, lifting his sword. But before he could strike, the king's great blade lashed down, splitting helmet and skull. The man fell before him, but the others were hardy rogues. They gave tongue like wolves and surged about the long figure in the gray mail, and the clamor and din of steel drowned the cries of the circling raven.

Conan did not shout. His eyes coals of blue fire and his lips smiling bleakly, he lashed right and left with his two-handed sword. For all his size he was quick as a cat on his feet, and he was constantly in motion, presenting a moving target so that thrusts and swings cut empty air oftener than not. Yet when he struck he was perfectly balanced, and his blows fell with devastating power. Three of the four were down, dying in their own blood, and the fourth was bleeding from half a dozen wounds, stumbling in headlong retreat as he parried frantically, when Conan's spur caught in the surcoat of one of the fallen men.

The king stumbled, and before he could catch himself the Nemedian, with the frenzy of desperation, rushed him so savagely that Conan staggered and fell sprawling over the corpse. The Nemedian croaked in triumph and sprang forward, lifting his great sword with both hands over his right shoulder, as he braced his legs wide for the stroke – and then, over the prostrate king, something huge and hairy shot like a thunderbolt full on the soldier's breast, and his yelp of triumph turned to a shriek of death.

Conan, scrambling up, saw the man lying dead with his throat torn out, and a great grey wolf stood over him, head sunk as it smelt the blood that formed a pool on the grass.

The king turned as the old woman spoke to him. She stood

straight and tall before him, and in spite of her ragged garb, her features, clear-cut and aquiline, and her keen black eyes, were not those of a common peasant woman. She called to the wolf and it trotted to her side like a great dog and rubbed its giant shoulder against her knee, while it gazed at Conan with great green lambent eyes. Absently she laid her hand upon its mighty neck, and so the two stood regarding the king of Aquilonia. He found their steady gaze disquieting, though there was no hostility in it.

'Men say King Conan died beneath the stones and dirt when the cliffs crumbled by Valkia,' she said in a deep, strong, resonant voice.

'So they say,' he growled. He was in no mood for controversy, and he thought of those armored riders who were pushing nearer every moment. The raven above him cawed stridently, and he cast an involuntary glare upward, grinding his teeth in a spasm of nervous irritation.

Up on the ledge the white horse stood with drooping head. The old woman looked at it, and then at the raven; and then she lifted a strange weird cry as she had before. As if recognizing the call, the raven wheeled, suddenly mute, and raced eastward. But before it got out of sight, the shadow of mighty wings fell across it. An eagle soared up from the tangle of trees, and rising above it, swooped and struck the black messenger to the earth. The strident voice of betrayal was stilled forever.

'Crom!' muttered Conan, staring at the old woman. 'Are you a magician, too?'

'I am Zelata,' she said. 'The people of the valleys call me a witch. Was that child of the night guiding armed men on your trail?'

'Aye.' She did not seem to think the answer fantastic. 'They cannot be far behind me.'

'Lead your horse and follow me, King Conan,' she said briefly.

Without comment he mounted the rocks and brought his horse down to the glade by a circuitous path. As he came he saw the eagle reappear, dropping lazily down from the sky, and rest an instant on Zelata's shoulder, spreading its great wings lightly so as not to crush her with its weight.

Without a word she led the way, the great wolf trotting at her side, the eagle soaring above her. Through deep thickets and along tortuous ledges poised over deep ravines she led him, and finally along a narrow precipice-edged path

66

to a curious dwelling of stone, half hut, half cavern, beneath a cliff hidden among the gorges and crags. The eagle flew to the pinnacle of this cliff, and perched there like a motionless sentinel.

Still silent, Zelata stabled the horse in a near-by cave, with leaves and grass piled high for provender, and a tiny spring bubbling in the dim recesses.

In the hut she seated the king on a rude, hide-covered bench, and she herself sat upon a low stool before the tiny fireplace, while she made a fire of tamarisk chunks and prepared a frugal meal. The great wolf drowsed beside he , facing the fire, his huge head sunk on his paws, his ears twi hing in his dreams.

'You do not fear to sit in the hut of a witch?' she asked, breaking her silence at last.

An impatient shrug of his gray-mailed shoulders was her guest's only reply. She gave into his hands a wooden dish heaped with dried fruits, cheese, and barley bread, and a great pot of the heady upland beer, brewed from barley grown in the high valleys.

'I have found the brooding silence of the glens more pleasing than the babble of city streets,' she said. 'The children of the wild are kinder than the children of men.' Her hand briefly stroked the ruff of the sleeping wolf. 'My children were afar from me today, or I had not needed your sword, my king. They were coming at my call.'

'What grudge had those Nemedian dogs against you?' Conan demanded.

'Skulkers from the invading army straggle all over the countryside, from the frontier to Tarantia,' she answered. 'The foolish villagers in the valleys told them that I had a store of gold hidden away, so as to divert their attention from their villages. They demanded treasure from me, and my answers angered them. But neither skulkers nor the men who pursue you, nor any raven will find you here.'

He shook his head, eating ravenously.

'I'm for Tarantia.'

She shook her head.

'You thrust your head into the dragon's jaws. Best seek refuge abroad. The heart is gone from your kingdom.'

'What do you mean?' he demanded. 'Battles have been lost before, yet wars won. A kingdom is not lost by a single defeat.'

'And you will go to Tarantia?'

'Aye. Prospero will be holding it against Amalric.'

'Are you sure?'

'Hell's devils, woman!' he exclaimed wrathfully. 'What else?'

She shook her head. 'I feel that it is otherwise. Let us see. Not lightly is the veil rent; yet I will rend it a little, and show you your capital city."

Conan did not see what she cast upon the fire, but the wolf whimpered in his dreams, and a green smoke gathered up and billowed into the hut. And as he watched, the walls and ceiling of the hut seemed to widen, to grow remote and vanish, merging with infinite immensities; the smoke rolled about him, blotting out everything. And in it forms moved and faded, and stood out in startling clarity.

He stared at the familiar towers and streets of Tarantia, where a mob seethed and screamed, and at the same time he was somehow able to see the banners of Nemedia moving inexorably westward through the smoke and flame of a pillaged land. In the great square of Tarantia the frantic throng milled and yammered, screaming that the king was dead, that the barons were girding themselves to divide the land between them, and that the rule of a king, even of Valerius, was better than anarchy. Prospero, shining in his armor, rode among them, trying to pacify them, bidding them trust Count Trocero, urging them to man the wall and aid his knights in defending the city. They turned on him, shrieking with fear and unreasoning rage, howling that he was Trocero's butcher, a more evil foe than Amalric himself. Offal and stones were hurled at his knights.

A slight blurring of the picture, that might have denoted a passing of time, and then Conan saw Prospero and his knights filing out of the gates and spurring southward. Behind him the city was in an uproar.

'Fools!' muttered Conan thickly. 'Fools! Why could they not trust Prospero? Zelata, if you are making game of me, with some trickery—'

'This has passed,' answered Zelata imperturbably, though somberly. 'It was the evening of the day that has passed when Prospero rode out of Tarantia, with the hosts of Amalric almost within sight. From the walls men saw the flame of their pillaging. So I read it in the smoke. At sunset the Nemedians rode into Tarantia, unopposed. Look! even now, in the royal hall of Tarantia—'

Abruptly Conan was looking into the great coronation

hall. Valerius stood on the regal dais, clad in ermine robes, and Amalric, still in his dusty, blood-stained armor, placed a rich and gleaming circlet on his yellow locks – the crown of Aquilonia! The people cheered; long lines of steel-clad Nemedian warriors looked grimly on, and nobles long in disfavor at Conan's court strutted and swaggered with the emblem of Valerius on their sleeves.

'Crom!' It was an explosive imprecation from Conan's lips as he started up, his great fists clenched into hammers, the veins on his temples knotting, his features convulsed. 'A Nemedian placing the crown of Aquilonia on that renegade – in the royal hall of Tarantia!'

As if dispelled by his violence, the smoke faded, and he saw Zelata's black eyes gleaming at him through the mist.

'You have seen – the people of your capital have forfeited the freedom you won for them by sweat and blood; they have sold themselves to the slavers and the butchers. They have shown that they do not trust their destiny. Can you rely upon them for the winning back of your kingdom?–

'They thought I was dead,' he grunted, recovering some of his poise. 'I have no son. Men can't be governed by a memory. What if the Nemedians have taken Tarantia? There still remain the provinces, the barons, and the people of the countrysides. Valerius has won an empty glory.'

'You are stubborn, as befits a fighter. I cannot show you the future, I cannot show you all the past. Nay, I show you nothing. I merely make you see windows opened in the veil by powers unguessed. Would you look into the past for a clue of the present?'

'Aye.' He seated himself abruptly.

Again the green smoke rose and billowed. Again images unfolded before him, this time alien and seemingly irrelevant. He saw great towering black walls, pedestals half hidden in the shadows upholding images of hideous, half-bestial gods. Men moved in the shadows, dark, wiry men, clad in red, silken loincloths. They were bearing a green jade sarcophagus along a gigantic black corridor. But before he could tell much about what he saw, the scene shifted. He saw a cavern, dim, shadowy, and haunted with a strange intangible horror. On an altar of black stone stood a curious golden vessel, shaped like the shell of a scallop. Into this cavern came some of the same dark, wiry

69

men who had borne the mummy-case. They seized the golden vessel, and then the shadows swirled around them and what happened he could not say. But he saw a glimmer in a whorl of darkness, like a ball of living fire. Then the smoke was only smoke, drifting up from the fire of tamarisk chunks, thinning and fading.

'But what does this portend?' he demanded, bewildered. 'What I saw in Tarantia I can understand. But what means this glimpse of Zamorian thieves sneaking through a subterranean temple of Set, in Stygia? And that cavern — I've never seen or heard of anything like it, in all my wanderings. If you can show me that much, these shreds of vision which mean nothing, disjointed, why can you not show me all that is to occur?'

Zelata stirred the fire without replying.

'These things are governed by immutable laws,' she said at last. 'I cannot make you understand; I do not altogether understand myself, though I have sought wisdom in the silences of the high places for more years than I can remember. I cannot save you, though I would if I might. Man must, at last, work out his own salvation. Yet perhaps wisdom may come to me in dreams, and in the morn I may be able to give the clue to the enigma.'

'What enigma?' he demanded.

'The mystery that confronts you, whereby you have lost a kingdom,' she answered. And then she spread a sheepskin upon the floor before the hearth. 'Sleep,' she said briefly.

Without a word he stretched himself upon it, and sank into restless but deep sleep through which phantoms moved silently and monstrous shapeless shadows crept. Once, limned against a purple sunless horizon, he saw the mighty walls and towers of a great city such as rose nowhere on the waking earth he knew. Its colossal pylons and purple minarets lifted toward the stars, and over it, floating like a giant mirage, hovered the bearded countenance of the man Xaltotun.

Conan woke in the chill whiteness of early dawn, to see Zelata crouched beside the tiny fire. He had not awakened once in the night, and the sound of the great wolf leaving or entering should have roused him. Yet the wolf was there, beside the hearth, with its shaggy coat wet with dew, and with more than dew. Blood glistened wetly amid the thick fell, and there was a cut upon its shoulder.

Zelata nodded, without looking around, as if reading the thoughts of her royal guest.

'He has hunted before dawn, and red was the hunting. I think the man who hunted a king will hunt no more, neither man nor beast.'

Conan stared at the great beast with strange fascination as he moved to take the food Zelata offered him.

'When I come to my throne again I won't forget,' he said briefly. 'You've befriended me – by Crom, I can't remember when I've lain down and slept at the mercy of man or woman as I did last night. But what of the riddle you would read me this morn?'

A long silence ensued, in which the crackle of the tamarisks was loud on the hearth.

'Find the heart of your kingdom,' she said at last. 'There lies your defeat and your power. You fight more than mortal man. You will not press the throne again unless you find the heart of your kingdom.'

'Do you mean the city of Tarantia?' he asked.

She shook her head. 'I am but an oracle, through whose lips the gods speak. My lips are sealed by them lest I speak too much. You must find the heart of your kingdom. I can say no more. My lips are opened and sealed by the gods.'

Dawn was still white on the peaks when Conan rode westward. A glance back showed him Zelata standing in the door of her hut, inscrutable as ever, the great wolf beside her.

A gray sky arched overhead, and a moaning wind was chill with a promise of winter. Brown leaves fluttered slowly down from the bare branches, sifting upon his mailed shoulders.

All day he pushed through the hills, avoiding roads and villages. Toward nightfall he began to drop down from the heights, tier by tier, and saw the broad plains of Aquilonia spread out beneath him.

Villages and farms lay close to the foot of the hills on the western side of the mountains, for, for half a century, most of the raiding across the frontier had been done by the Aquilonians. But now only embers and ashes showed where farm huts and villas had stood.

In the gathering darkness, Conan rode slowly on. There was little fear of discovery, which he dreaded from friend as well as foe. The Nemedians had remembered old scores on their westward drive, and Valerius had made no attempt to restrain his allies. He did not count on winning the love of the common people. A vast swath of desolation had been cut through the country from the foothills westward. Conan cursed as he rode over blackened expanses that had been rich fields, and saw the gaunt gable-ends of burned houses jutting against the sky. He moved through an empty and deserted land, like a ghost out of a forgotten and outworn past.

The speed with which the army had traversed the land showed what little resistance it had encountered. Yet had Conan been leading his Aquilonians, the invading army would have been forced to buy every foot they gained with their blood. The bitter realization permeated his soul; he was not the representative of a dynasty. He was only a lone adventurer. Even the drop of dynastic blood Valerius boasted had more hold on the minds of men than the memory of Conan and the freedom and power he had given the kingdom.

No pursuers followed him down out of the hills. He watched for wandering or returning Nemedian troops, but he met none. Skulkers gave him a wide path, supposing him to be one of the conquerors, what of his harness. Groves and rivers were far more plentiful on the western side of the mountains, and coverts for concealment were not lacking.

So he moved across the pillaged land, halting only to rest his horse, eating frugally of the food Zelata had given him, until, on a dawn when he lay hidden on a river bank where willows and oaks grew thickly, he glimpsed, afar, across the rolling plains dotted with rich groves, the blue and golden towers of Tarantia.

He was no longer in a deserted land, but one teeming with varied life. His progress thenceforth was slow and cautious, through thick woods and unfrequented byways. It was dusk when he reached the plantation of Servius Galannus.

8 – DYING EMBERS

THE COUNTRYSIDE about Tarantia had escaped the fearful ravaging of the more easterly provinces. There were evidences of the march of a conquering army in broken hedges, plundered fields, and looted granaries, but torch and steel had not been loosed wholesale.

There was but one grim splotch on the landscape – a charred expanse of ashes and blackened stone, where, Conan knew, had once stood the stately villa of one of his staunchest supporters.

The king dared not openly approach the Galannus farm, which lay only a few miles from the city. In the twilight he rode through an extensive woodland, until he sighted a keeper's lodge through the trees. Dismounting and tying his horse, he approached the thick, arched door with the intention of sending the keeper after Servius. He did not know what enemies the manor house might be sheltering. He had seen no troops, but they might be quartered all over the countryside. But as he drew near, he saw the door open and a compact figure in silk hose and richly embroidered doublet stride forth and turn up a path that wound away through the woods.

'Servius!'

At the low call the master of the plantation wheeled with a startled exclamation. His hand flew to the short hunting-sword at his hip, and he recoiled from the tall gray steel figure standing in the dusk before him.

'Who are you?' he demanded. 'What is your – *Mitra!*'

His breath hissed inward and his ruddy face paled. 'Avaunt!' he ejaculated. 'Why have you come back from the gray lands of death to terrify me? I was always your true liegeman in your lifetime—'

'As I still expect you to be,' answered Conan. 'Stop trembling, man; I'm flesh and blood.'

Sweating with uncertainty, Servius approached and stared into the face of the mail-clad giant, and then, convinced of the reality of what he saw, he dropped to one knee and doffed his plumed cap.

'Your Majesty! Truly, this is a miracle passing belief! The great bell in the citadel has tolled your dirge, days agone. Men said you died at Valkia, crushed under a million tons of earth and broken granite.'

'It was another in my harness,' grunted Conan. 'But let us talk later. If there is such a thing as a joint of beef on your board—'

'Forgive me, my lord!' cried Servius, springing to his feet. 'The dust of travel is gray on your mail, and I keep you

73

standing here without rest or sup! Mitra! I see well enough now that you are alive, but I swear, when I turned and saw you standing all gray and dim in the twilight, the marrow of my knees turned to water. It is an ill thing to meet a man you thought dead in the woodland at dusk.'

'Bid the keeper see to my steed, which is tied behind yonder oak,' requested Conan, and Servius nodded, drawing the king up the path. The patrician, recovering from his supernatural fright, had become extremely nervous.

'I will send a servant from the manor,' he said. 'The keeper is in his lodge – but I dare not trust even my servants in these days. It is better that only I know of your presence.'

Approaching the great house that glimmered dimly through the trees, he turned aside into a little-used path that ran between close-set oaks whose intertwining branches formed a vault overhead, shutting out the dim light of the gathering dusk. Servius hurried on through the darkness without speaking, and with something resembling panic in his manner, and presently led Conan through a small side-door into a narrow, dimly illuminated corridor. They traversed this in haste and silence, and Servius brought the king into a spacious chamber with a high, oak-beamed ceiling and richly paneled walls. Logs flamed in the wide fireplace, for there was a frosty edge to the air, and a great meat pasty in a stone platter stood smoking on a broad mahogany board. Servius locked the massive door and extinguished the candles that stood in a silver candlestick on the table, leaving the chamber illuminated only by the fire on the hearth.

'Your pardon, Your Majesty,' he apologized. 'These are perilous times; spies lurk everywhere. It were better than none be able to peer through the windows and recognize you. This pasty, however, is just from the oven, as I intended supping on my return from talk with my keeper. If Your Majesty would deign—'

'The light is sufficient,' grunted Conan, seating himself with scant ceremony, and drawing his poniard.

He dug ravenously into the luscious dish, and washed it down with great gulps of wine from grapes grown in Servius's vineyards. He seemed oblivious to any sense of peril, but Servius shifted uneasily on his settle by the fire, nervously fingering the heavy gold chain about his neck. He glanced continually at the diamond panes of the casement, gleaming dimly in the firelight, and cocked his ear toward the door, as if half expecting to hear the pad of furtive feet in the corridor without.

Finishing his meal, Conan rose and seated himself on another settle before the fire.

'I won't jeopardize you long by my presence, Servius,' he said abruptly. 'Dawn will find me far from your plantation.'

'My lord—' Servius lifted his hands in expostulation, but Conan waved his protests aside.

'I know your loyalty and your courage. Both are above reproach. But if Valerius has usurped my throne, it would be death for you to shelter me, if you were discovered.'

'I am not strong enough to defy him openly,' admitted Servius. 'The fifty men-at-arms I could lead to battle would be but a handful of straws. You saw the ruins of Emilius Scavonus's plantation?'

Conan nodded, frowning darkly.

'He was the strongest patrician in this province, as you know. He refused to give his allegiance to Valerius. The Nemedians burned him in the ruins of his own villa. After that the rest of us saw the futility of resistance, especially as the people of Tarantia refused to fight. We submitted and Valerius spared our lives, though he levied a tax upon us that will ruin many. But what could we do? We thought you were dead. Many of the barons had been slain, others taken prisoner. The army was shattered and scattered. You have no heir to take the crown. There was no one to lead us—'

'Was there not Count Trocero of Poitain?' demanded Conan harshly.

Servius spread his hands helplessly.

'It is true that his general Prospero was in the field with a small army. Retreating before Amalric, he urged men to rally to his banner. But with your Majesty dead, men remembered old wars and civil brawls, and how Trocero and his Poitanians once rode through these provinces even as Amalric was riding now, with torch and sword. The barons were jealous of Trocero. Some men – spies of Valerius perhaps – shouted that the Count of Poitain intended seizing the crown for himself. Old sectional hates flared up again. If we had had one man with dynastic blood in his veins we would have crowned and followed him against Nemedia. But we had none.

'The barons who followed you loyally would not follow one of their own number, each holding himself as good as his neighbor, each fearing the ambitions of the others. You were the cord that held the fagots together. When the cord was cut, the fagots fell apart. If you had had a son, the barons would have rallied loyally to him. But there was no point for their patriotism to focus upon.

'The merchants and commoners, dreading anarchy and a return of feudal days when each baron was his own law, cried out that any king was better than none, even Valerius, who was at least of the blood of the old dynasty. There was no one to oppose him when he rode up at the head of his steel-clad hosts, with the scarlet dragon of Nemedia floating over him, and rang his lance against the gates of Tarantia.

'Nay, the people threw open the gates and knelt in the dust before him. They had refused to aid Prospero in holding the city. They said they had rather be ruled by Valerius than by Trocero. They said – truthfully – that the barons would not rally to Trocero, but that many would accept Valerius. They said that by yielding to Valerius they would escape the devastation of civil war, and the fury of the Nemedians. Prospero rode southward with his ten thousand knights, and the horsemen of the Nemedians entered the city a few hours later. They did not follow him. They remained to see that Valerius was crowned in Tarantia.'

'Then the old witch's smoke showed the truth,' muttered Conan, feeling a queer chill along his spine. 'Amalric crowned Valerius?'

'Aye, in the coronation hall, with the blood of slaughter scarcely dried on his hands.'

'And do the people thrive under his benevolent rule?' asked Conan with angry irony.

'He lives like a foreign prince in the midst of a conquered land,' answered Servius bitterly. 'His court is filled with Nemedians, the palace troops are of the same breed, and a large garrison of them occupy the citadel. Aye, the hour of the Dragon has come at last.

'Nemedians swagger like lords through the streets. Women are outraged and merchants plundered daily, and Valerius either can, or will, make no attempt to curb them. Nay, he is but their puppet, their figurehead. Men of sense knew he would be, and the people are beginning to find it out.

'Amalric has ridden forth with a strong army to reduce the outlying provinces where some of the barons have defied him. But there is no unity among them. Their jealousy of each other is stronger than their fear of Amalric. He will crush them one by one. Many castles and cities, realizing that, have sent in their submission. Those who resist fare miserably.

The Nemedians are glutting their long hatred. And their ranks are swelled by Aquilonians whom fear, gold, or necessity of occupation are forcing into their armies. It is a natural consequence.'

Conan nodded somberly, staring at the red reflections of the firelight on the richly carven oaken panels.

'Aquilonia has a king instead of the anarchy they feared,' said Servius at last. 'Valerius does not protect his subjects against his allies. Hundreds who could not pay the ransom imposed upon them have been sold to the Kothic slave-traders.'

Conan's head jerked up and a lethal flame lit his blue eyes. He swore gustily, his mighty hands knotting into iron hammers.

'Aye, white men sell white men and white women, as it was in the feudal days. In the palaces of Shem and of Turan they will live out the lives of slaves. Valerius is king, but the unity for which the people looked, even though of the sword, is not complete.

'Gunderland in the north and Poitain in the south are yet unconquered, and there are unsubdued provinces in the west, where the border barons have the backing of the Bossonian bowmen. Yet these outlying provinces are no real menace to Valerius. They must remain on the defensive, and will be lucky if they are able to keep their independence. Here Valerius and his foreign knights are supreme.'

'Let him make the best of it then,' said Conan grimly. 'His time is short. The people will rise when they learn that I'm alive. We'll take Tarantia back before Amalric can return with his army. Then we'll sweep these dogs from the kingdom.'

Servius was silent. The crackle of the fire was loud in the stillness.

'Well,' exclaimed Conan impatiently, 'why do you sit with your head bent, staring at the hearth? Do you doubt what I have said?'

Servius avoided the king's eye.

'What mortal man can do, you will do, Your Majesty,' he answered. 'I have ridden behind you in battle, and I know that no mortal being can stand before your sword.'

'What then?'

Servius drew his fur-trimmed jupon closer about him, and shivered in spite of the flame.

'Men say your fall was occasioned by sorcery,' he said presently.

'What then?'

'What mortal can fight against sorcery? Who is this veiled man who communes at midnight with Valerius and his allies, as men say, who appears and disappears so mysteriously? Men say in whispers that he is a great magician who died thousands of years ago, but has returned from death's gray lands to overthrow the king of Aquilonia and restore the dynasty of which Valerius is heir.'

'What matter?' exclaimed Conan angrily. 'I escaped from the devil-haunted pits of Belverus, and from diabolism in the mountains. If the people rise—'

Servius shook his head.

'Your staunchest supporters in the eastern and central provinces are dead, fled, or imprisoned. Gunderland is far to the north, Poitain far to the south. The Bossonians have retired to their marches far to the west. It would take weeks to gather and concentrate these forces, and before that could be done, each levy would be attacked separately by Amalric and destroyed.'

'But an uprising in the central provinces would tip the scales for us!' exclaimed Conan. 'We could seize Tarantia and hold it against Amalric until the Gundermen and Poitanians could get here.'

Servius hesitated, and his voice sank to a whisper.

'Men say you died accursed. Men say this veiled stranger cast a spell upon you to slay you and break your army. The great bell has tolled your dirge. Men believe you to be dead. And the central provinces would not rise, even if they knew you lived. They would not dare. Sorcery defeated you at Valkia. Sorcery brought the news to Tarantia, for that very night men were shouting of it in the streets.

'A Nemedian priest loosed black magic again in the streets of Tarantia to slay men who still were loyal to your memory. I myself saw it. Armed men dropped like flies and died in the streets in a manner no man could understand. And the lean priest laughed and said: "I am only Altaro, only an acolyte of Orastes, who is but an acolyte of him who wears the veil; not mine is the power; the power but works through me."'

'Well,' said Conan harshly, 'is it not better to die honorably than to live in infamy? Is death worse than oppression, slavery, and ultimate destruction?'

'When the fear of sorcery is in, reason is out,' replied Servius. 'The fear of the central provinces is too great to allow them to rise for you. The outlying provinces would fight for you – but the same sorcery that smote your army at Valkia would smite you again. The Nemedians hold the broadest, richest, and most thickly populated sections of Aquilonia, and they cannot be defeated by the forces which might still be at your command. You would be sacrificing your loyal subjects uselessly. In sorrow I say it, but it is true: King Conan, you are a king without a kingdom.'

Conan stared into the fire without replying. A smoldering log crashed down among the flames without a bursting shower of sparks. It might have been the crashing ruin of his kingdom.

Again Conan felt the presence of a grim reality behind the veil of material illusion. He sensed again the inexorable drive of a ruthless fate. A feeling of furious panic tugged at his soul, a sense of being trapped, and a red rage that burned to destroy and kill.

'Where are the officials of my court?' he demanded at last.

'Pallantides was sorely wounded at Valkia, was ransomed by his family, and now lies in his castle at Attalus. He will be fortunate if he ever rides again. Publius, the chancellor, has fled the kingdom in disguise, no man knows whither. The council has been disbanded. Some were imprisoned, some banished. Many of your loyal subjects have been put to death. Tonight, for instance, the Countess Albiona dies under the headsman's ax.'

Conan started and stared at Servius with such anger smoldering in his blue eyes that the patrician shrank back.

'Why?'

'Because she would not become the mistress of Valerius. Her lands are forfeit, her henchmen sold into slavery, and at midnight, in the Iron Tower, her head must fall. Be advised, my king – to me you will ever be my king – and flee before you are discovered. In these days none is safe. Spies and informers creep among us, betraying the slightest deed or word of discontent as treason and rebellion. If you make yourself known to your subjects it will only end in your capture and death.

'My horses and all the men that I can trust are at your disposal. Before dawn we can be far from Tarantia, and well on our way toward the border. If I cannot aid you to recover your kingdom, I can at least follow you into exile.'

Conan shook his head. Servius glanced uneasily at him as he sat staring into the fire, his chin propped on his mighty fist.

The firelight gleamed redly on his steel mail, on his baleful eyes. They burned in the firelight like the eyes of a wolf. Servius was again aware, as in the past, and now more strongly than ever, of something alien about the king. That great frame under the mail mesh was too hard and supple for a civilized man; the elemental fire of the primitive burned in those smoldering eyes. Now the barbaric suggestion about the king was more pronounced, as if in his extremity the outward aspects of civilization were stripped away, to reveal the primordial core. Conan was reverting to his pristine type. He did not act as a civilized man would act under the same conditions, nor did his thoughts run in the same channels. He was unpredictable. It was only a stride from the king of Aquilonia to the skin-clad slayer of the Cimmerian hills.

'I'll ride to Poitain, if it may be,' Conan said at last. 'But I'll ride alone. And I have one last duty to perform as king of Aquilonia.'

'What do you mean, Your Majesty?' asked Servius, shaken by a premonition.

'I'm going into Tarantia after Albiona tonight,' answered the king. 'I've failed all my other loyal subjects, it seems – if they take her head, they can have mine too.'

'This is madness!' cried Servius, staggering up and clutching his throat, as if he already felt the noose closing about it.

'There are secrets to the Tower which few know,' said Conan. 'Anyway, I'd be a dog to leave Albiona to die because of her loyalty to me. I may be a king without a kingdom, but I'm not a man without honor.'

'It will ruin us all!' whispered Servius.

'It will ruin no one but me if I fail. You've risked enough. I ride alone tonight. This is all I want you to do: procure me a patch for my eye, a staff for my hand, and garments such as travelers wear.'

9 – 'IT IS THE KING OR HIS GHOST!'

MANY MEN PASSED through the great arched gates of Tarantia between sunset and midnight – belated travelers, merchants from afar with heavily laden mules, free workmen from the surrounding farms and vineyards. Now that Valerius was supreme in the central provinces, there was no rigid scrutiny of the folk who flowed in a steady stream through the wide gates. Discipline had been relaxed. The Nemedian soldiers who stood on guard were half drunk, and much too busy watching for handsome peasant girls and rich merchants who could be bullied to notice workmen or dusty travelers, even one tall wayfarer whose worn cloak could not conceal the hard lines of his powerful frame.

This man carried himself with an erect, aggressive bearing that was too natural for him to realize it himself, much less dissemble it. A great patch covered one eye, and his leather coif, drawn low over his brows, shadowed his features. With a long thick staff in his muscular brown hand, he strode leisurely through the arch where the torches flared and guttered, and, ignored by the tipsy guardsmen, emerged upon the wide streets of Tarantia.

Upon these well-lighted thoroughfares the usual throngs went about their business, and shops and stalls stood open, with their wares displayed. One thread ran a constant theme through the pattern. Nemedian soldiers, singly or in clumps, swaggered through the throngs, shouldering their way with studied arrogance. Women scurried from their path, and men stepped aside with darkened brows and clenched fists. The Aquilonians were a proud race, and these were their hereditary enemies.

The knuckles of the tall traveler knotted on his staff, but, like the others, he stepped aside to let the men in armor have the way. Among the motley and varied crowd he did not attract much attention in his drab, dusty garments. But once, as he passed a sword-seller's stall and the light that streamed from its wide door fell full upon him, he thought he felt an intense stare upon him, and turning quickly, saw a man in the brown jerkin of a free workman regarding him fixedly. This man turned away with undue haste, and vanished in the shifting throng. But Conan turned into a narrow by-street and quickened his pace. It might have been idle curiosity; but he could take no chances.

The grim Iron Tower stood apart from the citadel, amid a maze of narrow streets and crowding houses where the meaner structures, appropriating a space from which the more fastidious shrank, had invaded a portion of the city alien to them. The Tower was in reality a castle, an ancient, formidable pile of heavy stone and black iron, which had itself served as the citadel in an earlier, ruder century.

Not a long distance from it, lost in a tangle of partly deserted tenements and warehouses, stood an ancient watch-tower, so old and forgotten that it did not appear on the maps of the city for a hundred years back. Its original purpose had been forgotten, and nobody, of such as saw it at all, noticed that the apparently ancient lock which kept it from being appropriated as sleeping-quarters by beggars and thieves, was in reality comparatively new and extremely powerful, cunningly disguised into an appearance of rusty antiquity. Not half a dozen men in the kingdom had ever known the secret of that tower.

No keyhole showed in the massive, green-crusted lock. But Conan's practiced fingers, stealing over it, pressed here and there knobs invisible to the casual eye. The door silently opened inward and he entered solid blackness, pushing the door shut behind him. A light would have showed the tower empty, a bare, cylindrical shaft of massive stone.

Groping in a corner with the sureness of familiarity, he found the projections for which he was feeling on a slab of the stone that composed the floor. Quickly he lifted it, and without hesitation lowered himself into the aperture beneath. His feet felt stone steps leading downward into what he knew was a narrow tunnel that ran straight toward the foundations of the Iron Tower, three streets away.

The bell on the citadel, which tolled only at the midnight hour or for the death of a king, boomed suddenly. In a dimly lighted chamber in the Iron Tower a door opened and a form emerged into a corridor. The interior of the Tower was as forbidding as its external appearance. Its massive stone walls were rough, unadorned. The flags of the floor were worn deep by generations of faltering feet, and the vault of the ceiling was gloomy in the dim light of torches set in niches.

The man who trudged down that grim corridor was in appearance in keeping with his surroundings. He was a tall, powerfully-built man, clad in close-fitting black silk. Over his head was drawn a black hood which fell about his shoulders, having two holes for his eyes. From his shoulders hung a loose, black cloak, and over one shoulder he bore a heavy ax, the shape of which was that of neither tool nor weapon.

As he went down the corridor, a figure came hobbling up it, a bent, surly old man, stooping under the weight of his pike and a lantern he bore in one hand.

'You are not as prompt as your predecessor, master heads-man,' he grumbled. 'Midnight has just struck, and masked men have gone to milady's cell. They await you.'

'The tones of the bell still echo among the towers,' answered the executioner. 'If I am not so quick to leap and run at the beck of Aquilonians as was the dog who held this office before me, they shall find my arm no less ready. Get you to your duties, old watchman, and leave me to mine. I think mine is the sweeter trade, by Mitra, for you tramp cold corridors and peer at rusty dungeon doors, while I lop off the fairest head in Tarantia this night.'

The watchman limped on down the corridor, still grumbling, and the headsman resumed his leisurely way. A few strides carried him around a turn in the corridor, and he absently noted that at his left a door stood partly open. If he had thought, he would have known that that door had been opened since the watchman passed; but thinking was not his trade. He was passing the unlocked door before he realized that aught was amiss, and then it was too late.

A soft tigerish step and the rustle of a cloak warned him, but before he could turn, a heavy arm hooked about his throat from behind, crushing the cry before it could reach his lips. In the brief instant that was allowed him he realized with a surge of panic the strength of his attacker, against which his own brawny thews were helpless. He sensed without seeing the poised dagger.

'Nemedian dog!' muttered a voice thick with passion in his ear. 'You've cut off your last Aquilonian head!'

And that was the last thing he ever heard.

In a dank dungeon, lighted only by a guttering torch, three men stood about a young woman who knelt on the rush-strewn flags staring wildly up at them. She was clad only in a scanty shift; her golden hair fell in lustrous ripples about her white shoulders, and her wrists were bound behind her. Even in the uncertain torchlight, and in spite of her disheveled condition and pallor of fear, her beauty was striking. She knelt mutely, staring with wide eyes up at her tormentors. The men were closely masked and cloaked. Such a deed as this needed masks, even in a conquered land. She knew them all, never-theless; but what she knew would harm no one – after that night.

'Our merciful sovereign offers you one more chance, Countess,' said the tallest of the three, and he spoke Aqui-

Ionian without an accent. 'He bids me say that if you soften your proud, rebellious spirit, he will still open his arms to you. If not—' he gestured towards a grim wooden block in the center of the cell. It was blackly stained, and showed many deep nicks as if a keen edge, cutting through some yielding substance, had sunk into the wood.

Albiona shuddered and turned pale, shrinking back. Every fiber in her vigorous young body quivered with the urge of life. Valerius was young, too, and handsome. Many women loved him, she told herself, fighting with herself for life. But she could not speak the word that would ransom her soft young body from the block and the dripping ax. She could not reason the matter. She only knew that when she thought of the clasp of Valerius's arms, her flesh crawled with an abhorrence greater than the fear of death. She shook her head helplessly, compelled by an impulsion more irresistible than the instinct to live.

'Then there is no more to be said!' exclaimed one of the others impatiently, and he spoke with a Nemedian accent. 'Where is the headsman?'

As if summoned by the word, the dungeon door opened silently, and a great figure stood framed in it, like a black shadow from the underworld.

Albiona voiced a low, involuntary cry at the sight of that grim shape, and the others stared silently for a moment, perhaps themselves daunted with superstitious awe at the silent, hooded figure. Through the coif the eyes blazed like coals of blue fire, and as those eyes rested on each man in turn, he felt a curious chill travel down his spine.

Then the tall Aquilonian roughly seized the girl and dragged her to the block. She screamed uncontrollably and fought hopelessly against him, frantic with terror, but he ruthlessly forced her to her knees, and bent her yellow head down to the bloody block.

'Why do you delay, headsman?' he exclaimed angrily. 'Perform your task!'

He was answered by a short, gusty boom of laughter that was indescribably menacing. All in the dungeon froze in their places, staring at the hooded shape – the two cloaked figures, the masked man bending over the girl, the girl herself on her knees, twisting her imprisoned head to look upward.

'What means this unseemly mirth, dog?' demanded the Aquilonian uneasily.

The man in the black garb tore his hood from his head and

84

flung it to the ground; he set his back to the closed door and lifted the headsman's ax.

'Do you know me, dogs?' he rumbled. 'Do you know me?'

The breathless silence was broken by a scream.

'The king!' shrieked Albiona, wrenching herself free from the slackened grasp of her captor. 'Oh, Mitra, *the king!*'

The three men stood like statues, and then the Aquilonian started and spoke, like a man who doubts his own senses.

'Conan!' he ejaculated. 'It *is* the king, or his ghost! What devil's work is this?'

'Devil's work to match devils!' mocked Conan, his lips laughing but hell flaming in his eyes. 'Come, fall to, my gentlemen. You have your swords, and I this cleaver. Nay, I think this butcher's tool fits the work at hand, my fair lords!'

'At him!' muttered the Aquilonian, drawing his sword. 'It is Conan and we must kill or be killed!'

And like men waking from a trance, the Nemedians drew their blades and rushed on the king.

The headsman's ax was not made for such work, but the king wielded the heavy, clumsy weapon as lightly as a hatchet, and his quickness of foot, as he constantly shifted his position, defeated their purpose of engaging him all three at once.

He caught the sword of the first man on his ax-head and crushed in the wielder's breast with a murderous counter-stroke before he could step back or parry. The remaining Nemedian, missing a savage swipe, had his brains dashed out before he could recover his balance, and an instant later the Aquilonian was backed into a corner, desperately parrying the crashing strokes that rained about him, lacking opportunity even to scream for help.

Suddenly Conan's long left arm shot out and ripped the mask from the man's head, disclosing the pallid features.

'Dog!' grated the king. 'I thought I knew you. Traitor! Damned renegade! Even this base steel is too honorable for your foul head. Nay, die as thieves die!'

The ax fell in a devastating arc, and the Aquilonian cried out and went to his knees, grasping the severed stump of his right arm from which blood spouted. It had been shorn away at the elbow, and the ax, unchecked in its descent, had gashed deeply into his side, so that his entrails bulged out.

'Lie there and bleed to death,' grunted Conan, casting the ax away disgustedly. 'Come, Countess!'

Stooping, he slashed the cords that bound her wrists and lifting her as if she had been a child, strode from the dungeon.

She was sobbing hysterically, with her arms thrown about his corded neck in a frenzied embrace.

'Easy all,' he muttered. 'We're not out of this yet. If we can reach the dungeon where the secret door opens on stairs that lead to the tunnel — devil take it, they've heard that noise, even through these walls.'

Down the corridor arms clanged and the tramp and shouting of men echoed under the vaulted roof. A bent figure came hobbling swiftly along, lantern held high, and its light shone full on Conan and the girl. With a curse the Cimmerian sprang toward him, but the old watchman, abandoning both lantern and pike, scuttled away down the corridor, screeching for help at the top of his cracked voice. Deeper shouts answered him.

Conan turned swiftly and ran the other way. He was cut off from the dungeon with the secret lock and the hidden door through which he had entered the Tower, and by which he had hoped to leave, but he knew this grim building well. Before he was king he had been imprisoned in it.

He turned off into a side passage and quickly emerged into another, broader corridor, which ran parallel to the one down which he had come, and which was at the moment deserted. He followed this only a few yards, when he again turned back, down another side passage. This brought him back into the corridor he had left, but at a strategic point. A few feet farther up the corridor there was a heavy bolted door, and before it stood a bearded Nemedian in corselet and helmet, his back to Conan as he peered up the corridor in the direction of the growing tumult and wildly waving lanterns.

Conan did not hesitate. Slipping the girl to the ground, he ran at the guard swiftly and silently, sword in hand. The man turned just as the king reached him, bawled in surprise and fright and lifted his pike; but before he could bring the clumsy weapon into play, Conan brought down his sword on the fellow's helmet with a force that would have felled an ox. Helmet and skull gave way together and the guard crumpled to the floor.

In an instant Conan had drawn the massive bolt that barred the door — too heavy for one ordinary man to have manipulated — and called hastily to Albiona, who ran staggering to him. Catching her up unceremoniously with one arm, he bore her through the door and into the outer darkness.

They had come into a narrow alley, black as pitch, walled by the side of the Tower on one hand, and the sheer stone

86

back of a row of buildings on the other. Conan, hurrying through the darkness as swiftly as he dared, felt the latter wall for doors or windows, but found none.

The great door clanged open behind them, and men poured out, with torches gleaming on breastplates and naked swords. They glared about, bellowing, unable to penetrate the darkness which their torches served to illuminate for only a few feet in any direction, and then rushed down the alley at random – heading in the direction opposite to that taken by Conan and Albiona.

'They'll learn their mistake quick enough,' he muttered, increasing his pace. 'If we ever find a crack in this infernal wall – damn! The street watch!'

Ahead of them a faint glow became apparent, where the alley opened into a narrow street, and he saw dim figures looming against it with a glimmer of steel. It was indeed the street watch, investigating the noise they had heard echoing down the alley.

'Who goes there?' they shouted, and Conan gritted his teeth at the hated Nemedian accent.

'Keep behind me,' he ordered the girl. 'We've got to cut our way through before the prison guards come back and pin us between them.'

And grasping his sword, he ran straight at the oncoming figures. The advantage of surprise was his. He could see them, limned against the distant glow, and they could not see him coming at them out of the black depths of the alley. He was among them before they knew it, smiting with the silent fury of a wounded lion.

His one chance lay in hacking through before they could gather their wits. But there were half a score of them, in full mail, hard-bitten veterans of the border wars, in whom the instinct for battle could take the place of bemused wits. Three of them were down before they realized that it was only one man who was attacking them, but even so their reaction was instantaneous. The clangor of steel rose deafeningly, and sparks flew as Conan's sword crashed on basinet and hauberk. He could see better than they, and in the dim light his swiftly moving figure was an uncertain mark. Flailing swords cut empty air or glanced from his blade, and when he struck, it was with the fury and certainty of a hurricane.

But behind him sounded the shouts of the prison guards, returning up the alley at a run, and still the mailed figures before him barred his way with a bristling wall of steel. In an instant the guards would be on his back – in desperation he redoubled his strokes, flailing like a smith on an anvil, and then was suddenly aware of a diversion. Out of nowhere behind the watchmen rose a score of black figures and there was a sound of blows, murderously driven. Steel glinted in the gloom, and men cried out, struck mortally from behind. In an instant the alley was littered with writhing forms. A dark, cloaked shape sprang toward Conan, who heaved up his sword, catching a gleam of steel in the right hand. But the other was extended to him empty and a voice hissed urgently: 'This way, Your Majesty! Quickly!'

With a muttered oath of surprise, Conan caught up Albiona in one massive arm, and followed his unknown befriender. He was not inclined to hesitate, with thirty prison guardsmen closing in behind him.

Surrounded by mysterious figures he hurried down the alley, carrying the countess as if she had been a child. He could tell nothing of his rescuers except that they wore dark cloaks and hoods. Doubt and suspicion crossed his mind, but at least they had struck down his enemies, and he saw no better course than to follow them.

As if sensing his doubt, the leader touched his arm lightly and said: 'Fear not, King Conan; we are your loyal subjects.' The voice was not familiar, but the accent was Aquilonian of the central provinces.

Behind them the guards were yelling as they stumbled over the shambles in the mud, and they came pelting vengefully down the alley, seeing the vague dark mass moving between them and the light of the distant street. But the hooded men turned suddenly toward the seemingly blank wall, and Conan saw a door gape there. He muttered a curse. He had traversed that alley by day, in times past, and had never noticed a door there. But through it they went, and the door closed behind them with the click of a lock. The sound was not reassuring, but his guides were hurrying him on, moving with the precision of familiarity, guiding Conan with a hand at either elbow. It was like traversing a tunnel, and Conan felt Albiona's lithe limbs trembling in his arms. Then somewhere ahead of them an opening was faintly visible, merely a somewhat less black arch in the blackness, and through this they filed.

After that there was a bewildering succession of dim courts and shadowy alleys and winding corridors, all traversed in utter silence, until at last they emerged into a broad lighted chamber, the location of which Conan could not even guess, for their devious route had confused even his primitive sense of direction.

10 – A COIN FROM ACHERON

NOT ALL his guides entered the chamber. When the door closed, Conan saw only one man standing before him – a slim figure, masked in a black cloak with a hood. This the man threw back, disclosing a pale oval of a face, with calm, delicately chiseled features.

The king set Albiona on her feet, but she still clung to him and stared apprehensively about her. The chamber was a large one, with marble walls partly covered with black velvet hangings and thick rich carpets on the mosaic floor, laved in the soft golden glow of bronze lamps.

Conan instinctively laid a hand on his hilt. There was blood on his hand, blood clotted about the mouth of his scabbard, for he had sheathed his blade without cleansing it.

'Where are we?' he demanded.

The stranger answered with a low, profound bow in which the suspicious king could detect no trace of irony.

'In the temple of Asura, Your Majesty.'

Albiona cried out faintly and clung closer to Conan, staring fearfully at the black, arched doors, as if expecting the entry of some grisly shape of darkness.

'Fear not, my lady,' said their guide. 'There is nothing here to harm you, vulgar superstition to the contrary. If your monarch was sufficiently convinced of the innocency of our religion to protect us from the persecution of the ignorant, then certainly one of his subjects need have no apprehensions.'

'Who are you?' demanded Conan.

'I am Hadrathus, priest of Asura. One of my followers recognized you when you entered the city, and brought the word to me.'

Conan grunted profanely.

'Do not fear that others discovered your identity,' Hadrathus assured him. 'Your disguise would have deceived any but a follower of Asura, whose cult it is to seek below the aspect of illusion. You were followed to the watch tower, and some of my people went into the tunnel to aid you if you returned by that route. Others, myself among them, surrounded the tower. And now, King Conan, it is yours to command. Here in the temple of Asura you are still king.'

'Why should you risk your lives for me?' asked the king.

'You were our friend when you sat upon your throne,' answered Hadrathus. 'You protected us when the priests of Mitra sought to scourge us out of the land.'

Conan looked about him curiously. He had never before visited the temple of Asura, had not certainly known that there was such a temple in Tarantia. The priests of the religion had a habit of hiding their temples in a remarkable fashion. The worship of Mitra was overwhelmingly predominant in the Hyborian nations, but the cult of Asura persisted, in spite of official ban and popular antagonism. Conan had been told dark tales of hidden temples where intense smoke drifted up incessantly from black altars where kidnaped humans were sacrificed before a great coiled serpent, whose fearsome head swayed forever in the haunted shadows.

Persecution caused the followers of Asura to hide their temples with cunning art, and to veil their rituals in obscurity; and this secrecy, in turn, evoked more monstrous suspicions and tales of evil.

But Conan's was the broad tolerance of the barbarian, and he had refused to persecute the followers of Asura or to allow the people to do so on no better evidence than was presented against them, rumors and accusations that could not be proven. 'If they are black magicians,' he had said, 'how will they suffer you to harry them? If they are not, there is no evil in them. Crom's devils! Let men worship what gods they will.'

At a respectful invitation from Hadrathus he seated himself on an ivory chair, and motioned Albiona to another, but she preferred to sit on a golden stool at his feet, pressing close against his thigh, as if seeking security in the contact. Like most orthodox followers of Mitra, she had intuitive horror of the followers and cult of Asura, instilled in her infancy and childhood by wild tales of human sacrifice and anthropomorphic gods shambling through shadowy temples.

Hadrathus stood before them, his uncovered head bowed.

'What is your wish, Your Majesty?'

'Food, first,' he grunted, and the priest smote a golden gong with a silver wand.

Scarcely had the mellow notes ceased echoing when four hooded figures came through a curtained doorway bearing a great four-legged silver platter of smoking dishes and crystal vessels. This they set before Conan, bowing low, and the king wiped his hands on the damask, and smacked his lips with unconcealed relish.

'Beware, Your Majesty!' whispered Albiona. 'These folk eat human flesh!'

'I'll stake my kingdom that this is nothing but honest roast beef,' answered Conan. 'Come, lass, fall to! You must be hungry after the prison fare.'

Thus advised, and with the example before her of one whose word was the ultimate law to her, the countess complied, and ate ravenously though daintily, while her liege lord tore into the meat joints and guzzled the wine with as much gusto as if he had not already eaten once that night.

'Your priests are shrewd, Hadrathus,' he said, with a great beef-bone in his hands and his mouth full of meat. 'I'd welcome your service in my campaign to regain my kingdom.'

Slowly Hadrathus shook his head, and Conan slammed the beef-bone down on the table in a gust of impatient wrath.

'Crom's devils! What ails the men of Aquilonia? First Servius – now you! Can you do nothing but wag your idiotic heads when I speak of ousting these dogs?'

Hadrathus sighed and answered slowly: 'My lord, it is ill to say, and I fain would say otherwise. But the freedom of Aquilonia is at a end. Nay, the freedom of the whole world may be at an end! Age follows age in the history of the world, and now we enter an age of horror and slavery, as it was long ago.'

'What do you mean?' demanded the king uneasily.

Hadrathus dropped into a chair and rested his elbows on his thighs, staring at the floor.

'It is not alone the rebellious lords of Aquilonia and the armies of Nemedia which are arrayed against you,' answered Hadrathus. 'It is sorcery – grisly black magic from the grim youth of the world. An awful shape has risen out of the shades of the Past, and none can stand before it.'

'What do you mean?' Conan repeated.

'I speak of Xaltotun of Acheron, who died three thousand years ago, yet walks the earth today.'

Conan was silent, while in his mind floated an image – the image of a bearded face of calm inhuman beauty. Again he was haunted by a sense of uneasy familiarity. Acheron – the sound of the word roused instinctive vibrations of memory and associations in his mind.

'Acheron,' he repeated. 'Xaltotun of Acheron – man, are you mad? Acheron has been a myth for more centuries than I can remember. I've often wondered if it ever existed at all.'

'It was a black reality,' answered Hadrathus, 'an empire of black magicians, steeped in evil now long forgotten. It was finally overthrown by the Hyborian tribes of the west. The wizards of Acheron praticed foul necromancy, thaumaturgy of the most evil kind, grisly magic taught them by devils. And of all the sorcerers of that accursed kingdom, none was so great as Xaltotun of Python.'

'Then how was he ever overthrown?' asked Conan skeptically.

'By some means a source of cosmic power which he jealously guarded was stolen and turned against him. That source has been returned to him, and he is invincible.'

Albiona, hugging the headsman's black cloak about her, stared from the priest to the king, not understanding the conversation. Conan shook his head angrily.

'You are making game of me,' he growled. 'If Xaltotun has been dead three thousand years, how can this man be he? It's some rogue who's taken the old one's name.'

Hadrathus leaned to an ivory table and opened a small gold chest which stood there. From it he took something which glinted dully in the mellow light – a broad gold coin of antique minting.

'You have seen Xaltotun unveiled? Then look upon this. It is a coin which was stamped in ancient Acheron, before its fall. So pervaded with sorcery was that black empire, that even this coin has its uses in making magic.'

Conan took it and scowled down at it. There was no mistaking its great antiquity. Conan had handled many coins in the years of his plunderings, and had a good practical knowledge of them. The edges were worn and the inscription almost obliterated. But the countenance stamped on one side was still clear-cut and distinct. And Conan's breath sucked in between his clenched teeth. It was not cool in the chamber, but he felt a prickling of his scalp, an icy contraction of his flesh. The countenance was that of a bearded man, inscrutable, with a calm inhuman beauty.

'By Crom! It's he!' muttered Conan. He understood, now, the sense of familiarity that the sight of the bearded man had roused in him from the first. He had seen a coin like this once before, long ago in a far land.

With a shake of his shoulders he growled: 'The likeness is only a coincidence — or if he's shrewd enough to assume a forgotten wizard's name, he's shrewd enough to assume his likeness.' But he spoke without conviction. The sight of that coin had shaken the foundation of his universe. He felt that reality and stability were crumbling into an abyss of illusion and sorcery. A wizard was understandable; but this was diabolism beyond sanity.

'We cannot doubt that it is indeed Xaltotun of Python,' said Hadrathus. 'He it was who shook down the cliffs at Valkia, by his spells that enthrall the elementals of the earth — he it is who sent the creature of darkness into your tent before dawn.'

Conan scowled at him. 'How did you know that?'

'The followers of Asura have secret channels of knowledge. That does not matter. But do you realize the futility of sacrificing your subjects in a vain attempt to regain your crown?'

Conan rested his chin on his fist, and stared grimly into nothing. Albiona watched him anxiously, her mind groping bewildered in the mazes of the problem that confronted him.

'Is there no wizard in the world who could make magic to fight Xaltotun's magic?' he asked at last.

Hadrathus shook his head. 'If there were, we of Asura would know of him. Men say our cult is a survival of the ancient Stygian serpent-worship. That is a lie. Our ancestors came from Vendhya, beyond the Sea of Vilayet and the blue Himelian mountains. We are sons of the East, not the South, and we have knowledge of all the wizards of the East, who are greater than the wizards of the West. And not one of them but would be a straw in the wind before the black might of Xaltotun.'

'But he was conquered once,' persisted Conan.

'Aye; a cosmic source was turned against him. But now that source is again in his hands, and he will see that it is not stolen again.'

'And what is this damnable source?' demanded Conan irritably.

'It is called the Heart of Ahriman. When Acheron was overthrown, the primitive priest who had stolen it and turned it against Xaltotun hid it in a haunted cavern and built a small temple over the cavern. Thrice thereafter the temple was rebuilt, each time greater and more elaborately than before, but always on the site of the original

93

shrine, though men forgot the reason therefor. Memory of the hidden symbol faded from the minds of common men, and was preserved only in priestly books and esoteric volumes. Whence it came no one knows. Some say it is the veritable heart of a god, others that it is a star that fell from the skies long ago. Until it was stolen, none had looked upon it for three thousand years.

'When the magic of the Mitran priests failed against the magic of Xaltotun's acolyte, Altaro, they remembered the ancient legend of the Heart, and the high priest and an acolyte went down into the dark and terrible crypt below the temple into which no priest had descended for three thousand years. In the ancient iron-bound volumes which speak of the Heart in their cryptic symbolism, it is also told of a creature of darkness left by the ancient priest to guard it.

'Far down in a square chamber with arched doorways leading off into immeasurable blackness, the priest and his acolytes found a black stone altar that glowed dimly with inexplicable radiance.

'On that altar lay a curious gold vessel like a double-valved sea-shell which clung to the stone like a barnacle. But it gaped open and empty. The Heart of Ahriman was gone. While they stared in horror, the keeper of the crypt, the creature of darkness, came upon them and mangled the high priest so that he died. But the acolyte fought off the being – a mindless, soulless waif of the pits brought long ago to guard the Heart – and escaped up the long black narrow stairs carrying the dying priest, who, before he died, gasped out the news to his followers, bade them submit to a power they could not overcome, and commanded secrecy. But the word has been whispered about among the priests, and we of Asura learned of it.'

'And Xaltotun draws his power from this symbol?' asked Conan, still skeptical.

'No. His power is drawn from the black gulf. But the Heart of Ahriman came from some far universe of flaming light, and against it the powers of darkness cannot stand, when it is in the hands of an adept. It is like a sword that might smite at him, not a sword with which he can smite. It restores life, and can destroy life. He has stolen it, not to use against his enemies, but to keep them from using it against him.'

'A shell-shaped bowl of gold on a black altar in a deep cavern,' Conan muttered, frowning as he sought to capture

94

the illusive image. 'That reminds me of something I have heard or seen. But what, in Crom's name, *is* this notable Heart?'

'It is in the form of a great jewel, like a ruby, but pulsing with blinding fire with which no ruby ever burned. It glows like living flame—'

But Conan sprang suddenly up and smote his right fist into his left palm like a thunderclap.

'Crom!' he roared. 'What a fool I've been! The Heart of Ahriman! The heart of my kingdom! Find the heart of my kingdom, Zelata said. By Ymir, it was the jewel I saw in the green smoke, the jewel which Tarascus stole from Xaltotun while he lay in the sleep of the black lotus!'

Hadrathus was also on his feet, his calm dropped from him like a garment.

'What are you saying? The Heart stolen from Xaltotun?'

'Aye!' Conan boomed. 'Tarascus feared Xaltotun and wanted to cripple his power, which he thought resided in the Heart. Maybe he thought the wizard would die if the Heart was lost. By Crom – ahhh!' With a savage grimace of disappointment and disgust he dropped his clenched hand to his side.

'I forgot. Tarascus gave it to a thief to throw into the sea. By this time the fellow must be almost to Kordava. Before I can follow him he'll take ship and consign the Heart to the bottom of the ocean.'

'The sea will not hold it!' exclaimed Hadrathus, quivering with excitement. 'Xaltotun would himself have cast it into the sea long ago, had he not known that the first storm would carry it ashore. But on what unknown beach might it not land!'

'Well,' Conan was recovering some of his resilient confidence, 'there's no assurance that the thief will throw it away. If I know thieves – and I should, for I was a thief in Zamora in my early youth – he won't throw it away. He'll sell it to some rich trader. By Crom!' He strode back and fourth in his growing excitement. 'It's worth looking for! Zelata bade me find the heart of my kingdom, and all else she showed me proved to be truth. Can it be that the power to conquer Xaltotun lurks in that crimson bauble?'

'Aye! My head upon it!' cried Hadrathus, his face lightened with fevor, his eyes blazing, his fists clenched. 'With it in our hands we can dare the powers of Xaltotun! I swear it! If we can recover it, we have an even chance of recovering your crown and driving the invaders from our portals. It is not the swords of Nemedia that Aquilonia fears, but the black arts of Xaltotun.'

Conan looked at him for a space, impressed by the priest's fire.

'It's like a quest in a nightmare,' he said at last. 'Yet your words echo the thought of Zelata, and all else she said was truth. I'll seek for this jewel.'

'It holds the destiny of Aquilonia,' said Hadrathus with conviction. 'I will send men with you—'

'Nay!' exclaimed the king impatiently, not caring to be hampered by priests on his quest, however skilled in esoteric arts. 'This is a task for a fighting-man. I go alone. First to Poitain, where I'll leave Albiona with Trocero. Then to Kordava, and to the sea beyond, if necessary. It may be that, even if the thief intends carrying out Tarascus's order, he'll have some difficulty finding an outbound ship at this time of the year.'

'And if you find the Heart,' cried Hadrathus, 'I will prepare the way for your conquest. Before you return to Aquilonia I will spread the word through secret channels that you live and are returning with a magic stronger than Xaltotun's. I will have men ready to rise on your return. They *will* rise, if they have assurance that they will be protected from the black arts of Xaltotun.'

'And I will aid you on your journey.'

He rose and struck the gong.

'A secret tunnel leads from beneath this temple to a place outside the city wall. You shall go to Poitain on a pilgrim's boat. None will dare molest you.'

'As you will.' With a definite purpose in mind Conan was afire with impatience and dynamic energy. 'Only let it be done swiftly.'

In the meantime events were moving not slowly elsewhere in the city. A breathless messenger had burst into the palace where Valerius was amusing himself with his dancing-girls, and throwing himself on his knees, gasped out a garbled story of a bloody prison break and the escape of a lovely captive. He bore also the news that Count Thespius, to whom the execution of Albiona's sentence had been entrusted, was dying and begged for a word with Valerius before he passed.

Hurriedly cloaking himself, Valerius accompanied the

man through various winding ways, and came to a chamber where Thespius lay. There was no doubt that the count was dying; bloody froth bubbled from his lips at each shuddering gasp. His severed arm had been bound to stop the flow of blood, but even without that, the gash in his side was mortal.

Alone in the chamber with the dying man, Valerius swore softly.

'By Mitra, I had believed that only one man ever lived who could strike such a blow.'

'Valerius!' gasped the dying man. 'He lives! Conan lives!'

'What are you saying?' ejaculated the other.

'I swear by Mitra!' gurgled Thespius, gagging on the blood that gushed to his lips. 'It was he who carried off Albiona! He is not dead – no phantom come back from Hell to haunt us. He is flesh and blood, and more terrible than ever. The alley behind the tower is full of dead men. Beware, Valerius – he has come back – to slay us all—'

A strong shudder shook the blood-smeared figure, and Count Thespius went limp.

Valerius frowned down at the dead man, cast a swift glance about the empty chamber, and stepping swiftly to the door, cast it open suddenly. The messenger and a group of Nemedian guardsmen stood several paces down the corridor. Valerius muttered something that might have indicated satisfaction.

'Have all gates been closed?' he demanded.

'Yes, Your Majesty.'

'Triple the guards at each. Let no one enter or leave the city without strictest investigation. Set men scouring the streets and searching the quarters. A very valuable prisoner has escaped, with the aid of an Aquilonian rebel. Did any of you recognize the man?'

'No, Your Majesty. The old watchman had a glimpse of him, but could only say that he was a giant, clad in the black garb of the executioner, whose naked body we found in an empty cell.'

'He is a dangerous man,' said Valerius. 'Take no chances with him. You all know the Countess Albiona. Search for her, and if you find her, kill her and her companion instantly. Do not try to take them alive.'

Returning to his palace chamber, Valerius summoned before him four men of curious and alien aspect. They were tall, gaunt, of yellowish skin, and immobile countenances. They were very similar in appearence, clad alike in long black robes beneath which their sandaled feet were just visible. Their features were shadowed by their hoods. They stood before Valerius with their hands in their wide sleeves, their arms folded. Valerius looked at them without pleasure. In his far journeyings he had encountered many strange races.

'When I found you starving in the Khitan jungles,' he said abruptly, 'exiles from your kingdom, you swore to serve me. You have served me well enough, in your abominable way. One more service I require, and then I set you free of your oath.

'Conan the Cimmerian, king of Aquilonia, still lives, in spite of Xaltotun's sorcery – or perhaps because of it. I know not. The dark mind of that resurrected devil is too devious and subtle for a mortal man to fathom. But while Conan lives I am not safe. The people accepted me as the lesser of two evils, when they thought he was dead. Let him reappear and the throne will be rocking under my feet in revolution before I can lift my hand.

'Perhaps my allies mean to use him to replace me, if they decide I have served my purpose. I do not know. I do know that this planet is too small for two kings of Aquilonia. Seek the Cimmerian. Use your uncanny talents to ferret him out wherever he hides or runs. He has many friends in Tarantia. He had aid when he carried off Albiona. It took more than one man, even such a man as Conan, to wreak all that slaughter in the alley outside the tower. But no more. Take your staffs and strike his trail. Where that trail will lead you, I know not. But find him! And when you find him, slay him!'

The four Khitans bowed together, and still unspeaking, turned and padded noiselessly from the chamber.

11 – SWORDS OF THE SOUTH

DAWN THAT ROSE over the distant hills shone on the sails of a small craft that dropped down the river which curves to within a mile of the walls of Tarantia, and loops southward like a great shining serpent. This boat differed from the ordinary craft plying the broad Khorotas – fishermen and merchant barges loaded with rich goods. It was long and slender, with a high, curving prow, and was black as ebony, with white skulls painted along the gunwales. Amidships rose a small cabin, the windows closely masked. Other craft gave the ominously painted boat a wide berth; for it was obviously one of those 'pilgrim boats' that carried a lifeless follower of Asura on his last mysterious pilgrimage southward to where, far beyond the Poitanian mountains, the river flowed at last into the blue ocean. In that cabin undoubtedly lay the corpse of the departed worshipper. All men were familiar with the sight of those gloomy craft; and the most fanatical votary of Mitra would not dare touch or interfere with their somber voyages.

Where the ultimate destination lay, men did not know. Some said Stygia; some a nameless island lying beyond the horizon; others said it was in the glamorous and mysterious land of Vendhya where the dead came home at last. But none knew certainly. They only knew that when a follower of Asura died, the corpse went southward down the great river, in a black boat rowed by a giant slave, and neither boat nor corpse nor slave was ever seen again; unless, indeed, certain dark tales were true, and it was always the same slave who rowed the boats southward.

The man who propelled this particular boat was as huge and brown as the others, though closer scrutiny might have revealed the fact that the hue was the result of carefully applied pigments. He was clad in leather loincloth and sandals, and he handled the long sweep and oars with unusual skill and power. But none approached the grim boat closely, for it was well known that the followers of Asura were accursed, and that these pilgrim boats were loaded with dark magic. So men swung their boats wide and muttered an incantation as the dark craft slid past, and they never dreamed that they were thus assisting in the flight of their king and the Countess Albiona.

It was a strange journey, in that black, slim craft down the great river for nearly two hundred miles to where the Khorotas swings eastward, skirting the Poitanian mountains. Like a dream the ever-changing panorama glided past. During the day Albiona lay patiently in the little cabin, as quietly as the corpse she pretended to be. Only late at night, after the pleasure boats with their fair occupants lounging on silken cushions in the flare of torches held by slaves had left the river, before dawn brought the hurrying fisher-boats, did the girl venture out. Then she held the long sweep, cunningly bound in place by ropes to aid her, while Conan snatched a few hours of sleep. But the king needed little rest. The fire of his desire drove him relentlessly, and his powerful frame was equal to the grinding test. Without halt or pause they drove southward.

So down the river they fled, through nights when the flowing current mirrored the million stars, and through days of golden sunlight, leaving winter behind them as they sped southward. They passed cities in the night, above which throbbed and pulsed the reflection of the myriad lights, lordly river villas and fertile groves. So at last the blue mountains of Poitain rose above them, tier above tier, like ramparts of the gods, and the great river, swerving from those turreted cliffs, swept thunderously through the marching hills with many a rapid and foaming cataract.

Conan scanned the shore-line closely, and finally swung the long sweep and headed inshore at a point where a neck of land jutted into the water, and fir trees grew in a curiously symmetrical ring about a gray, strangely shaped rock.

'How these boats ride those falls we hear roaring ahead of us is more than I can see,' he grunted. 'Hadrathus said they did – but here's where we halt. He said a man would be waiting for us with horses, but I don't see anyone. How word of our coming could have preceded us I don't know anyway.'

He drove inshore and bound the prow to an arching root in the low bank, and then, plunging into the water, washed the brown paint from his skin and emerged dripping, and in his natural color. From the cabin he brought forth a suit of Aquilonian ring-mail which Hadrathus had procured for him, and his sword. These he donned while Albiona put on garments suitable for mountain travel. And when Conan was fully armed, and turned to look toward the shore, he started and his hand went to his sword. For on the shore, under the trees, stood a black-coated figure holding the reins of a white palfrey and a bay warhorse.

'Who are you?' demanded the king.

The other bowed low.

'A follower of Asura. A command came. I obeyed.'

'How, "came"?' inquired Conan, but the other merely bowed again.

'I have come to guide you through the mountains to the first Poitanian stronghold.'

'I don't need a guide,' answered Conan. 'I know these hills well. I thank you for the horses, but the countess and I will attract less attention alone than if we were accompanied by an acolyte of Asura.'

The man bowed profoundly, and giving the reins into Conan's hands, stepped into the boat. Casting off, he floated down the swift current, toward the distant roar of the unseen rapids. With a baffled shake of his head, Conan lifted the countess into the palfrey's saddle, and then mounted the war-horse and reined toward the summits that castellated the sky.

The rolling country at the foot of the towering mountains was now a borderland, in a state of turmoil, where the barons reverted to feudal practices, and bands of outlaws roamed unhindered. Poitain had not formally declared her separation from Aquilonia, but she was now, to all intents, a self-contained kingdom, ruled by her hereditary count, Trocero. The rolling south country had submitted nominally to Valerius, but he had not attempted to force the passes guarded by strongholds where the crimson leopard banner of Poitain waved defiantly.

The king and his fair companion rode up the long blue slopes in the soft evening. As they mounted higher, the rolling country spread out like a vast purple mantle far beneath them, shot with the shine of rivers and lakes, the yellow glint of broad fields, and the white gleam of distant towers. Ahead of them and far above, they glimpsed the first of the Poitanian holds – a strong fortress dominating a narrow pass, the crimson banner streaming against the clear blue sky.

Before they reached it, a band of knights in burnished armor rode from among the trees, and their leader sternly ordered the travelers to halt. They were tall men, with the dark eyes and raven locks of the south.

'Halt, sir, and state your business, and why you ride toward Poitain.'

'Is Poitain in revolt, then,' asked Conan, watching the

other closely, 'that a man in Aquilonian harness is halted and questioned like a foreigner?'

'Many rogues ride out of Aquilonia these days,' answered the other coldly. 'As for revolt, if you mean the repudiation of a usurper, then Poitain is in revolt. We had rather serve the memory of a dead man than the scepter of a living dog.'

Conan swept off his helmet, and shaking back his black mane, stared full at the speaker. The Poitanian started violently and went livid.

'Saints of heaven!' he gasped. 'It is the king – *alive!*'

The others stared wildly, then a roar of wonder and joy burst from them. They swarmed about Conan, shouting their war-cries and brandishing their swords in their extreme emotion. The acclaim of Poitanian warriors was a thing to terrify a timid man.

'Oh, but Trocero will weep tears of joy to see you, sire!' cried one.

'Aye, and Prospero!' shouted another. 'The general has been like one wrapped in a mantle of melancholy, and curses himself night and day that he did not reach the Valkia in time to die beside his king!'

'Now we will strike for empery!' yelled another, whirling his great sword about his head. 'Hail, Conan, *king of Poitain!*'

The clangor of bright steel about him and the thunder of their acclaim frightened the birds that rose in gay-hued clouds from the surrounding trees. The hot southern blood was afire, and they desired nothing but for their new-found sovereign to lead them to battle and pillage.

'What is your command, sire?' they cried. 'Let one of us ride ahead and bear the news of your coming into Poitain! Banners will wave from every tower, roses will carpet the road before your horse's feet, and all the beauty and chivalry of the south will give you the honor due you—'

Conan shook his head.

'Who could doubt your loyalty? But winds blow over these mountains into the countries of my enemies, and I would rather these didn't know that I lived – yet. Take me to Trocero, and keep my identity a secret.'

So what the knights would have made a triumphal procession was more in the nature of a secret flight. They traveled in haste, speaking to no one, except for a whisper to the captain on duty at each pass; and Conan rode among them with his vizor lowered.

The mountains were uninhabited save by outlaws and garrisons of soldiers who guarded the passes. The pleasure-loving Poitanians had no need nor desire to wrest a hard and scanty living from their stern breasts. South of the ranges the rich and beautiful plains of Poitain stretched to the river Alimane; but beyond the river lay the land of Zingara.

Even now, when winter was crisping the leaves beyond the mountains, the tall rich grass waved upon the plains where grazed the horses and cattle for which Poitain was famed. Palm trees and orange groves smiled in the sun, and the gorgeous purple and gold and crimson towers of castles and cities reflected the golden light. It was a land of warmth and plenty, of beautiful women and ferocious warriors. It is not only the hard lands that breed hard men. Poitain was surrounded by covetous neighbors and her sons learned hardihood in incessant wars. To the north the land was guarded by the mountains, but to the south only the Alimane separated the plains of Poitain from the plains of Zingara, and not once but a thousand times had that river run red. To the east lay Argos and beyond that Ophir, proud kingdoms and avaricious. The knights of Poitain held their lands by the weight and edge of their swords, and little of ease and idleness they knew.

So Conan came presently to the castle of Count Trocero ...

Conan sat on a silken divan in a rich chamber whose filmy curtains the warm breeze billowed. Trocero paced the floor like a panther, a lithe, restless man with the waist of a woman and the shoulders of a swordsman, who carried his years lightly.

'Let us proclaim you king of Poitain!' urged the count. 'Let those northern pigs wear the yoke to which they have bent their necks. The south is still yours. Dwell here and rule us, amid the flowers and the palms.'

But Conan shook his head. 'There is no nobler land on earth than Poitain. But it cannot stand alone, bold as are its sons.'

'It *did* stand alone, for generations,' retorted Trocero, with the quick jealous pride of his breed. 'We were not always a part of Aquilonia.'

'I know. But conditions are not as they were then, when all kingdoms were broken into principalities which warred with each other. The days of dukedoms and free cities are past, the days of empires are upon us. Rulers are dreaming imperial dreams, and only in unity is there strength.'

'Then let us unite Zingara with Poitain,' argued Trocero. 'Half a dozen princes strive against each other, and the country is torn asunder by civil wars. We will conquer it, province by province, and add it to your dominions. Then with the aid of the Zingarans we will conquer Argos and Ophir. *We* will build an empire—'

Again Conan shook his head. 'Let others dream imperial dreams. I but wish to hold what is mine. I have no desire to rule an empire welded together by blood and fire. It's one thing to seize a throne with the aid of its subjects and rule them with their consent. It's another to subjugate a foreign realm and rule it by fear. I don't wish to be another Valerius. No, Trocero, I'll rule all Aquilonia and no more, or I'll rule nothing.'

'Then lead us over the mountains and we will smite the Nemedians.'

Conan's fierce eyes glowed with appreciation.

'No, Trocero. It would be a vain sacrifice. I've told you what I must do to regain my kingdom. I must find the Heart of Ahriman.'

'But this is madness!' protested Trocero. 'The maunderings of a heretical priest, the mumblings of a mad witch-woman.'

'You were not in my tent before Valkia,' answered Conan grimly, involuntarily glancing at his right wrist, on which blue marks still showed faintly. 'You didn't see the cliffs thunder down to crush the flower of my army. No, Trocero, I've been convinced. Xaltotun's no mortal man, and only with the Heart of Ahriman can I stand against him. So I'm riding to Kordava, alone.'

'But that is dangerous,' protested Trocero.

'Life is dangerous,' rumbled the king. 'I won't go as king of Aquilonia, or even as a knight of Poitain, but as a wandering mercenary, as I rode in Zingara in the old days. Oh, I have enemies enough south of the Alimane, in the lands and the waters of the south. Many who won't know me as king of Aquilonia will remember me as Conan of the Barachan pirates, or Amra of the black corsairs. But I have friends, too, and men who'll aid me for their own private reasons.' A faintly reminiscent grin touched his lips.

Trocero dropped his hands helplessly and glanced at Albiona, who sat on a near-by divan.

'I understand your doubts, my lord,' said she. 'But I too saw the coin in the temple of Asura, and look you, Hadrathus said it was dated five hundred years *before* the fall of Acheron. If Xaltotun, then, is the man pictured on the coin, as his Majesty swears he is, that means he was no common wizard, even in his other life, for the years of his life were numbered in centuries, not as the lives of other men are numbered.'

Before Trocero could reply, a respectful rap was heard on the door and a voice called: 'My lord, we have caught a man skulking about the castle, who says he wishes to speak with your guest. I await your orders.'

'A spy from Aquilonia!' hissed Trocero, catching at his dagger, but Conan lifted his voice and called: 'Open the door and let me see him.'

The door was opened and a man was framed in it, grasped on either hand by stern-looking men-at-arms. He was a slender man, clad in a dark hooded robe.

'Are you a follower of Asura?' asked Conan.

The man nodded, and the stalwart men-at-arms looked shocked and glanced hesitantly at Trocero.

'The word came southward,' said the man. 'Beyond the Alimane we cannot aid you, for our sect goes no farther southward, but stretches eastward with the Khorotas. But this I have learned: the thief who took the Heart of Ahriman from Tarascus never reached Kordava. In the mountains of Poitain he was slain by robbers. The jewel fell into the hands of their chief, who, not knowing its true nature, and being harried after the destruction of his band by Poitanian knights, sold it to the Kothic merchant Zorathus.'

'Ha!' Conan was on his feet, galvanized. 'And what of Zorathus?'

'Four days ago he crossed the Alimane, headed for Argos, with a small band of armed servants.'

'He's a fool to cross Zingara in such times,' said Trocero.

'Aye, times are troublous across the river. But Zorathus is a bold man, and reckless in his way. He is in great haste to reach Messantia, where he hopes to find a buyer for the jewel. Perhaps he hopes to sell it finally in Stygia. Perhaps he guesses at its true nature. At any rate, instead of following the long road that winds along the borders of Poitain and so at last comes into Argos far from Messantia, he has struck straight across eastern Zingara, following the shorter and more direct route.'

Conan smote the table with his clenched fist so that the great board quivered.

105

'Then, by Crom, fortune has at last thrown the dice for me! A horse, Trocero, and the harness of a Free Companion! Zorathus has a long start, but not too long for me to overtake him, if I follow him to the end of the world!'

12 – THE FANG OF THE DRAGON

AT DAWN Conan waded his horse across the shallows of the Alimane and struck the wide caravan trail which ran southeastward, and behind him, on the farther bank, Trocero sat upon his horse silently at the head of his steel-clad knights, with the crimson leopard of Poitain floating its long folds over him in the morning breeze. Silently they sat, those dark-haired men in shining steel, until the figure of their king had vanished in the blue of distance that whitened toward sunrise.

Conan rode a great black stallion, the gift of Trocero. He no longer wore the armor of Aquilonia. His harness proclaimed him a veteran of the Free Companies, who were of all races. His headpiece was a plain basinet, dented and battered. The leather and mail-mesh of his hauberk were worn and shiny as if by many campaigns, and the scarlet cloak flowing carelessly from his mailed shoulders was tattered and stained. He looked the part of the hired fighting-man, who had known all vicissitudes of fortune, plunder and wealth one day, an empty purse and a close-drawn belt the next.

And more than looking the part, he felt the part; the awakening of old memories, the resurge of the wild, mad, glorious days of old before his feet were set on the imperial path when he was a wandering mercenary, roistering, brawling, guzzling, adventuring, with no thought for the morrow, and no desire save sparkling ale, red lips, and a keen sword to swing on all the battlefields of the world.

Unconsciously he reverted to the old ways; a new swagger became evident in his bearing, in the way he sat his horse; half-forgotten oaths rose naturally to his lips, and as he rode he hummed old songs that he had roared in chorus with his reckless companions in many a tavern and on many a dusty road or bloody field.

It was an unquiet land through which he rode. The companies of cavalry which usually patrolled the river, alert for raids out of Poitain, were nowhere in evidence. Internal strife had left the borders unguarded. The long white road stretched bare from horizon to horizon. No laden camel trains or rumbling wagons or lowing herds moved along it now; only occasional groups of horsemen in leather and steel, hawk-faced, hard-eyed men, who kept together and rode warily. These swept Conan with their searching gaze but rode on, for the solitary rider's harness promised no plunder, but only hard strokes.

Villages lay in ashes and deserted, the fields and meadows idle. Only the boldest would ride the roads these days, and the native population had been decimated in the civil wars, and by raids from across the river. In more peaceful times the road was thronged with merchants riding from Poitain to Messantia in Argos, or back. But now these found it wiser to follow the road that led east through Poitain, and then turned south down across Argos. It was longer, but safer. Only an extremely reckless man would risk his life and goods on this road through Zingara.

The southern horizon was fringed with flame by night, and in the day straggling pillars of smoke drifted upward; in the cities and plains to the south men were dying, thrones were toppling, and castles going up in flames. Conan felt the old tug of the professional fighting-man, to turn his horse and plunge into the fighting, the pillaging, and the looting as in the days of old. Why should he toil to regain the rule of a people which had already forgotten him? – why chase a will-o'-the-wisp, why pursue a crown that was lost for ever? Why should he not seek forgetfulness, lose himself in the red tides of war and rapine that had engulfed him so often before? Could he not, indeed, carve out another kingdom for himself? The world was entering an age of iron, an age of war and imperialistic ambition; some strong man might well rise above the ruins of nations as a supreme conqueror. Why should it not be himself? So his familiar devil whispered in his ear, and the phantoms of his lawless and bloody past crowded upon him. But he did not turn aside; he rode onward, following a quest that grew dimmer and dimmer as he advanced, until sometimes it seemed that he pursued a dream that never was.

He pushed the black stallion as hard as he dared, but the long white road lay bare before him, from horizon to horizon. It was a long start Zorathus had, but Conan rode steadily on, knowing that he was traveling faster than the burdened merchants could travel. And so he came to the castle of Count Valbroso, perched like a vulture's eyrie on a bare hill overlooking the road.

Valbroso rode down with his men-at-arms, a lean, dark man with glittering eyes and a predatory beak of a nose. He wore black plate-armor and was followed by thirty spearmen, black-mustached hawks of the border wars, as avaricious and ruthless as himself. Of late the toll of the caravans had been slim, and Valbroso cursed the civil wars that stripped the roads of their fat traffic, even while he blessed them for the free hand they allowed him with his neighbors.

He had not hoped for much from the solitary rider he had glimpsed from his tower, but all was grist that came to his mill. With a practiced eye he took in Conan's worn mail and dark, scarred face, and his conclusions were the same as those of the riders who had passed the Cimmerian on the road – an empty purse and a ready blade.

'Who are you, knave?' he demanded.

'A mercenary, riding for Argos,' answered Conan. 'What matter names?'

'You are riding in the wrong direction for a Free Companion,' grunted Valbroso. 'Southward the fighting is good and also the plundering. Join my company. You won't go hungry. The road remains bare of fat merchants to strip, but I mean to take my rogues and fare southward to sell our swords to whichever side seems strongest.'

Conan did not at once reply, knowing that if he refused outright, he might be instantly attacked by Valbroso's men-at-arms. Before he could make up his mind, the Zingaran spoke again:

'You rogues of the Free Companies always know tricks to make men talk. I have a prisoner – the last merchant I caught, by Mitra, and the only one I've seen for a week – and the knave is stubborn. He has an iron box, the secret of which defies us, and I've been unable to persuade him to open it. By Ishtar, I thought I knew all the modes of persuasion there are, but perhaps you, as a veteran Free Companion, know some that I do not. At any rate come with me and see what you may do.'

Valbroso's words instantly decided Conan. That sounded a great deal like Zorathus. Conan did not know the merchant, but any man who was stubborn enough to try to traverse the Zingaran roads in times like these would very probably be stubborn enough to defy torture.

108

He fell in beside Valbroso and rode up the straggling road to the top of the hill where the gaunt castle stood. As a man-at-arms he should have ridden behind the count, but force of habit made him careless and Valbroso paid no heed. Years of life on the border had taught the count that the frontier is not the royal court. He was aware of the independence of the mercenaries, behind whose swords many a king had trodden the throne-path.

There was a dry moat, half filled with debris in some places. They clattered across the drawbridge and through the arch of the gate. Behind them the portcullis fell with a sullen clang. They came into a bare courtyard, grown with straggling grass, and with a well in the middle. Shacks for the men-at-arms straggled about the bailey wall, and women, slatternly or decked in gaudy finery, looked from the doors. Fighting-men in rusty mail tossed dice on the flags under the arches. It was more like a bandit's hold than the castle of a nobleman.

Valbroso dismounted and motioned Conan to follow him. They went through a doorway and along a vaulted corridor, where they were met by a scarred, hard-looking man in mail descending a stone staircase – evidently the captain of the guard.

'How, Beloso,' quoth Valbroso; 'has he spoken?'

'He is stubborn,' muttered Beloso, shooting a glance of suspicion at Conan.

Valbroso ripped out an oath and stamped furiously up the winding stair, followed by Conan and the captain. As they mounted, the groans of a man in mortal agony became audible. Valbroso's torture-room was high above the court, instead of in a dungeon below. In that chamber, where a gaunt, hairy beast of a man in leather breeks squatted gnawing a beef-bone voraciously, stood the machines of torture – racks, boots, hooks and all the implements that the human mind devises to tear flesh, break bones, and rend and rupture veins and ligaments.

On a rack a man was stretched naked, and a glance told Conan that he was dying. The unnatural elongation of his limbs and body told of unhinged joints and unnameable ruptures. He was a dark man, with an intelligent, aquiline face and quick dark eyes. They were glazed and bloodshot now with pain, and the dew of agony glistened on his face. His lips were drawn back from blackened gums.

'There is the box.' Viciously Valbroso kicked a small but heavy iron chest that stood on the floor near by. It was intricately carved, with tiny skulls and writhing dragons curiously intertwined, but Conan saw no catch or hasp that might serve to unlock the lid. The marks of fire, of ax and sledge and chisel showed on it but as scratches.

'This is the dog's treasure box,' said Valbroso angrily. 'All men of the south know of Zorathus and his iron chest. Mitra knows what is in it. But he will not give up its secret.'

Zorathus! It was true, then; the man he sought lay before him. Conan's heat beat suffocatingly as he leaned over the writhing form, though he exhibited no evidence of his painful eagerness.

'Ease those ropes, knave!' he ordered the torturer harshly, and Valbroso and his captain stared. In the forgetfulness of the moment Conan had used his imperial tone, and the brute in leather instinctively obeyed the knife-edge of command in that voice. He eased away gradually, for else the slackening of the ropes had been as great a torment to the torn joints as further stretching.

Catching up a vessel of wine that stood near by, Conan placed the rim to the wretch's lips. Zorathus gulped spasmodically, the liquid slopping over his heaving breast.

Into the bloodshot eyes came a gleam of recognition, and the froth-smeared lips parted. From them issued a racking whimper in the Kothic tongue.

'Is this death, then? Is the long agony ended? For this is King Conan who died at Valkia, and I am among the dead.'

'You're not dead,' said Conan. 'But you're dying. You'll be tortured no more. I'll see to that. But I can't help you further. Yet before you die, tell me how to open your iron box!'

'My iron box,' mumbled Zorathus in delirious disjointed phrases. 'The chest forged in unholy fires among the flaming mountains of Khrosha; the metal no chisel can cut. How many treasures has it borne, across the width and the breadth of the world! But no such treasure as it now holds.'

'Tell me how to open it,' urged Conan. 'It can do you no good, and it may aid me.'

'Aye, you are Conan,' muttered the Kothian. 'I have seen you sitting on your throne in the great public hall of Tarantia, with your crown on your head and the scepter in your hand. But you are dead; you died at Valkia. And now I know my own end is at hand.'

'What does the dog say?' demanded Valbroso impatiently, not understanding Kothic. 'Will he tell us how to open the box?'

As if the voice roused a spark of life in the twisted breast, Zorathus rolled his bloodshot eyes toward the speaker.

'Only Valbroso will I tell,' he gasped in Zingaran. 'Death is upon me. Lean close to me, Valbroso!'

The count did so, his dark face lit with avarice; behind him his saturnine captain, Beloso, crowded closer.

'Press the seven skulls on the rim, one after another,' gasped Zorathus. 'Press then the head of the dragon that writhes across the lid. Then press the sphere in the dragon's claws. That will release the secret catch.'

'Quick, the box!' cried Valbroso with an oath.

Conan lifted it and set it on a dais, and Valbroso shouldered him aside.

'Let me open it!' cried Beloso, starting forward.

Valbroso cursed him back, his greed blazing in his black eyes.

'None but me shall open it!' he cried.

Conan, whose hand had instinctively gone to his hilt, glanced at Zorathus. The man's eyes were glazed and blood-shot, but they were fixed on Valbroso with burning intensity; and was there the shadow of a grim twisted smile on the dying man's lips? Not until the merchant knew he was dying had he given up the secret. Conan turned to watch Valbroso, even as the dying man watched him.

Along the rim of the lid seven skulls were carved among intertwining branches of strange trees. An inlaid dragon writhed its way across the top of the lid, amid ornate arabesques. Valbroso pressed the skulls in fumbling haste, and as he jammed his thumb down on the carved head of the dragon he swore sharply and snatched his hand away, shaking it in irritation.

'A sharp point on the carvings,' he snarled. 'I've pricked my thumb.'

He pressed the gold ball clutched in the dragon's talons, and the lid flew abruptly open. Their eyes were dazzled by a golden flame. It seemed to their dazed minds that the carven box was full of glowing fire that spilled over the rim and dripped through the air in quivering flakes. Beloso cried out and Valbroso sucked in his breath. Conan stood speechless, his brain snared by the blaze.

'Mitra, what a jewel!' Valbroso's hand dived into the

111

chest, came out with a great pulsing crimson sphere that filled the room with a lambent glow. In its glare Valbroso looked like a corpse. And the dying man on the loosened rack laughed wildly and suddenly.

'Fool!' he screamed. 'The jewel is yours! I give you death with it! The scratch on your thumb – look at the dragon's head, Valbroso!'

They all wheeled, stared. Something tiny and dully gleaming stood up from the gaping, carved mouth.

'The dragon's fang!' shrieked Zorathus. 'Steeped in the venom of the black Stygian scorpion! Fool – fool to open the box of Zorathus with your naked hand! Death! You are a dead man now!'

And with bloody foam on his lips he died.

Valbroso staggered, crying out. 'Ah, Mitra, I burn!' he shrieked. 'My veins race with liquid fire! My joints are bursting asunder! Death! Death!' And he reeled and crashed headlong. There was an instant of awful convulsions, in which the limbs were twisted into hideous and unnatural positions, and then in that posture the man froze, his glassy eyes staring sightlessly upward, his lips drawn back from blackened gums.

'Dead!' muttered Conan, stooping to pick up the jewel where it rolled on the floor from Valbroso's rigid hand. It lay on the floor like a quivering pool of sunset fire.

'Dead!' muttered Beloso, with madness in his eyes. And then he moved.

Conan was caught off guard, his eyes dazzled, his brain dazed by the blaze of the great gem. He did not realize Beloso's intention until something crashed with terrible force upon his helmet. The glow of the jewel was splashed with redder flame, and he went to his knees under the blow.

He heard a rush of feet, a bellow of ox-like agony. He was stunned but not wholly senseless, and realized that Beloso had caught up the iron box and crashed it down on his head as he stooped. Only the basinet had saved his skull. He staggered up, drawing his sword, trying to shake the dimness out of his eyes. The room swam to his dizzy gaze. But the door was open and fleet footsteps were dwindling down the winding stair. On the floor the brutish torturer was gasping out his life with a great gash under his breast. And the Heart of Ahriman was gone.

Conan reeled out of the chamber, sword in hand, blood streaming down his face from under his helmet. He ran

112

drunkenly down the steps, hearing a clang of steel in the courtyard below, shouts, then the frantic drum of hoofs. Rushing into the bailey, he saw the men-at-arms milling about confusedly, while women screeched. The postern gate stood open and a soldier lay across his pike with his head split. Horses, still bridled and saddled, ran neighing about the court, Conan's black stallion among them.

'He's mad!' howled a woman, wringing her hands as she rushed brainlessly about. 'He came out of the castle like a mad dog, hewing right and left! Beloso's mad! Where's Lord Valbroso?'

'Which way did he go?' roared Conan.

All turned and stared at the stranger's blood-stained face and naked sword.

'Through the postern!' shrilled a woman, pointing eastward, and another bawled: 'Who is this rogue?'

'Beloso has killed Valbroso!' yelled Conan, leaping and seizing the stallion's mane, as the men-at-arms advanced uncertainly on him. A wild outcry burst forth at his news, but their reaction was exactly as he had anticipated. Instead of closing the gates to take him prisoner, or pursuing the fleeing slayer to avenge their lord, they were thrown into even greater confusion by his words. Wolves bound together only by fear of Valbroso, they owed no allegiance to the castle or to each other.

Swords began to clash in the courtyard, and women screamed. And in the midst of it all, none noticed Conan as he shot through the postern gate and thundered down the hill. The wide plain spread before him, and beyond the hill the caravan road divided; one branch ran south, the other east. And on the eastern road he saw another rider, bending low and spurring hard. The plain swam to Conan's gaze, the sunlight was a thick red haze and he reeled in his saddle, grasping the flowing mane with his hand. Blood rained on his mail, but grimly he urged the stallion on.

Behind him smoke began to pour out of the castle on the hill where the count's body lay forgotten and unheeded beside that of his prisoner. The sun was setting; against a lurid red sky the two black figures fled.

The stallion was not fresh, but neither was the horse ridden by Beloso. But the great beast responded mightily, calling on deep reservoirs of reserve vitality. Why the Zingaran fled from one pursuer Conan did not tax his bruised brain to guess. Perhaps unreasoning panic rode Beloso, born of the madness

113

that lurked in that blazing jewel. The sun was gone; the white road was a dim glimmer through a ghostly twilight fading into purple gloom far ahead of him.

The stallion panted, laboring hard. The country was changing in the gathering dusk. Bare plains gave way to clumps of oaks and alders. Low hills mounted up in the distance. Stars began to blink out. The stallion gasped and reeled in his course. But ahead rose a dense wood that stretched to the hills on the horizon, and between it and himself Conan glimpsed the dim form of the fugitive. He urged on the distressed stallion, for he saw that he was overtaking his prey, yard by yard. Above the pound of the hoofs a strange cry rose from the shadows, but neither pursuer nor pursued gave heed.

As they swept in under the branches that overhung the road, they were almost side by side. A fierce cry rose from Conan's lips as his sword went up; a pale oval of a face was turned toward him, a sword gleamed in a half-seen hand, and Beloso echoed the cry – and then the weary stallion, with a lurch and a groan, missed his footing in the shadows and went heels over head, hurling his dazed rider from the saddle. Conan's throbbing head crashed against a stone, and the stars were blotted out in a thicker night.

How long Conan lay senseless he never knew. His first sensation of returning consciousness was that of being dragged by one arm over rough and stony ground, and through dense underbrush. Then he was thrown carelessly down, and perhaps the jolt brought back his senses.

His helmet was gone, his head ached abominably, he felt a qualm of nausea, and blood was clotted thickly among his black locks. But with the vitality of a wild thing life and consciousness surged back into him, and he became aware of his surroundings.

A broad red moon was shining through the trees, by which he knew that it was long after midnight. He had lain senseless for hours, long enough to have recovered from that terrible blow Beloso had dealt him, as well as the fall which had rendered him senseless. His brain felt clearer than it had felt during that mad ride after the fugitive.

He was not lying beside the white road, he noticed with a start of surprise, as his surroundings began to record themselves on his perceptions. The road was nowhere in sight. He lay on the grassy earth, in a small glade hemmed in by a black wall of tree stems and tangled branches. His face and hands were scratched and lacerated as if he had been dragged through brambles. Shifting his body he looked about him. And then he started violently – something was squatting over him. . . .

At first Conan doubted his consciousness, thought it was but a figment of delirium. Surely it could not be real, that strange, motionless gray being that squatted on its haunches and stared down at him with unblinking soulless eyes.

Conan lay and stared, half expecting it to vanish like a figure of a dream, and then a chill of recognition crept along his spine. Half-forgotten memories surged back, of grisly tales whispered of the shapes that haunted these uninhabited forests at the foot of the hills that mark the Zingaran-Argossean border. *Ghouls*, men called them, eaters of human flesh, spawn of darkness, children of unholy matings of a lost and forgotten race with the demons of the underworld. Somewhere in these primitive forests were the ruins of an ancient, accursed city, men whispered, and among its tombs slunk gray, anthropomorphic shadows – Conan shuddered strongly.

He lay staring at the malformed head that rose dimly above him, and cautiously he extended a hand toward the dagger at his hip. With a horrible cry that the man involuntarily echoed, the monster was at his throat.

Conan threw up his right arm, and the dog-like jaws closed on it, driving the mail links into the hard flesh. The misshapen yet manlike hands clutched for his throat, but he evaded them with a heave and roll of his whole body, at the same time drawing his dagger with his left hand.

They tumbled over and over on the grass, smiting and tearing. The muscles coiling under that gray corpse-like skin were stringy and hard as steel wires, exceeding the strength of a man. But Conan's thews were iron too, and his mail saved him from the gnashing fangs and ripping claws long enough for him to drive home his dagger, again and again and again. The horrible vitality of the semi-human monstrosity seemed inexhaustible, and the king's skin crawled at the feel of that slick, clammy flesh. He put all his loathing and savage revulsion behind the plunging blade, and suddenly the monster heaved up convulsively beneath him as the point found its grisly heart, and then lay still.

Conan rose, shaken with nausea. He stood in the center of the glade, uncertainly, dagger in hand. He had not lost his instinctive sense of direction, as far as the points of the compass were concerned, but he did not know in which direction the road lay. He had no way of knowing in which direction the ghoul had dragged him. Conan glared at the silent, black, moon-dappled woods which ringed him, and felt cold moisture bead his flesh. He was without a horse and lost in these haunted woods, and that staring, deformed thing at his feet was a mute evidence of the horrors that lurked in the forest. He stood almost holding his breath in his painful intensity, straining his ears for some crack of twig or rustle of grass.

When a sound did come he started violently. Suddenly out on the night air broke the scream of a terrified horse. His stallion! There were panthers in the wood – or – ghouls ate beasts as well as men.

He broke savagely through the brush in the direction of the sound, whistling shrilly as he ran, his fear drowned in berserk rage. If his horse was killed, there went his last chance of following Beloso and recovering the jewel. Again the stallion screamed with fear and fury, somewhere nearer. There was a sound of lashing heels, and something that was struck heavily and gave way.

Conan burst out into the wide white road without warning, and saw the stallion plunging and rearing in the moonlight, his ears laid back, his eyes and teeth flashing wickedly. He lashed out with his heels at a slinking shadow that ducked and bobbed about him – and then about Conan other shadows moved: gray, furtive shadows that closed in on all sides. A hideous charnel-house scent reeked up in the night air.

A gleam among the dead leaves that carpeted the ground caught Conan's eye. It was his broadsword, lying where he had dropped it when his horse fell, and reflecting the rays of the moon. With a curse, the king caught up the weapon and hewed right and left. Dripping fangs flashed in the moonlight, foul paws caught at him, but he hacked his way through to the stallion, caught the rein, leaped into the saddle. His sword rose and fell, a frosty arc in the moon, showering blood as it split misshapen heads, clove shambling bodies. The stallion reared, biting and kicking. They burst through and thundered down the road. On either hand, for a short space, flitted gray abhorrent shadows. Then these fell behind, and Conan, topping a wooded crest, saw a vast expanse of bare slopes sweeping up and away before him.

13 – 'A GHOST OUT OF THE PAST'

SOON AFTER SUNRISE Conan crossed the Argossean border. Of Beloso he had seen no trace. Either the captain had made good his escape while the king lay senseless, or had fallen prey to the grim man-eaters of the Zingaran forest. But Conan had seen no signs to indicate the latter possibility. The fact that he had lain unmolested for so long seemed to indicate that the monsters had been engrossed in futile pursuit of the captain. And if the man lived, Conan felt certain that he was riding along the road somewhere ahead of him. Unless he had intended going into Argos he would never have taken the eastward road in the first place.

The helmeted guards at the frontier did not question the Cimmerian. A single wandering mercenary required no passport or safe-conduct, especially when his unadorned mail showed him to be in the service of no lord. Through the low, grassy hills where streams murmured and oak groves dappled the sward with lights and shadows he rode, following the long road that rose and fell away ahead of him over dales and rises in the blue distance. It was an old, old road, this highway from Poitain to the sea.

Argos was at peace; laden ox-wains rumbled along the road, and men with bare, brown, brawny arms toiled in orchards and fields that smiled away under the branches of the roadside trees. Old men on settles before inns under spreading oak branches called greetings to the wayfarer.

From the men that worked the fields, from the garrulous old men in the inns where he slaked his thirst with great leathern jacks of foaming ale, from the sharp-eyed silk-clad merchants he met upon the road, Conan sought for news of Beloso.

Stories were conflicting, but this much Conan learned: that a lean, wiry Zingaran with the dangerous black eyes and mustache of the western folk was somewhere on the road ahead of him, and apparently making for Messantia. It was a logical destination; all the sea-ports of Argos were cosmopolitan, in strong contrast with the inland provinces, and Messantia was the most polyglot of all. Craft of all the maritime nations rode in its harbor, and refugees and fugitives from many lands gathered there. Laws were lax; for Messantia thrived on the trade of the sea, and her citizens found it profitable to be somewhat blind in their dealings with seamen. It was not only legitimate trade that flowed into Messantia; smugglers and buccaneers played their part. All this Conan knew well, for had he not, in the days of old when he was a Barachan pirate, sailed by night into the harbor of Messantia to discharge strange cargoes? Most of the pirates of the Barachan Isles – small islands off the southwestern coast of Zingara – were Argossean sailors, and as long as they confined their attentions to the shipping of other nations, the authorities of Argos were not too strict in their interpretation of sea-laws.

But Conan had not limited his activities to those of the Barachans. He had also sailed with the Zingaran buccaneers, and even with those wild black corsairs that swept up from the far south to harry the northern coasts, and this put him beyond the pale of any law. If he were recognized in any of the ports of Argos it would cost him his head. But without hesitation he rode on to Messantia, halting day or night only to rest the stallion and to snatch a few winks of sleep for himself.

He entered the city unquestioned, merging himself with the throngs that poured continually in and out of this great commercial center. No walls surrounded Messantia. The sea and the ships of the sea guarded the great southern trading city.

It was evening when Conan rode leisurely through the streets that marched down to the waterfront. At the ends of these streets he saw the wharves and the masts and sails of ships. He smelled salt water for the first time in years, heard the thrum of cordage and the creak of spars in the breeze that was kicking up whitecaps out beyond the headlands. Again the urge of far wandering tugged at his heart.

But he did not go on to the wharves. He reined aside and rode up a steep flight of wide, worn stone steps, to a broad street where ornate white mansions overlooked the waterfront and the harbor below. Here dwelt the men who had grown rich from the hard-won fat of the seas – a few old sea-captains who had found treasure afar, many traders and merchants who never trod the naked decks nor knew the roar of tempest or sea-fight.

Conan turned in his horse at a certain gold-worked gate, and rode into a court where a fountain tinkled and pigeons fluttered from marble coping to marble flagging. A page in jagged silken jupon and hose came forward inquiringly. The merchants of Messantia dealt with many strange and rough characters, but most of these smacked of the sea. It was strange that a mercenary trooper should so freely ride into the court of a lord of commerce.

'The merchant Publio dwells here?' It was more statement than question, and something in the timbre of the voice caused the page to doff his feathered chaperon as he bowed and replied: 'Aye, so he does, my captain.'

Conan dismounted and the page called a servitor, who came running to receive the stallion's rein.

'Your master is within?' Conan drew off his gauntlets and slapped the dust of the road from cloak and mail.

'Aye, my captain. Whom shall I announce?'

'I'll announce myself,' grunted Conan. 'I know the way well enough. Bide you here.'

And obeying that peremptory command the page stood still, staring after Conan as the latter climbed a short flight of marble steps, and wondering what connection his master might have with this giant fighting-man who had the aspect of a northern barbarian.

Menials at their task halted and gaped open-mouthed as Conan crossed a wide, cool balcony overlooking the court and entered a broad corridor through which the sea-breeze swept. Half-way down this he heard a quill scratching and turned into a broad room whose many wide casements overlooked the harbor.

Publio sat at a carved teakwood desk writing on rich parchment with a golden quill. He was a short man, with a massive head and quick dark eyes. His blue robe was of the finest watered silk, trimmed with cloth-of-gold, and from his thick white throat hung a heavy gold chain.

As the Cimmerian entered, the merchant looked up with a gesture of annoyance. He froze in the midst of his gesture. His mouth opened; he stared as at a ghost out of the past. Unbelief and fear glimmered in his wide eyes.

'Well,' said Conan, 'have you no word of greeting, Publio?'

Publio moistened his lips.

'Conan!' he whispered incredulously. 'Mitra! Conan! Amra!'

'Who else?' The Cimmerian unclasped his cloak and threw it with his gauntlets down upon the desk. 'How, man?' he exclaimed irritably. 'Can't you at least offer me a beaker of wine? My throat's caked with the dust of the highway.'

'Aye, wine!' echoed Publio mechanically. Instinctively his hand reached for a gong, then recoiled as from a hot coal, and he shuddered.

While Conan watched him with a flicker of grim amusement in his eyes, the merchant rose and hurriedly shut the door, first craning his neck up and down the corridor to be sure that no slave was loitering about. Then, returning, he took a gold vessel of wine from a near-by table and was about to fill a slender goblet when Conan impatiently took the vessel from him and, lifting it with both hands, drank deep and with gusto.

'Aye, it's Conan, right enough,' muttered Publio. 'Man, are you mad?'

'By Crom, Publio,' said Conan, lowering the vessel but retaining it in his hands, 'you dwell in different quarters than of old. It takes an Argossean merchant to wring wealth out of a little waterfront shop that stank of rotten fish and cheap wine.'

'The old days are past,' muttered Publio, drawing his robe about him with a slight involuntary shudder. 'I have put off the past like a worn-out cloak.'

'Well,' retorted Conan, 'you can't put *me* off like an old cloak. It isn't much I want of you, but that much I do want. And you can't refuse me. We had too many dealings in the old days. Am I such a fool that I'm not aware that this fine mansion was built on my sweat and blood? How many cargoes from my galleys passed through your shop?'

'All merchants of Messantia have dealt with the sea-rovers at one time or another,' mumbled Publio nervously.

'But not with the black corsairs,' answered Conan grimly.

'For Mitra's sake, be silent!' ejaculated Publio, sweat starting out on his brow. His fingers jerked at the gilt-worked edge of his robe.

'Well, I only wished to recall it to your mind,' answered Conan. 'Don't be so fearful. You took plenty of risks in the past, when you were struggling for life and wealth in that lousy little shop down by the wharves, and were hand-and-glove with every buccaneer and smuggler and pirate from here to the Barachan Isles. Prosperity must have softened you.'

'I am respectable,' began Publio.

'Meaning you're rich as hell,' snorted Conan. 'Why? Why did you grow wealthy so much quicker than your competitors? Was it because you did a big business in ivory and ostrich feathers, copper and skins and pearls and hammered gold ornaments, and other things from the coast of Kush? And where did you get them so cheaply, while other merchants were paying their weight in silver to the Stygians for them? I'll tell you, in case you've forgotten: you bought them from me, at considerably less than their value, and I took them from the tribes of the Black Coast, and from the ships of the Stygians – I, and the black corsairs.'

'In Mitra's name, cease!' begged Publio. 'I have not forgotten. But what are you doing here? I am the only man in Argos who knew that the king of Aquilonia was once Conan the buccaneer, in the old days. But word has come southward of the overthrow of Aquilonia and the death of the king.'

'My enemies have killed me a hundred times by rumors,' grunted Conan. 'Yet here I sit and guzzle wine of Kyros.' And he suited the action to the word.

Lowering the vessel, which was now nearly empty, he said: 'It's but a small thing I ask of you, Publio. I know that you're aware of everything that goes on in Messantia. I want to know if a Zingaran named Beloso, or he might call himself anything, is in this city. He's tall and lean and dark like all his race, and it's likely he'll seek to sell a very rare jewel.'

Publio shook his head.

'I have not heard of such a man. But thousands come and go in Messantia. If he is here my agents will discover him.'

'Good. Send them to look for him. And in the meantime have my horse cared for, and have food served me here in this room.'

Publio assented volubly, and Conan emptied the wine vessel, tossed it carelessly into a corner, and strode to a near-by casement, involuntarily expanding his chest as he breathed deep of the salt air. He was looking down upon the meandering waterfront streets. He swept the ships in the harbor with an appreciative glance, then lifted his head and stared beyond the bay, far into the blue haze of the distance where sea met sky. And his memory sped beyond that horizon, to the golden seas of the south, under flaming suns, where laws were not and life ran hotly. Some vagrant scent of spice or palm woke clear-etched images of strange coasts where mangroves grew and drums thundered, of ships locked in battle and decks running blood, of smoke and flame and the crying of slaughter. . . . Lost in his thoughts, he scarcely noticed when Publio stole from the chamber.

Gathering up his robe, the merchant hurried along the corridors until he came to a certain chamber where a tall, gaunt man with a scar upon his temple wrote continually upon parchment. There was something about this man which made his clerkly occupation seem incongruous. To him Publio spoke abruptly:

'Conan has returned!'

'Conan?' The gaunt man started up and the quill fell from his fingers. 'The corsair?'

'Aye!'

The gaunt man went livid. 'Is he mad? If he is discovered here we are ruined! They will hang a man who shelters or trades with a corsair as quickly as they'll hang the corsair himself! What if the governor should learn of our past connections with him?'

'He will not learn,' answered Publio grimly. 'Send your men into the markets and wharfside dives and learn if one Beloso, a Zingaran, is in Messantia. Conan said he had a gem, which he will probably seek to dispose of. The jewel merchants should know of him, if any do. And here is another task for you: pick up a dozen or so desperate villains who can be trusted to do away with a man and hold their tongues afterward. You understand me?'

'I understand.' The other nodded slowly and somberly.

'I have not stolen, cheated, lied and fought my way up from the gutter to be undone by a ghost out of my past,' muttered Publio, and the sinister darkness of his countenance at that moment would have surprised the wealthy nobles and ladies who bought their silks and pearls from his many stalls. But when he returned to Conan a short time later, bearing in his own hands a platter of fruit and meats, he presented a placid face to his unwelcome guest.

Conan still stood at the casement, staring down into the harbor at the purple and crimson and vermilion and scarlet sails of galleons and carracks and galleys and dromonds.

'There's a Stygian galley, if I'm not blind,' he remarked, pointing to a long, low, slim black ship lying apart from the others, anchored off the low broad sandy beach that curved round to the distant headland. 'Is there peace, then, between Stygia and Argos?'

'The same sort that has existed before,' answered Publio, setting the platter on the table with a sigh of relief, for it was heavily laden; he knew his guest of old. 'Stygian ports are temporarily open to our ships, as ours to theirs. But may no craft of mine meet their cursed galleys out of sight of land! That galley crept into the bay last night. What its masters wish I do not know. So far they have neither bought nor sold. I distrust those dark-skinned devils. Treachery had its birth in that dusky land.'

'I've made them howl,' said Conan carelessly, turning from the window. 'In my galley manned by black corsairs I crept to the very bastions of the sea-washed castles of black-walled Khemi by night, and burned the galleons anchored there. And speaking of treachery, mine host, suppose you taste these viands and sip a bit of this wine, just to show me that your heart is on the right side.'

Publio complied so readily that Conan's suspicions were lulled, and without further hesitation he sat down and devoured enough for three men.

And while he ate, men moved through the markets and along the waterfront, searching for a Zingaran who had a jewel to sell or who sought for a ship to carry him to foriegn lands. And a tall gaunt man with a scar on his temple sat with his elbows on a wine-stained table in a squalid cellar with a brass lantern hanging from a smoke-blackened beam overhead, and held converse with ten desperate rogues whose sinister countenances and ragged garments proclaimed their profession.

And as the first stars blinked out, they shone on a strange band spurring their mounts along the white road that led to Messantia from the west. They were four men, tall, gaunt, clad in black, hooded robes, and they did not speak. They forced their steeds mercilessly onward, and those steeds were gaunt as themselves, and sweat-stained and weary as if from long travel and far wandering.

14 - THE BLACK HAND OF SET

CONAN WOKE FROM a sound sleep as quickly and instantly as a cat. And like a cat he was on his feet with his sword out before the man who had touched him could so much as draw back.

'What word, Publio?' demanded Conan, recognizing his host. The gold lamp burned low, casting a mellow glow over the thick tapestries and the rich coverings of the couch whereon he had been reposing.

Publio, recovering from the start given him by the sudden action of his awakening guest, replied: 'The Zingaran has been located. He arrived yesterday, at dawn. Only a few hours ago he sought to sell a huge, strange jewel to a Shemitish merchant, but the Shemite would have naught to do with it. Men say he turned pale beneath his black beard at the sight of it, and closing his stall, fled as from a thing accursed.'

'It must be Beloso,' muttered Conan, feeling the pulse in his temples pounding with impatient eagerness. 'Where is he now?'

'He sleeps in the house of Servio.'

'I know that dive of old,' grunted Conan. 'I'd better hasten before some of these waterfront thieves cut his throat for the jewel.'

He took up his cloak and flung it over his shoulders, then donned a helmet Publio had procured for him.

'Have my steed saddled and ready in the court,' said he. 'I may return in haste. I shall not forget this night's work, Publio.'

A few moments later Publio, standing at a small outer door, watched the king's tall figure receding down the shadowy street.

'Farewell to you, corsair,' muttered the merchant. 'This must be a notable jewel, to be sought by a man who has just lost a kingdom. I wish I had told my knaves to let him secure it before they did their work. But then, something might have gone awry. Let Argos forget Amra, and let my dealings with him be lost in the dust of the past. In the alley behind the house of Servio – that is where Conan will cease to be a peril to me.'

Servio's house, a dingy, ill-famed den, was located close to the wharves, facing the waterfront. It was a shambling building of stone and heavy ship-beams, and a long narrow alley wandered up alongside it. Conan made his way along the alley, and as he approached the house he had an uneasy feeling that he was being spied upon. He stared hard into the shadows of the squalid buildings, but saw nothing, though once he caught the faint rasp of cloth or leather against flesh.

But that was nothing unusual. Thieves and beggars prowled these alleys all night, and they were not likely to attack him, after one look at his size and harness.

But suddenly a door opened in the wall ahead of him, and he slipped into the shadow of an arch. A figure emerged from the open door and moved along the alley, not furtively, but with a natural noiselessness like that of a jungle beast. Enough starlight filtered into the alley to silhouette the man's profile dimly as he passed the doorway where Conan lurked. The stranger was a Stygian. There was no mistaking that hawk-faced, shaven head, even in the starlight, nor the mantle over the broad shoulders. He passed on down the alley in the direction of the beach, and once Conan thought he must be carrying a lantern among his garments, for he caught a flash of lambent light, just as the man vanished.

But the Cimmerian forgot the stranger as he noticed that the door through which he had emerged still stood open. Conan had intended entering by the main entrance and forcing Servio to show him the room where the Zingaran slept. But if he could get into the house without attracting anyone's attention, so much the better.

A few long strides brought him to the door, and as his hand fell on the lock he stifled an involuntary grunt. His practiced fingers, skilled among the thieves of Zamora long ago, told him that the lock had been forced, apparently by some terrific pressure from the outside that had twisted and bent the heavy iron bolts, tearing the very sockets loose from the jambs. How such damage could have been wrought so violently without awakening everyone in the neighborhood Conan could not imagine, but he felt sure that it had been done that night. A broken lock, if discovered, would not go unmended in the house of Servio, in this neighborhood of thieves and cutthroats.

Conan entered stealthily, poniard in hand, wondering how he was to find the chamber of the Zingaran. Groping in total darkness, he halted suddenly. He sensed death in that room, as a wild beast senses it – not as peril threatening him, but a dead thing, something freshly slain. In the darkness his foot hit and recoiled from something heavy and yielding. With a sudden premonition he groped along the wall until he found the shelf that supported the brass lamp, with its flint, steel and tinder beside it. A few seconds later a flickering, uncertain light sprang up, and he stared narrowly about him.

A bunk built against the rough stone wall, a bare table and a bench completed the furnishings of the squalid chamber. An inner door stood closed and bolted. And on the hard-beaten dirt floor lay Beloso. On his back he lay, with his head drawn back between his shoulders so that he seemed to stare with his wide glassy eyes at the sooty beams of the cobwebbed ceiling. His lips were drawn back from his teeth in a frozen grin of agony. His sword lay near him, still in its scabbard. His shirt was torn open, and on his brown, muscular breast was the print of a black hand, thumb and four fingers plainly distinct.

Conan glared in silence, feeling the short hairs bristle at the back of his neck.

'Crom!' he muttered. 'The black hand of Set!'

He had seen that mark of old, the death-mark of the black priests of Set, the grim cult that ruled in dark-Stygia. And suddenly he remembered that curious flash he had seen emanating from the mysterious Stygian who had emerged from this chamber.

'The Heart, by Crom!' he muttered. 'He was carrying it under his mantle. He stole it. He burst that door by his magic, and slew Beloso. He was a priest of Set.'

A quick investigation confirmed at least part of his suspicions. The jewel was not on the Zingaran's body. An uneasy feeling rose in Conan that this had not happened by chance, or without design; a conviction that that mysterious Stygian galley had come into the harbor of Messantia on a definite mission. How could the priests of Set know that the Heart had come southward? Yet the thought was no more fantastic than the necromancy that could slay an armed man by the touch of an open, empty hand.

A stealthy footfall outside the door brought him round like a great cat. With one motion he extinguished the lamp and drew his sword. His ears told him that men were out there in the darkness, were closing in on the doorway. As his eyes became accustomed to the sudden darkness, he could make out dim figures ringing the entrance. He could not guess their identity, but as always he took the initiative – leaping suddenly forth from the doorway without awaiting the attack.

His unexpected movement took the skulkers by surprise. He sensed and heard men close about him, saw a dim masked figure in the starlight before him; then his sword crunched home, and he was fleeting away down the alley before the slower-thinking and slower-acting attackers could intercept him.

As he ran he heard, somewhere ahead of him, a faint creak of oar-locks, and he forgot the men behind him. A boat was moving out into the bay! Gritting his teeth he increased his speed, but before he reached the beach he heard the rasp and creak of ropes, and the grind of the great sweep in its socket.

Thick clouds, rolling up from the sea, obscured the stars. In thick darkness Conan came upon the strand, straining his eyes out across the black restless water. Something was moving out there – a long, low, black shape that receded in the darkness, gathering momentum as it went. To his ears came the rhythmical clack of long oars. He ground his teeth in helpless fury. It was the Stygian galley and she was racing out to sea, bearing with her the jewel that meant to him the throne of Aquilonia.

With a savage curse he took a step toward the waves that lapped against the sands, catching at his hauberk and intending to rip it off and swim after the vanishing ship. Then the crunch of a heel in the sand brought him about. He had forgotten his pursuers.

Dark figures closed in on him with a rush of feet through the sands. The first went down beneath the Cimmerian's flailing sword, but the others did not falter. Blades whickered dimly about him in the darkness or rasped on his mail. Blood and entrails spilled over his hand and someone screamed as he ripped murderously upward. A muttered voice spurred on the attack, and that voice sounded vaguely familiar. Conan plowed through the clinging, hacking shapes toward the voice. A faint light gleaming momentarily through the drifting clouds showed him a tall, gaunt man with a great livid scar on his temple. Conan's sword sheared through his skull as through a ripe melon.

Then an ax, swung blindly in the dark, crashed on the king's basinet, filling his eyes with sparks of fire. He lurched and lunged, felt his sword sink deep and heard a shriek of agony. Then he stumbled over a corpse, and a bludgeon knocked the dented helmet from his head; the next instant the club fell full on his unprotected skull.

The king of Aquilonia crumpled into the wet sands. Over him wolfish figures panted in the gloom.

'Strike off his head,' muttered one.

'He's dead,' grunted another. 'His skull's split. Help me

tie up my wounds before I bleed to death. The tide will wash him into the bay.'

'Help me strip him,' urged another. 'His harness will fetch a few pieces of silver. And haste. Tiberio is dead, and I hear seamen singing as they reel along the strand. Let us be gone.'

There followed hurried activity in the darkness, and then the sound of quickly receding footsteps. The tipsy singing of the seamen grew louder.

In his chamber, Publio, nervously pacing back and forth before a window that overlooked the shadowed bay, whirled suddenly, his nerves tingling. To the best of his knowledge the door had been bolted from within; but now it stood open and four men filed into the chamber. At the sight of them his flesh crawled. Many strange beings Publio had seen in his lifetime, but none before like these. They were tall and gaunt, black-robed, and their faces were dim yellow ovals in the shadows of their coifs. He could not tell much about their features and was unreasoningly glad that he could not. Each bore a long, curiously mottled staff.

'Who are you?' he demanded, and his voice sounded brittle and hollow. 'What do you wish here?'

'Where is Conan, he who was king of Aquilonia?' demanded the tallest of the four in a passionless monotone that made Publio shudder. It was like the hollow tone of a Khitan temple bell.

'I do not know what you mean,' stammered the merchant, his customary poise shaken by the uncanny aspect of his visitors. 'I know no such man.'

'He has been here,' returned the other with no change of inflection. 'His horse is in the courtyard. Tell us where he is before we do you an injury.'

'Gebal!' shouted Publio frantically, recoiling until he crouched against the wall. '*Gebal!*'

The four Khitans watched him without emotion or change of expression.

'If you summon your slave he will die,' warned one of them, which only served to terrify Publio more than ever.

'Gebal!' he screamed. 'Where are you, curse you? Thieves are murdering your master!'

Swift footsteps padded in the corridor outside, and Gebal burst into the chamber – a Shemite, of medium height and mightily muscled build, his curled blue-black beard bristling, and a short leaf-shaped sword in his hand.

He stared in stupid amazement at the four invaders, unable to understand their presence; dimly remembering that he had drowsed unexplainably on the stair he was guarding and up which they must have come. He had never slept on duty before. But his master was shrieking with a note of hysteria in his voice, and the Shemite drove like a bull at the strangers, his thickly muscled arm drawing back for the disemboweling thrust. But the stroke was never dealt.

A black-sleeved arm shot out, extending the long staff. Its end but touched the Shemite's brawny breast and was instantly withdrawn. The stroke was horribly like the dart and recovery of a serpent's head.

Gebal halted short in his headlong plunge, as if he had encountered a solid barrier. His bull head toppled forward on his breast, the sword slipped from his fingers, and then he *melted* slowly to the floor. It was as if all the bones of his frame had suddenly become flabby. Publio turned sick.

'Do not shout again,' advised the tallest Khitan. 'Your servants sleep soundly, but if you waken them they will die, and you with them. Where is Conan?'

'He is gone to the house of Servio, near the waterfront, to search for the Zingaran Beloso,' gasped Publio, all his power of resistance gone out of him. The merchant did not lack courage; but these uncanny visitants turned his marrow to water. He started convulsively at a sudden noise of footsteps hurrying up the stair outside, loud in the ominous stillness.

'Your servant?' asked the Khitan.

Publio shook his head mutely, his tongue frozen to his palate. He could not speak.

One of the Khitans caught up a silken cover from a couch and threw it over the corpse. Then they melted behind the tapestry, but before the tallest man disappeared, he murmured: 'Talk to this man who comes, and send him away quickly. If you betray us, neither he nor you will live to reach that door. Make no sign to show him that you are not alone.' And lifting his staff suggestively, the yellow man faded behind the hangings.

Publio shuddered and choked down a desire to retch. It might have been a trick of the light, but it seemed to him that occasionally those staffs moved slightly of their own accord, as if possessed of an unspeakable life of their own.

He pulled himself together with a mighty effort, and presented a composed aspect to the ragged ruffian who burst into the chamber.

'We have done as you wished, my lord,' this man exclaimed. 'The barbarian lies dead on the sands at the water's edge.'

Publio felt a movement in the arras behind him, and almost burst from fright. The man swept heedlessly on.

'Your secretary, Tiberio, is dead. The barbarian slew him, and four of my companions. We bore their bodies to the rendezvous. There was nothing of value on the barbarian except a few silver coins. Are there any further orders?'

'None!' gasped Publio, white about the lips. 'Go!'

The desperado bowed and hurried out, with a vague feeling that Publio was a man both of weak stomach and few words.

The four Khitans came from behind the arras.

'Of whom did this man speak?' the taller demanded.

'Of a wandering stranger who did me an injury,' panted Publio.

'You lie,' said the Khitan calmly. 'He spoke of the king of Aquilonia. I read it in your expression. Sit upon that divan and do not move or speak. I will remain with you while my three companions go search for the body.'

So Publio sat and shook with terror of the silent, inscrutable figure which watched him, until the three Khitans filed back into the room, with the news that Conan's body did not lie upon the sands. Publio did not know whether to be glad or sorry.

'We found the spot where the fight was fought,' they said. 'Blood was on the sand. But the king was gone.'

The fourth Khitan drew imaginary symbols upon the carpet with his staff, which glistened scalily in the lamplight.

'Did you read naught from the sands?' he asked.

'Aye,' they answered. 'The king lives, and he has gone southward in a ship.'

The tall Khitan lifted his head and gazed at Publio, so that the merchant broke into a profuse sweat.

'What do you wish of me?' he stuttered.

'A ship,' answered the Khitan. 'A ship well manned for a long voyage.'

'For how long a voyage?' stammered Publio, never thinking of refusing.

130

'To the ends of the world, perhaps,' answered the Khitan, 'or to the molten seas of Hell that lie beyond the sunrise.'

15 THE RETURN OF THE CORSAIR

CONAN'S FIRST SENSATION of returning consciousness was that of motion; under him was no solidity, but a ceaseless heaving and plunging. Then he heard wind humming through cords and spars, and knew he was aboard a ship even before his blurred sight cleared. He heard a mutter of voices and then a dash of water deluged him, jerking him sharply into full animation. He heaved up with a sulfurous curse, braced his legs, and glared about him, with a burst of coarse guffaws in his ears and the reek of unwashed bodies in his nostrils.

He was standing on the poop deck of a long galley, which was running before the wind that whipped down from the north, her striped sail bellying against the taut sheets. The sun was just rising, in a dazzling blaze of gold and blue and green. To the left of the shoreline was a dim purple shadow. To the right stretched the open ocean. This much Conan saw at a glance that likewise included the ship itself.

It was long and narrow, a typical trading ship of the southern coasts, high of poop and stern, with cabins at either extremity. Conan looked down into the open waist, whence wafted that sickening, abominable odor. He knew it of old. It was the body-scent of the oarsmen, chained to their benches. They were all Negroes, forty men to each side, each confined by a chain locked about his waist, with the other end welded to a heavy ring set deep in the solid runway beam that ran between the benches from stem to stern. The life of a slave aboard an Argossean galley was a hell unfathomable. Most of these were Kushites, but some thirty of the blacks who now rested on their idle oars and stared up at the stranger with dull curiosity were from the far southern isles, the homelands of the corsairs. Conan recognized them by their straighter features and hair, their rangier, cleaner-limbed build. And he saw among them men who had followed him of old.

But all this he saw and recognized in one swift, all-embracing glance as he rose, before he turned his attention to the figures about him. Reeling momentarily on braced

131

legs, his fists clenched wrathfully, he glared at the figures clustered about him. The sailor who had drenched him stood grinning, the empty bucket still poised in his hand, and Conan cursed him with venom, instinctively reaching for his hilt. Then he discovered that he was weaponless and naked except for his short leather breeks.

'What lousy tub is this?' he roared. 'How did I come aboard here?'

The sailors laughed jeeringly – stocky, bearded Argosseans to a man – and one, whose richer dress and air of command proclaimed him captain, folded his arms and said domineeringly: 'We found you lying on the sands. Somebody had rapped you on the pate and taken your clothes. Needing an extra man, we brought you aboard.'

'What ship is this?' Conan demanded.

'The *Venturer*, out of Messantia, with a cargo of mirrors, scarlet silk cloaks, shields, gilded helmets, and swords to trade to the Shemites for copper and gold ore. I am Demetrio, captain of this vessel and your master henceforward.'

'Then I'm headed in the direction I wanted to go, after all', muttered Conan, heedless of that last remark. They were racing southeastward, following the long curve of the Argossean coast. These trading-ships never ventured far from the shoreline. Somewhere ahead of him he knew that low dark Stygian galley was speeding southward.

'Have you sighted a Stygian galley—' began Conan, but the beard of the burly, brutal-faced captain bristled. He was not in the least interested in any question his prisoner might wish to ask, and felt it high time he reduced this independent wastrel to his proper place.

'Get for'ard!' he roared. 'I've wasted time enough with you! I've done you the honor of having you brought to the poop to be revived, and answered enough of your infernal questions. Get off this poop! You'll work your way aboard this galley—'

'I'll buy your ship—' began Conan, before he remembered that he was a penniless wanderer.

A roar of rough mirth greeted these words, and the captain turned purple, thinking he sensed ridicule.

'You mutinous swine!' he bellowed, taking a threatening step forward, while his hand closed on the knife at his belt. 'Get for'ard before I have you flogged! You'll keep a civil tongue in your jaws, or by Mitra, I'll have you chained among the blacks to tug an oar!'

Conan's volcanic temper, never long at best, burst into explosion. Not in years, even before he was king, had a man spoken to him thus and lived.

'Don't lift your voice to me, you tar-breeched dog!' he roared in a voice as gusty as the sea-wind, while the sailors gaped dumbfounded. 'Draw that toy and I'll feed you to the fishes!'

'Who do you think you are?' gasped the captain.

'I'll show you!' roared the maddened Cimmerian, and he wheeled and bounded toward the rail, where weapons hung in their brackets.

The captain drew his knife and ran at him bellowing, but before he could strike, Conan gripped his wrist with a wrench that tore the arm clean out of the socket. The captain bellowed like an ox in agony, and then rolled clear across the deck as he was hurled contemptuously from his attacker. Conan ripped a heavy ax from the rail and wheeled cat-like to meet the rush of the sailors. They ran in, giving tongue like hounds, clumsy-footed and awkward in comparison to the pantherish Cimmerian. Before they could reach him with their knives he sprang among them, striking right and left too quickly for the eye to follow, and blood and brains spattered as two corpses struck the deck.

Knives flailed the air wildly as Conan broke through the stumbling, gasping mob and bounded to the narrow bridge that spanned the waist from poop to forecastle, just out of reach of the slaves below. Behind him the handful of sailors on the poop were floundering after him, daunted by the destruction of their fellows, and the rest of the crew — some thirty in all — came running across the bridge toward him, with weapons in their hands.

Conan bounded out on the bridge and stood poised above the upturned black faces, ax lifted, black mane blown in the wind.

'Who am I?' he yelled. 'Look, you dogs! Look, Ajonga, Yasunga, Laranga! *Who am I?*'

And from the waist rose a shout that swelled to a mighty roar: 'Amra! It is Amra! The Lion has returned!'

The sailors who caught and understood the burden of that awesome shout paled and shrank back, staring in sudden fear at the wild figure on the bridge. Was this in truth that bloodthirsty ogre of the southern seas who had so mysteriously vanished years ago, but who still lived in gory legends? The blacks were frothing crazy now, shaking and tearing at their chains and shrieking the name of Amra like an invocation. Kushites who had never seen Conan before took up the yell. The slaves in the pen under the after-cabin began to batter at the walls, shrieking like the damned.

Demetrio, hitching himself along the deck on one hand and his knees, livid with the agony of his dislocated arm, screamed: 'In and kill him, dogs, before the slaves break loose!'

Fired to desperation by that word, the most dread to all galleymen, the sailors charged on to the bridge from both ends. But with a lion-like bound, Conan left the bridge and hit like a cat on his feet on the runway between the benches.

'Death to the masters!' he thundered, and his ax rose and fell crashingly full on a shackle-chain, severing it like matchwood. In an instant a shrieking slave was free, splintering his oar for a bludgeon. Men were racing frantically along the bridge above, and all hell and bedlam broke loose on the *Venturer*. Conan's ax rose and fell without pause, and with every stroke a frothing, screaming black giant broke free, mad with hate and the fury of freedom and vengeance.

Sailors leaping down into the waist to grapple or smite at the naked, white giant hewing like one possessed at the shackles, found themselves dragged down by hands of slaves yet unfreed, while others, their broken chains whipping and snapping about their limbs, came up out of the waist like a blind, black torrent, screaming like fiends, smiting with broken oars and pieces of iron, tearing and rending with talons and teeth. In the midst of the mêlée the slaves in the pen broke down the walls and came surging up on the decks, and with fifty blacks freed of their benches Conan abandoned his iron-hewing and bounded up on the bridge to add his notched ax to the bludgeons of his partizans.

Then it was massacre. The Argosseans were strong, sturdy, fearless like all their race, trained in the brutal school of the sea. But they could not stand against these maddened giants, led by the tigerish barbarian. Blows and abuse and hellish suffering were avenged in one red gust of fury that raged like a typhoon from one end of the ship to the other, and when it had blown itself out, but one white man lived aboard the *Venturer*, and that was the blood-stained giant about whom the chanting blacks thronged to cast themselves prostrate on the bloody deck and beat their heads against the boards in an ecstasy of hero-worship.

Conan, his mighty chest heaving and glistening with sweat, the red ax gripped in his blood-smeared hand, glared about him as the first chief of men might have glared in some primordial dawn, and shook back his black mane. In that moment he was not king of Aquilonia; he was again lord of the black corsairs, who had hacked his way to lordship through flame and blood.

'Amra! Amra!' chanted the delirious blacks, those who were left to chant. 'The Lion has returned! Now will the Stygians howl like dogs in the night, and the black dogs of Kush will howl! Now will villages burst in flames and ships founder! *Aie*, there will be wailing of women and the thunder of the spears!'

'Cease this yammering, dogs!' Conan roared in a voice that drowned the clap of the sail in the wind. 'Ten of you go below and free the oarsmen who are yet chained. The rest of you man the sweeps and bend to oars and halyards. Crom's devils, don't you see we've drifted inshore during the fight? Do you want to run aground and be retaken by the Argosseans? Throw these carcasses overboard. Jump to it, you rogues, or I'll notch your hides for you!'

With shouts and laughter and wild singing they leaped to do his commands. The corpses, white and black, were hurled overboard, where triangular fins were already cutting the water.

Conan stood on the poop, frowning down at the black men who watched him expectantly. His heavy brown arms were folded, his black hair, grown long in his wanderings, blew in the wind. A wilder and more barbaric figure never trod the bridge of a ship, and in this ferocious corsair few of the courtiers of Aquilonia would have recognized their king.

'There's food in the hold!' he roared. 'Weapons in plenty for you, for this ship carried blades and harness to the Shemites who dwell along the coast. There are enough of us to work ship, aye, and to fight! You rowed in chains for the Argossean dogs: will you row as free men for Amra?'

'*Aye!*' they roared. 'We are thy children! Lead us where you will!'

'Then fall to and clean out that waist,' he commanded. 'Free men don't labor in such filth. Three of you come with

135

me to break out food from the after-cabin. By Crom, I'll pad out your ribs before this cruise is done !'

Another yell of approbation answered him, as the half-starved blacks scurried to do his bidding. The sail bellied as the wind swept over the waves with renewed force, and the white crests danced along the sweep of the wind. Conan planted his feet to the heave of the deck, breathed deep and spread his mighty arms. King of Aquilonia he might no longer be; king of the blue ocean he was still.

16 – BLACK-WALLED KHEMI

THE *Venturer* swept southward like a living thing, her oars pulled now by free and willing hands. She had been transformed from a peaceful trader into a war-galley, insofar as the transformation was possible. Men sat at the benches now with swords at their sides and gilded helmets on their kinky heads. Shields were hung along the rails, and sheaves of spears, bows, and arrows adorned the mast. Even the elements seemed to work for Conan now; the broad purple sail bellied to a stiff breeze that held day by day, needing little aid from the oars.

But though Conan kept a man on the masthead day and night, they did not sight a long, low, black galley fleeing southward ahead of them. Day by day the blue waters rolled empty to their view, broken only by fishing-craft which fled like frightened birds before them, at sight of the shields hung along the rail. The season for trading was practically over for the year, and they sighted no other ships.

When the lookout did sight a sail, it was to the north, not the south. Far on the skyline behind them appeared a racing-galley, with full spread of purple sail. The blacks urged Conan to turn and plunder it, but he shook his head. Somewhere south of him a slim black galley was racing towards the ports of Stygia. That night, before darkness shut down, the lookout's last glimpse showed him the racing-galley on the horizon, and at dawn it was still hanging on their tail, afar off, tiny in the distance. Conan wondered if it was following him, though he could think of no logical reason for such a supposition. But he paid little heed. Each day that carried him farther southward filled him with fiercer impatience. Doubts never assailed him. As he believed in the rise and set of the sun he believed that a priest of Set had stolen the Heart of Ahriman. And where would a priest of Set carry it but to Stygia? The blacks sensed his eagerness, and toiled as they had never toiled under the lash, though ignorant of his goal. They anticipated a red career of pillage and plunder and were content. The men of the southern isles knew no other trade; and the Kushites of the crew joined whole-heartedly in the prospect of looting their own people, with the callousness of their race. Blood-ties meant little; a victorious chieftain and personal gain everything.

Soon the character of the coastline changed. No longer they sailed past steep cliffs with blue hills marching behind them. Now the shore was the edge of broad meadowlands which barely rose above the water' edge and swept away and away into the hazy distance. Here were few harbors and fewer ports, but the green plain was dotted with the cities of the Shemites; green sea, lapping the rim of the green plains, and the zikkurats of the cities gleaming whitely in the sun, some small in the distance.

Through the grazing-lands moved the herds of cattle, and squat, broad riders with cylindrical helmets and curled blue-black beards, with bows in their hands. This was the shore of the lands of Shem, where there was no law save as each city-state could enforce its own. Far to the eastward, Conan knew, the meadowlands gave way to desert, where there were no cities and the nomadic tribes roamed unhindered.

Still as they plied southward, past the changeless panorama of city-dotted meadowland, at last the scenery again began to alter. Clumps of tamarind appeared, the palm groves grew denser. The shoreline became more broken, a marching rampart of green fronds and trees, and behind them rose bare, sandy hills. Streams poured into the sea, and along their moist banks vegetation grew thick and of vast variety.

So at last they passed the mouth of a broad river that mingled its flow with the ocean, and saw the great black walls and towers of Khemi rise against the southern horizon.

The river was the Styx, the real border of Stygia. Khemi was Stygia's greatest port, and at that time her most important city. The king dwelt at more ancient Luxur, but in Khemi reigned the priest-craft; though men said the center of their dark religion lay far inland, in a mysterious, deserted city near the bank of the Styx. This river, springing from

137

some nameless source far in the unknown lands south of Stygia, ran northward for a thousand miles before it turned and flowed westward for some hundreds of miles, to empty at last into the ocean.

The *Venturer*, showing no lights, stole past the point in the night, and before dawn discovered her, anchored in a small bay a few miles south of the city. It was surrounded by marsh, a green tangle of mangroves, palms and lianas, swarming with crocodiles and serpents. Discovery was extremely unlikely. Conan knew the place of old; he had hidden there before, in his corsair days.

As they slid silently past the city whose great black bastions rose on the jutting prongs of land which locked the harbor, torches gleamed and smoldered luridly, and to their ears came the low thunder of drums. The port was not crowded with ships, as were the harbors of Argos. The Stygians did not base their glory and power upon ships and fleets. Trading-vessels and war-galleys, indeed, they had, but not in proportion to their inland strength. Many of their craft plied up and down the great river, rather than along the sea-coasts.

The Stygians were an ancient race, a dark, inscrutable people, powerful and merciless. Long ago their rule had stretched far north of the Styx, beyond the meadowlands of Shem, and into the fertile uplands now inhabited by the people of Koth and Ophir and Argos. Their borders had marched with those of ancient Acheron. But Acheron had fallen, and the barbaric ancestors of the Hyborians had swept southward in wolfskins and horned helmets, driving the ancient rulers of the land before them. The Stygians had not forgotten.

All day the *Venturer* lay at anchor in the tiny bay, walled in with green branches and tangled vines through which flitted gay-plumed, harsh-voiced birds, and among which glided bright-scaled, silent reptiles. Towards sundown a small boat crept out and down along the shore, seeking and finding that which Conan desired – a Stygian fisherman in his shallow, flat-prowed boat.

They brought him to the deck of the *Venturer* – a tall, dark, rangily built man, ashy with fear of his captors, who were ogres of that coast. He was naked except for his silken breeks, for, like the Hyrkanians, even the commoners and slaves of Stygia wore silk; and in his boat was a wide mantle

138

such as these fishermen flung about their shoulders against the chill of the night.

He fell to his knees before Conan, expecting torture and death.

'Stand on your legs, man, and quit trembling,' said the Cimmerian impatiently, who found it difficult to understand abject terror. 'You won't be harmed. Tell me but this: has a galley, a black racing-galley returning from Argos, put into Khemi within the last few days?'

'Aye, my lord,' answered the fisherman. 'Only yesterday at dawn the priest Thutothmes returned from a voyage far to the north. Men say he has been to Messantia.'

'What did he bring from Messantia?'

'Alas, my lord, I know not.'

'Why did he go to Messantia?' demanded Conan.

'Nay, my lord, I am but a common man. Who am I to know the minds of the priests of Set? I can only speak what I have seen and what I have heard men whisper along the wharves. Men say that news of great import came southward, though of what none knows; and it is well known that the lord Thutothmes put off in his black galley in great haste. Now he is returned, but what he did in Argos, or what cargo he brought back, none knows, not even the seamen who manned his galley. Men say that he has opposed Thoth-Amon, who is the master of all priests of Set, and dwells in Luxur, and that Thutothmes seeks hidden power to overthrow the Great One. But who am I to say? When priests war with one another a common man can but lie on his belly and hope neither treads upon him.'

Conan snarled in nervous exasperation at this servile philosophy, and turned to his men. 'I'm going alone to Khemi to find this thief Thutothmes. Keep this man prisoner, but see that you do him no hurt. Crom's devils, stop your yowling! Do you think we can sail into the harbor and take the city by storm? I must go alone.'

Silencing the clamor of protests, he doffed his own garments and donned the prisoner's silk breeches and sandals, and the band from the man's hair, but scorned the short fisherman's knife. The common men of Stygia were not allowed to wear swords, and the mantle was not voluminous enough to hide the Cimmerian's long blade, but Conan buckled to his hip a Ghatana knife, a weapon borne by the fierce desert men who dwelt to the south of the Stygians, a broad, heavy, slightly curved blade of fine steel, edged like a razor and long enough to dismember a man.

Then, leaving the Stygian guarded by the corsairs, Conan climbed into the fisher's boat.

'Wait for me until dawn,' he said. 'If I haven't come then, I'll never come, so hasten southward to your own homes.'

As he clambered over the rail they set up a doleful wail at his going, until he thrust his head back into sight to curse them into silence. Then, dropping into the boat, he grasped the oars and sent the tiny craft shooting over the waves more swiftly than its owner had ever propelled it.

17 – 'HE HAS SLAIN THE SACRED SON OF SET!'

THE HARBOR OF Khemi lay between two great jutting points of land that ran into the ocean. He rounded the southern point, where the great black castles rose like a man-made hill, and entered the harbor just at dusk, when there was still enough light for the watchers to recognize the fisherman's boat and mantle, but not enough to permit recognition of betraying details. Unchallenged he threaded his way among the great black war galleys lying silent and unlighted at anchor, and drew up to a flight of wide stone steps which mounted up from the water's edge. There he made his boat fast to an iron ring set in the stone, as numerous similar craft were tied. There was nothing strange in a fisherman leaving his boat there. None but a fisherman could find a use for such a craft, and they did not steal from one another.

No one cast him more than a casual glance as he mounted the long steps, unobtrusively avoiding the torches that flared at intervals above the lapping black water. He seemed but an ordinary, empty-handed fisherman, returning from a fruitless day along the coast. If one had observed him closely, it might have seemed that his step was somewhat too springy and sure, his carriage somewhat too erect and confident for a lowly fisherman. But he passed quickly, keeping in the shadows, and the commoners of Stygia were no more given to analysis than were the commoners of the less exotic races.

In build he was not unlike the warrior castes of the Stygians, who were a tall, muscular race. Bronzed by the sun, he was nearly at dark as many of them. His black hair, square-cut and confined by a copper band, increased the resemblance. The characteristics which set him apart from them were the subtle difference in his walk, and his alien features and blue eyes.

But the mantle was a good disguise, and he kept as much in the shadows as possible, turning away his head when a native passed him too closely.

But it was a desperate game, and he knew he could not long keep up the deception. Khemi was not like the seaports of the Hyborians, where types of every race swarmed. The only aliens here were Negro and Shemite slaves; and he resembled neither even as much as he resembled the Stygians themselves. Strangers were not welcome in the cities of Stygia; tolerated only when they came as ambassadors or licensed traders. But even then the latter were not allowed ashore after dark. And now there were no Hyborian ships in the harbor at all. A strange restlessness ran through the city, a stirring of ancient ambitions, a whispering none could define except those who whispered. This Conan felt rather than knew, his whetted primitive instincts sensing unrest about him.

If he were discovered his fate would be ghastly. They would slay him merely for being a stranger; if he were recognized as Amra, the corsair chief who had swept their coasts with steel and flame – an involuntary shudder twitched Conan's broad shoulders. Human foes he did not fear, or any death by steel or fire. But this was a black land of sorcery and nameless horror. Set the Old Serpent, men said, banished long ago from the Hyborian races, yet lurked in the shadows of the cryptic temples, and awful and mysterious were the deeds done in the nighted shrines.

He had drawn away from the waterfront streets with their broad steps leading down to the water, and was entering the long shadowy streets of the main part of the city. There was no such scene as was offered by any Hyborian city – no blaze of lamps and cressets, with gay-clad people laughing and strolling along the pavements, and shops and stalls wide open and displaying their wares.

Here the stalls were closed at dusk. The only lights along the streets were torches, flaring smokily at wide intervals. People walking the streets were comparatively few; they went hurriedly and unspeaking, and their numbers decreased with the lateness of the hour. Conan found the scene gloomy and unreal; the silence of the people, their furtive haste, the great black stone walls that rose on each side of the streets. There was a grim massiveness about Stygian architecture that was overpowering and oppressive.

Few lights showed anywhere except in the upper parts of the buildings. Conan knew that most of the people lay on the flat roofs, among the palms of artificial gardens under the stars. There was a murmur of weird music from somewhere. Occasionally a bronze chariot rumbled along the flags, and there was a brief glimpse of a tall, hawk-faced noble, with a silk cloak wrapped about him, and a gold band with a rearing serpent-head emblem confining his black mane; of the ebon, naked charioteer bracing his knotty legs against the straining of the fierce Stygian horses.

But the people who yet traversed the streets on foot were commoners, slaves, tradesmen, harlots, toilers, and they became fewer as he progressed. He was making toward the temple of Set, where he knew he would be likely to find the priest he sought. He believed he would know Thutothmes if he saw him, though his one glance had been in the semi-darkness of the Messantia alley. That the man he had seen there had been the priest he was certain. Only occultists high in the mazes of the hideous Black Ring possessed the power of the black hand that dealt death by its touch; and only such a man would dare defy Thoth-Amon, whom the western world knew only as a figure of terror and myth.

The street broadened, and Conan was aware that he was getting into the part of the city dedicated to the temples. The great structures reared their black bulks against the dim stars, grim, indescribably menacing in the flare of the few torches. And suddenly he heard a low scream from a woman on the other side of the street and somewhat ahead of him – a naked courtezan wearing the tall plumed headdress of her class. She was shrinking back against the wall, staring across at something he could not yet see. At her cry the few people on the street halted suddenly as if frozen. At the same instant Conan was aware of a sinister slithering ahead of him. Then about the dark corner of the building he was approaching poked a hideous, wedge-shaped head, and after it flowed coil after coil of rippling, darkly glistening trunk.

The Cimmerian recoiled, remembering tales he had heard – serpents were sacred to Set, god of Stygia, who men said was himself a serpent. Monsters such as this were kept in the temples of Set, and when they hungered, were allowed to crawl forth into the streets to take what prey they wished. Their ghastly feasts were considered a sacrifice to the scaly god.

The Stygians within Conan's sight fell to their knees, men and women, and passively awaited their fate. One the great serpent would select, would lap in scaly coils, crush to a red pulp and swallow as a rat-snake swallows a mouse. The others would live. That was the will of the gods.

But it was not Conan's will. The python glided toward him, its attention probably attracted by the fact that he was the only human in sight still standing erect. Gripping his great knife under his mantle, Conan hoped the slimy brute would pass him by. But it halted before him and reared up horrifically in the flickering torchlight, its forked tongue flickering in and out, its cold eyes glittering with the ancient cruelty of the serpent-folk. Its neck arched, but before it could dart, Conan whipped his knife from under his mantle and struck like a flicker of lightning. The broad blade split that wedge-shaped head and sheared deep into the thick neck.

Conan wrenched his knife free and sprang clear as the great body knotted and looped and whipped terrifically in its death throes. In the moment that he stood staring in morbid fascination, the only sound was the thud and swish of the snake's tail against the stones.

Then from the shocked votaries burst a terrible cry: 'Blasphemer! He has slain the sacred son of Set! Slay him! Slay! Slay!'

Stones whizzed about him and the crazed Stygians rushed at him, shrieking hysterically, while from all sides others emerged from their houses and took up the cry. With a curse Conan wheeled and darted into the black mouth of an alley He heard the patter of bare feet on the flags behind him as he ran more by feel than by sight, and the walls resounded to the vengeful yells of the pursuers. Then his left hand found a break in the wall, and he turned sharply into another, narrower alley. On both sides rose sheer black stone walls. High above him he could see a thin line of stars. These giant walls, he knew, were the walls of temples. He heard, behind him, the pack sweep past the dark mouth in full cry. Their shouts grew distant, faded away. They had missed the smaller alley and run straight on in the blackness. He too kept straight ahead, though the thought of encountering another of Set's 'sons' in the darkness brought a shudder from him.

143

Then somewhere ahead of him he caught a moving glow, like that of a crawling glow-worm. He halted, flattened himself against the wall and gripped his knife. He knew what it was: a man approaching with a torch. Now it was so close he could make out the dark hand that gripped it, and the dim oval of a dark face. A few more steps and the man would certainly see him. He sank into a tigerish crouch – the torch halted. A door was briefly etched in the glow, while the torch-bearer fumbled with it. Then it opened, the tall figure vanished through it, and darkness closed again on the alley. There was a sinister suggestion of furtiveness about that slinking figure, entering the alley-door in darkness; a priest, perhaps, returning from some dark errand.

But Conan groped toward the door. If one man came up that alley with a torch, others might come at any time. To retreat the way he had come might mean to run full into the mob from which he was fleeing. At any moment they might return, find the narrower alley, and come howling down it. He felt hemmed in by those sheer, unscalable walls, desirous of escape, even if escape meant invading some unknown building.

The heavy bronze door was not locked. It opened under his fingers and he peered through the crack. He was looking into a great square chamber of massive black stone. A torch smoldered in a niche in the wall. The chamber was empty. He glided through the lacquered door and closed it behind him.

His sandaled feet made no sound as he crossed the black marble floor. A teak door stood partly open, and gliding through this, knife in hand, he came out into a great, dim, shadowy place whose lofty ceiling was only a hint of darkness high above him, towards which the black walls swept upward. On all sides black-arched doorways opened into the great still hall. It was lit by curious bronze lamps that gave a dim weird light. On the other side of the great hall a broad black marble stairway, without a railing, marched upward to lose itself in gloom, and above him on all sides dim galleries hung like black stone ledges.

Conan shivered; he was in a temple of some Stygian god, if not Set himself, then someone only less grim. And the shrine did not lack an occupant. In the midst of the great hall stood a black stone altar, massive, somber, without carvings or ornament, and upon it coiled one of the great sacred serpents, its iridescent scales shimmering in the lamplight. It did not move, and Conan remembered stories that the priests

144

kept these creatures drugged part of the time. The Cimmerian took an uncertain step out from the door, then shrank back suddenly, not into the room he had just quitted, but into a velvet-curtained recess. He had heard a soft step somewhere near by.

From one of the black arches emerged a tall, powerful figure in sandals and silken loin-cloth, with a wide mantle trailing from his shoulders. But face and head were hidden by a monstrous mask, a helf-bestial, half-human countenance, from the crest of which floated a mass of ostrich plumes.

In certain ceremonies the Stygian priests went masked. Conan hoped the man would not discover him, but some instinct warned the Stygian. He turned abruptly from his destination, which apparently was the stair, and stepped straight to the recess. As he jerked aside the velvet hanging, a hand darted from the shadows, crushed the cry in his throat and jerked him headlong into the alcove, and the knife impaled him.

Conan's next move was the obvious one suggested by logic. He lifted off the grinning mask and drew it over his own head. The fisherman's mantle he flung over the body of the priest, which he concealed behind the hangings, and drew the priestly mantle about his own brawny shoulders. Fate had given him a disguise. All Khemi might well be searching for the blasphemer who dared defend himself against a sacred snake; but who would dream of looking for him under the mask of a priest?

He strode boldly from the alcove and headed for one of the arched doorways at random; but he had not taken a dozen strides when he wheeled again, all his senses edged for peril.

A band of masked figures filed down the stair, appareled exactly as he was. He hesitated, caught in the open, and stood still, trusting to his disguise, though cold sweat gathered on his forehead and the backs of his hands. No word was spoken. Like phantoms they descended into the great hall and moved past him toward a black arch. The leader carried an ebon staff which supported a grinning white skull, and Conan knew it was one of the ritualistic processions so inexplicable to a foreigner, but which played a strong – and often sinister – part in the Stygian religion. The last figure turned his head slightly toward the motionless Cimmerian, as if expecting him to follow. Not to do what was obviously expected of him would rouse instant suspicion. Conan fell in behind the last man and suited his gait to their measured pace.

They traversed a long, dark, vaulted corridor in which, Conan noticed uneasily, the skull on the staff glowed phosphorescently. He felt a surge of unreasoning, wild animal panic that urged him to rip out his knife and slash right and left at these uncanny figures, to flee madly from this grim, dark temple. But he held himself in check, fighting down the dim monstrous intuitions that rose in the back of his mind and peopled the gloom with shadowy shapes of horror; and presently he barely stifled a sigh of relief as they filed through a great double-valved door which was three times higher than a man, and emerged into the starlight.

Conan wondered if he dared fade into some dark alley; but hesitated, uncertain, and down the long dark street they padded silently, while such folk as they met turned their heads away and fled from them. The procession kept far out from the walls; to turn and bolt into any one of the alleys they passed would be too conspicuous. While he mentally fumed and cursed, they came to a low-arched gateway in the southern wall, and through this they filed. Ahead of them and about them lay clusters of low, flat-topped mud houses, and palm-groves, shadowy in the starlight. Now if ever, thought Conan, was his time to escape his silent companions.

But the moment the gate was left behind them those companions were no longer silent. They began to mutter excitedly among themselves. The measured, ritualistic gait was abandoned, the staff with its skull was tucked unceremoniously under the leader's arm, and the whole group broke ranks and hurried onward. And Conan hurried with them. For in the low murmur of speech he had caught a word that galvanized him. The word was "*Thutothmes!*"

18 – 'I AM THE WOMAN WHO NEVER DIED'

CONAN STARED with burning interest at his masked companions. One of them was Thutothmes, or else the destination of the band was a rendezvous with the man he sought. And he knew what that destination was, when beyond the palms he glimpsed a black triangular bulk looming against the shadowy sky.

They passed through the belt of huts and groves, and if any man saw them he was careful not to show himself. The huts were dark. Behind them the black towers of Khemi rose gloomily against the stars that were mirrored in the waters of the harbor; ahead of them the desert stretched away in dim darkness; somewhere a jackal yapped. The quick-passing sandals of the silent neophytes made no noise in the sand. They might have been ghosts, moving toward that colossal pyramid that rose out of the murk of the desert. There was no sound over all the sleeping land.

Conan's heart beat quicker as he gazed at the grim black wedge that stood etched against the stars, and his impatience to close with Thutothmes in whatever conflict the meeting might mean was not unmixed with a fear of the unknown. No man could approach one of those somber piles of black stone without apprehension. The very name was a symbol of repellent horror among the northern nations, and legends hinted that the Stygians did not build them; that they were in the land at whatever immeasurably ancient date the dark-skinned people came into the land of the great river.

As they approached the pyramid, he glimpsed a dim glow near the base, which presently resolved itself into a doorway, on either side of which brooded stone lions with the heads of women, cryptic, inscrutable, nightmares crystallized in stone. The leader of the band made straight for the doorway, in the deep well of which Conan saw a shadowy figure.

The leader paused an instant beside this dim figure, and then vanished into the dark interior, and one by one the others followed. As each masked priest passed through the gloomy portal he was halted briefly by the mysterious guardian and something passed between them, some word or gesture Conan could not make out. Seeing this, the Cimmerian purposely lagged behind, and stooping, pretended to be fumbling with the fastening of his sandal. Not until the last of the masked figures had disappeared did he straighten and approach the portal.

He was uneasily wondering if the guardian of the temple were human, remembering some tales he had heard. But his doubts were set at rest. A dim bronze cresset glowing just within the door lighted a long narrow corridor that ran away into blackness, and a man standing silent in the mouth of it, wrapped in a wide black cloak. No one else was in sight.

147

Obviously the masked priests had disappeared down the corridor.

Over the cloak that was drawn about his lower features, the Stygian's piercing eyes regarded Conan sharply. With his left hand he made a curious gesture. On a venture Conan imitated it. But evidently another gesture was expected; the Stygian's right hand came from under his cloak with a gleam of steel and his murderous stab would have pierced the heart of an ordinary man.

But he was dealing with one whose thews were nerved to the quickness of a jungle cat. Even as the dagger flashed in the dim light, Conan caught the dusky wrist and smashed his clenched fist against the Stygian's jaw. The man's head went back against the stone wall with a dull crunch that told of a fractured skull.

Standing for an instant above him, Conan listened intently. The cresset burned low, casting vague shadows about the door. Nothing stirred in the blackness beyond, though far away and below him, as it seemed, he caught the faint, muffled note of a gong.

He stooped and dragged the body behind the great bronze door which stood wide, opened inward, and then the Cimmerian went warily but swiftly down the corridor, toward what doom he did not even try to guess.

He had not gone far when he halted, baffled. The corridor split in two branches, and he had no way of knowing which the masked priests had taken. At a venture he chose the left. The floor slanted slightly downward and was worn smooth as by many feet. Here and there a dim cresset cast a faint nightmarish twilight. Conan wondered uneasily for what purpose these colossal piles had been reared, in what forgotten age. This was an ancient, ancient land. No man knew how many ages the black temples of Stygia had looked against the stars.

Narrow black arches opened occasionally to right and left, but he kept to the main corridor, although a conviction that he had taken the wrong branch was growing in him. Even with their start of him, he should have overtaken the priests by this time. He was growing nervous. The silence was like a tangible thing, and yet he had a feeling that he was not alone. More than once, passing a nighted arch he seemed to feel the glare of unseen eyes fixed upon him. He paused, half minded

148

to turn back to where the corridor had first branched. He wheeled abruptly, knife lifted, every nerve tingling.

A girl stood at the mouth of a smaller tunnel, staring fixedly at him. Her ivory skin showed her to be a Stygian of some ancient noble family, and like all such women she was tall, lithe, voluptuously figured, her hair a great pile of black foam, among which gleamed a sparkling ruby. But for her velvet sandals and a broad jewel-crusted girdle about her supple waist she was quite nude.

'What do you here?' she demanded.

To answer would betray his alien origin. He remained motionless, a grim, somber figure in the hideous mask with the plumes floating over him. His alert gaze sought the shadows behind her and found them empty. But there might be hordes of fighting-men within her call.

She advanced toward him, apparently without apprehension though with suspicion.

'You are not a priest,' she said. 'You are a fighting-man. Even with that mask that is plain. There is as much difference between you and a priest as there is between a man and a woman. By Set!' she exclaimed, halting suddenly, her eyes flaring wide. 'I do not believe you are even a Stygian!'

With a movement too quick for the eye to follow, his hand closed around her round throat, lightly as a caress.

'Not a sound out of you!' he muttered.

Her smooth ivory flesh was cold as marble, yet there was no fear in the wide, dark, marvelous eyes which regarded him.

'Do not fear,' she answered calmly. 'I will not betray you. But are you mad to come, a stranger and a foreigner, to the forbidden temple of Set?'

'I'm looking for the priest Thutothmes,' he answered. 'Is he in this temple?'

'Why do you seek him?' she parried.

'He has something of mine which was stolen.'

'I will lead you to him,' she volunteered, so promptly that his suspicions were instantly roused.

'Don't play with me, girl,' he growled.

'I do not play with you. I have no love for Thutothmes.'

He hesitated, then made up his mind; after all, he was as much in her power as she was in his.

'Walk beside me,' he commanded, shifting his grasp from her throat to her wrist. 'But walk with care. If you make a suspicious move—'

She led him down the slanting corridor, down and down,

until there were no more cressets, and he groped his way in darkness, aware less by sight than by feel and sense of the woman at his side. Once when he spoke to her, she turned her head toward him, and he was startled to see her eyes glowing like golden fire in the dark. Dim doubts and vague monstrous suspicions haunted his mind, but he followed her, through a labyrinthine maze of black corridors that confused even his primitive sense of direction. He mentally cursed himself for a fool, allowing himself to be led into that black abode of mystery; but it was too late to turn back now. Again he felt life and movement in the darkness about him, sensed peril and hunger burning impatiently in the blackness. Unless his ears deceived him he caught a faint sliding noise that ceased and receded at a muttered command from the girl.

She led him at last into a chamber lighted by a curious seven-branched candelabrum in which black candles burned weirdly. He knew they were far below the earth. The chamber was square, with walls and ceiling of polished black marble and furnished after the manner of the ancient Stygians; there was a couch of ebony, covered with black velvet, and on a black stone dais lay a carven mummy-case.

Conan stood waiting expectantly, staring at the various black arches which opened into the chamber. But the girl made no move to go farther. Stretching herself on the couch with feline suppleness, she intertwined her fingers behind her sleek head and regarded him from under long, drooping lashes.

'Well?' he demanded impatiently. 'What are you doing? Where's Thutothmes?'

'There is no haste,' she answered lazily. 'What is an hour – or a day, or a year, or a century, for that matter? Take off your mask. Let me see your features.'

With a grunt of annoyance Conan dragged off the bulky headpiece, and the girl nodded as if in approval as she scanned his dark scarred face and blazing eyes.

'There is strength in you – great strength; you could strangle a bullock.'

He moved restlessly, his suspicion growing. With his hand on his hilt he peered into the gloomy arches.

'If you've brought me into a trap,' he said, 'you won't live to enjoy your handiwork. Are you going to get off that couch and do as you promised, or do I have to—'

His voice trailed away. He was staring at the mummy-case, on which the countenance of the occupant was carved in ivory with the startling vividness of a forgotten art. There was a disquieting familiarity about that carven mask, and with something of a shock he realized what it was; there was a startling resemblance between it and the face of the girl lolling on the ebon couch. She might have been the model from which it was carved, but he knew the portrait was at least centuries old. Archaic hieroglyphics were scrawled across the lacquered lid, and, seeking back into his mind for tag ends of learning, picked up here and there as incidentals of an adventurous life, he spelled them out, and said aloud: 'Akivasha!'

'You have heard of Princess Akivasha?' inquired the girl on the couch.

'Who hasn't?' he grunted. The name of that ancient, evil, beautiful princess still lived the world over in song and legend, though ten thousand years had rolled their cycles since the daughter of Tuthamon had reveled in purple feasts amid the black halls of ancient Luxur.

'Her only sin was that she loved life and all the meanings of life,' said the Stygian girl. 'To win life she courted death. She could not bear to think of growing old and shriveled and worn, and dying at last as hags die. She wooed Darkness like a lover and his gift was life – life that, not being life as mortals know it, can never grow old and fade. She went into the shadows to cheat age and death—'

Conan glared at her with eyes that were suddenly burning slits. And he wheeled and tore the lid from the sarcophagus. It was empty. Behind him the girl was laughing and the sound froze the blood in his veins. He whirled back to her, the short hairs on his neck bristling.

'*You* are Akivisha!' he grated.

She laughed and shook back her burnished locks, spread her arms sensuously.

'I am Akivasha! I am the woman who never died, who never grew old! Who fools say was lifted from the earth by the gods, in the full bloom of her youth and beauty, to queen it forever in some celestial clime! Nay, it is in the shadows that mortals find immortality! Ten thousand years ago I died to live forever! Give me your lips, strong man!'

Rising lithely she came to him, rose on tiptoe and flung her arms about his massive neck. Scowling down into her upturned, beautiful countenance he was aware of a fearful fascination and an icy fear.

'Love me!' she whispered, her head thrown back, eyes closed and lips parted. 'Give me your blood to renew my youth and perpetuate my everlasting life! I will make you, too, immortal! I will teach you the wisdom of all the ages, all the secrets that have lasted out the eons in the blackness beneath these dark temples. I will make you king of that shadowy horde which revel among the tombs of the ancient when night veils the desert and bats flit across the moon. I am weary of priests and magicians, and captive girls dragged screaming through the portals of death. I desire a man. Love me, barbarian!'

She pressed her dark head down against his mighty breast, and he felt a sharp pang at the base of his throat. With a curse he tore her away and flung her sprawling across the couch.

'Damned vampire!' Blood was trickling from a tiny wound in his throat.

She reared up on the couch like a serpent poised to strike, all the golden fires of hell blazed in her wide eyes. Her lips drew back, revealing white pointed teeth.

'Fool!' she shrieked. 'Do you think to escape me? You will live and die in the darkness! I have brought you far below the temple. You can never find your way out alone. You can never cut your way through those which guard the tunnels. But for my protection the sons of Set would long ago have taken you into their bellies. Fool, I shall yet drink your blood!'

'Keep away from me or I'll slash you asunder,' he grunted, his flesh crawling with revulsion. 'You may be immortal, but steel will dismember you.'

As he backed toward the arch through which he had entered, the light went out suddenly. All the candles were extinguished at once, though he did not know how; for Akivasha had not touched them. But the vampire's laugh rose mockingly behind him, poison-sweet as the viols of hell, and he sweated as he groped in the darkness for the arch in a near-panic. His fingers encountered an opening and he plunged through it. Whether it was the arch through which he had entered he did not know, nor did he very much care. His one thought was to get out of the haunted chamber which had housed that beautiful, hideous, undead fiend for so many centuries.

His wanderings through those black, winding tunnels were a sweating nightmare. Behind him and about him he heard faint slitherings and glidings, and once the echo of that sweet, hellish laughter he had heard in the chamber of Akivasha. He slashed ferociously at sounds and movements he heard or imagined he heard in the darkness near him, and once his sword cut through some yielding tenuous substance that might have been cobwebs. He had a desperate feeling that he was being played with, lured deeper and deeper into ultimate night, before being set upon by demoniac talon and fang.

And through his fear ran the sickening revulsion of his discovery. The legend of Akivasha was so old, and among the evil tales told of her ran a thread of beauty and idealism, of everlasting youth. To so many dreamers and poets and lovers she was not alone the evil princess of Stygian legend, but the symbol of eternal youth and beauty, shining forever in some far realm of the gods. And this was the hideous reality. This foul perversion was the truth of that everlasting life. Through his physical revulsion ran a sense of a shattered dream of man's idolatry, its glittering gold proved slime and cosmic filth. A wave of futility swept over him, a dim fear of the falseness of all men's dreams and idolatries.

And now he knew that his ears were not playing him tricks. He was being followed, and his pursuers were closing in on him. In the darkness sounded shufflings and slidings that were never made by human feet; nor by the feet of any normal animal. The underworld had its bestial life too, perhaps. They were behind him. He turned to face them, though he could see nothing, and slowly backed away. Then the sounds ceased, even before he turned his head and saw, somewhere down the long corridor, a glow of light.

19 – IN THE HALL OF THE DEAD

CONAN MOVED cautiously in the direction of the light he had seen, his ear cocked over his shoulder, but there was no further sound of pursuit, though he *felt* the darkness pregnant with sentient life.

The glow was not stationary; it moved, bobbing grotesquely along. Then he saw the source. The tunnel he was traversing crossed another, wider corridor some distance ahead of him. And along this latter tunnel filed a bizarre procession – four tall, gaunt men in black, hooded robes, leaning on staffs. The leader held a torch above his head – a torch that burned with a curious steady glow. Like phantoms they passed across his limited range of vision and vanished, with only a fading glow to tell of their passing. Their appearance was indescribably eldritch. They were not Stygians, not like anything Conan had ever seen. He doubted if they were even humans. They were like black ghosts, stalking ghoulishly along the haunted tunnels.

But his position could be no more desperate than it was. Before the inhuman feet behind him could resume their slithering advance at the fading of the distant illumination, Conan was running down the corridor. He plunged into the other tunnel and saw, far down it, small in the distance, the weird procession moving in the glowing sphere. He stole noiselessly after them, then shrank suddenly back against the wall as he saw them halt and cluster together as if conferring on some matter. They turned as if to retrace their steps, and he slipped into the nearest archway. Groping in the darkness to which he had become so accustomed that he could all but see through it, he discovered that the tunnel did not run straight, but meandered, and he fell back beyond the first turn, so that the light of the strangers should not fall on him as they passed.

But as he stood there, he was aware of a low hum of sound from somewhere behind him, like the murmur of human voices. Moving down the corridor in that direction, he confirmed his first suspicion. Abandoning his original intention of following the ghoulish travelers to whatever destination might be theirs, he set out in the direction of the voices.

Presently he saw a glint of light ahead of him, and turning into the corridor from which it issued, saw a broad arch filled with a dim glow at the other end. On his left a narrow stone stair went upward, and instinctive caution prompted him to turn and mount that stair. The voices he heard were coming from beyond that flame-filled arch.

The sounds fell away beneath him as he climbed, and presently he came out through a low arched door into a vast open space glowing with a weird radiance.

He was standing on a shadowy gallery from which he looked down into a broad, dim-lit hall of colossal proportions. It was a hall of the dead, which few ever see but the silent priests of Stygia. Along the black walls rose tier above tier of carven, painted sarcophagi. Each stood in a niche in the dusky stone, and the tiers mounted up and up to be lost in the gloom above. Thousands of carven masks stared impassively down upon the group in the midst of the hall, rendered futile and insignificant by that vast array of the dead.

Of this group ten were priests, and though they had discarded their masks Conan knew they were the priests he had accompanied to the pyramid. They stood before a tall, hawk-faced man beside a black altar on which lay a mummy in rotting swathings. And the altar seemed to stand in the heart of a living fire which pulsed and shimmered, dripping flakes of quivering golden flame on the black stones about it. This dazzling glow emanated from a great red jewel which lay upon the altar, and in the reflection of which the faces of the priests looked ashy and corpse-like. As he looked, Conan felt the pressure of all the weary leagues and the weary nights and days of his long quest, and he trembled with the mad urge to rush among those silent priests, clear his way with mighty blows of naked steel, and grasp the red gem with passion-taut fingers. But he gripped himself with iron control, and crouched down in the shadow of the stone balustrade. A glance showed him that a stair led down into the hall from the gallery, hugging the wall and half hidden in the shadows. He glared into the dimness of the vast place, seeking other priests or votaries, but saw only the group about the altar.

In that great emptiness the voice of the man beside the altar sounded hollow and ghostly:

'. . . And so the word came southward. The night wind whispered it, the ravens croaked of it as they flew, and the grim bats told it to the owls and the serpents that lurk in hoary ruins. Werewolf and vampire knew, and the ebon-bodied demons that prowl by night. The sleeping Night of the World stirred and shook its heavy mane, and there began a throbbing of drums in deep darkness, and the echoes of far weird cries frightened men who walked by dusk. For the Heart of Ahriman had come again into the world to fulfill its cryptic destiny.

'Ask me not how I, Thutothmes of Khemi and the Night,

155

heard the word before Thoth-Amon who calls himself prince of all wizards. There are secrets not meet for such ears even as yours, and Thoth-Amon is not the only lord of the Black Ring.

'I knew, and I went to meet the Heart which came southward. It was like a magnet which drew me, unerringly. From death to death it came, riding on a river of human blood. Blood feeds it, blood draws it. Its power is greatest when there is blood on the hands that grasp it, when it is wrested by slaughter from its holder. Wherever it gleams, blood is spilt and kingdoms totter, and the forces of nature are put in turmoil.

'And here I stand, the master of the Heart, and have summoned you to come secretly, who are faithful to me, to share in the black kingdom that shall be. Tonight you shall witness the breaking of Thoth-Amon's chains which enslave us, and the birth of empire.

'Who am I, even I, Thutothmes, to know what powers lurk and dream in those crimson deeps? It holds secrets forgotten for three thousand years. But I shall learn. These shall tell me!'

He waved his hand toward the silent shapes that lined the hall.

'See how they sleep, staring through their carven masks! Kings, queens, generals, priests, wizards, the dynasties and the nobility of Stygia for ten thousand years! The touch of the Heart will awaken them from their long slumber. Long, long the Heart throbbed and pulsed in ancient Stygia. Here was its home in the centuries before it journeyed to Acheron. The ancients knew its full powers, and they will tell me when by its magic I restore them to life to labor for me.

'I will rouse them, will waken them, will learn their forgotten wisdom, the knowledge locked in those withered skulls. By the lore of the dead we shall enslave the living! Aye, kings and generals and wizards of old shall be our helpers and our slaves. Who shall stand before us?

'Look! This dried, shriveled thing on the altar was once Thothmekri, a high priest of Set, who died three thousand years ago. He was an adept of the Black Ring. He knew of the Heart. He will tell us of its powers.'

Lifting the great jewel, the speaker laid it on the withered breast of the mummy, and lifted his hand as he began an incantation. But the incantation was never finished. With his hand lifted and his lips parted he froze, glaring past his acolytes, and they wheeled to stare in the direction in which he was looking.

Through the black arch of a door four gaunt, black-robed shapes had filed into the great hall. Their faces were dim yellow ovals in the shadow of their hoods.

'Who are you?' ejaculated Thutothmes in a voice as pregnant with danger as the hiss of a cobra. 'Are you mad, to invade the holy shrine of Set?'

The tallest of the strangers spoke, and his voice was toneless as a Khitan temple bell.

'We follow Conan of Aquilonia.'

'He is not here,' answered Thutothmes, shaking back his mantle from his right hand with a curious menacing gesture, like a panther unsheathing his talons.

'You lie. He is in this temple. We tracked him from a corpse behind the bronze door of the outer portal through a maze of corridors. We were following his devious trail when we became aware of this conclave. We go now to take it up again. But first give us the Heart of Ahriman.'

'Death is the portion of madmen,' murmured Thutothmes, moving nearer the speaker. His priests closed in on cat-like feet, but the strangers did not appear to heed.

'Who can look upon it without desire?' said the Khitan. 'In Khitai we have heard of it. It will give us power over the people which cast us out. Glory and wonder dream in its crimson deeps. Give it to us, before we slay you.'

A fierce cry rang out as a priest leaped with a flicker of steel. Before he could strike, a scaly staff licked out and touched his breast, and he fell as a dead man falls. In an instant the mummies were staring down on a scene of blood and horror. Curved knives flashed and crimsoned, snaky staffs licked in and out, and whenever they touched a man, that man screamed and died.

At the first stroke Conan had bounded up and was racing down the stairs. He caught only glimpses of that brief, fiendish fight – saw men swaying, locked in battle and steaming blood; saw one Khitan, fairly hacked to pieces, yet still on his feet and dealing death, when Thutothmes smote him on the breast with his open, empty hand, and he dropped dead, though naked steel had not been enough to destroy his uncanny vitality.

By the time Conan's hurtling feet left the stair, the fight

was all but over. Three of the Khitans were down, slashed and cut to ribbons and disemboweled, but of the Stygians only Thutothmes remained on his feet.

He rushed at the remaining Khitan, his empty hand lifted like a weapon, and that hand was black as that of a Negro. But before he could strike, the staff in the tall Khitan's hand licked out, seeming to elongate itself as the yellow man thrust. The point touched the bosom of Thutothmes and he staggered; again and yet again the staff licked out, and Thutothmes reeled and fell dead, his features blotted out in a rush of blackness that made the whole of him the same hue as his enchanted hand.

The Khitan turned toward the jewel that burned on the breast of the mummy, but Conan was before him.

In a tense stillness the two faced each other, amid that shambles, with the carven mummies staring down upon them.

'Far have I followed you, O king of Aquilonia,' said the Khitan calmly. 'Down the long river, and over the mountains, across Poitain and Zingara and through the hills of Argos and down the coast. Not easily did we pick up your trail from Tarantia, for the priests of Asura are crafty. We lost it in Zingara, but we found your helmet in the forest below the border hills, where you had fought with the ghouls of the forests. Almost we lost the trail again tonight among these labyrinths.'

Conan reflected that he had been fortunate in returning from the vampire's chamber by another route than that by which he had been led to it. Otherwise he would have run full into these yellow fiends instead of sighting them from afar as they smelled out his spoor like human bloodhounds, with whatever uncanny gift was theirs.

The Khitan shook his head slightly, as if reading his mind.

'That is meaningless; the long trail ends here.'

'Why have you hounded me?' demanded Conan, poised to move in any direction with the celerity of a hairtrigger.

'It was a debt to pay,' answered the Khitan. 'To you who are about to die I will not withhold knowledge. We were vassals of the king of Aquilonia, Valerius. Long we served him, but of that service we are free now – my brothers by death, and I by the fulfillment of obligation. I shall return to Aquilonia with two hearts; for myself the Heart of Ahriman; for Valerius the heart of Conan. A kiss of the staff that was cut from the living Tree of Death—'

The staff licked out like the dart of a viper, but the slash of Conan's knife was quicker. The staff fell in writhing halves, there was another flicker of the keen steel like a jet of lightning, and the head of the Khitan rolled to the floor.

Conan wheeled and extended his hand toward the jewel – then he shrank back, his hair bristling, his blood congealing icily.

For no longer a withered brown thing lay on the altar. The jewel shimmered on the full, arching breast of a naked, living man who lay among the moldering bandages. Living? Conan could not decide. The eyes were like dark murky glass under which shone inhuman somber fires.

Slowly the man rose, taking the jewel in his hand. He towered beside the altar, dusky naked, with a face like a carven image. Mutely he extended his hand toward Conan, with the jewel throbbing like a living heart within it. Conan took it, with an eerie sensation of receiving gifts from the hand of the dead. He somehow realized that the proper incantations had not been made – the conjurement had not been completed – life had not been fully restored to this corpse.

'Who are you?' demanded the Cimmerian.

The answer came in a toneless monotone, like the dripping of water from stalactites in subterranean caverns. 'I was Thothmekri; I am dead.'

'Well, lead me out of this accursed temple, will you?' Conan requested, his flesh crawling.

With measured, mechanical steps the dead man moved toward a black arch. Conan followed him. A glance back showed him once again the vast, shadowy hall with its tiers of sarcophagi, the dead men sprawled about the altar; the head of the Khitan he had slain stared sightless up at the sweeping shadows.

The glow of the jewel illuminated the black tunnels like an ensorceled lamp, dripping golden fire. Once Conan caught a glimpse of ivory flesh in the shadows, believed he saw the vampire that was Akivasha shrinking back from the glow of the jewel; and with her, other less human shapes scuttled or shambled into the darkness.

The dead man strode straight on, looking neither to right nor left, his pace as changeless as the tramp of doom. Cold sweat gathered thick on Conan's flesh. Icy doubts assailed him. How could he know that this terrible figure out of the past was leading him to freedom? But he knew that, left to himself, he could never untangle this bewitched maze of corridors and tunnels. He followed his awful guide through blackness that loomed before and behind them and was filled with skulking shapes of horror and lunacy that cringed from the blinding glow of the Heart.

Then the bronze doorway was before him, and Conan felt the night wind blowing across the desert, and saw the stars, and the starlit desert across which streamed the great black shadow of the pyramid. Thotmekri pointed silently into the desert, and then turned and stalked soundlessly back in the darkness. Conan stared after that silent figure that receded into the blackness on soundless, inexorable feet as one that moves to a known and inevitable doom, or returns to everlasting sleep.

With a curse the Cimmerian leaped from the doorway and fled into the desert as if pursued by demons. He did not look back toward the pyramid, or toward the black towers of Khemi looming dimly across the sands. He headed southward toward the coast, and he ran as a man runs in ungovernable panic. The violent exertion shook his brain free of black cobwebs; the clean desert wind blew the nightmares from his soul and his revulsion changed to a wild tide of exultation before the desert gave way to a tangle of swampy growth through which he saw the black water lying before him and the *Venturer* at anchor.

He plunged through the undergrowth, hip-deep in the marshes; dived headlong into the deep water, heedless of sharks or crocodiles, and swam to the galley and was clambering up the chain onto the deck, dripping and exultant, before the watch saw him.

'Awake, you dogs!' roared Conan, knocking aside the spear the startled lookout thrust at his breast. 'Heave up the anchor! Lay to the doors! Give that fisherman a helmet full of gold and put him ashore! Dawn will soon be breaking, and before sunrise we must be racing for the nearest port of Zingara!'

He whirled about his head the great jewel, which threw off splashes of light that spotted the deck with golden fire.

WINTER HAD PASSED from Aquilonia. Leaves sprang out on the limbs of trees, and the fresh grass smiled to the touch of the warm southern breezes. But many a field lay idle and empty, many a charred heap of ashes marked the spot where proud villas or prosperous towns had stood. Wolves prowled openly along the grass-grown highways, and bands of gaunt, masterless men slunk through the forests. Only in Tarantia was feasting and wealth and pageantry.

Valerius ruled like one touched with madness. Even many of the barons who had welcomed his return cried out at last against him. His tax-gatherers crushed rich and poor alike; the wealth of a looted kingdom poured into Tarantia, which became less like the capital of a realm than the garrison of conquerors in a conquered land. Its merchants waxed rich, but it was a precarious prosperity; for none knew when he might be accused of treason on a trumped-up charge, and his property confiscated, himself cast into prison or brought to the bloody block.

Valerius made no attempt to conciliate his subjects. He maintained himself by means of the Nemedian soldiery and by desperate mercenaries. He knew himself to be a puppet of Amalric. He knew that he ruled only on the sufferance of the Nemedian. He knew that he could never hope to unite Aquilonia under his rule and cast off the yoke of his masters, for the outland provinces would resist him to the last drop of blood. And for that matter the Nemedians would cast him from his throne if he made any attempt to consolidate his kingdom. He was caught in his own vise. The gall of defeated pride corroded his soul, and he threw himself into a reign of debauchery, as one who lives from day to day, without thought or care for tomorrow.

Yet there was subtlety in his madness, so deep that not even Amalric guessed it. Perhaps the wild, chaotic years of wandering as an exile had bred in him a bitterness beyond common conception. Perhaps his loathing of his present position increased this bitterness to a kind of madness. At any event he lived with one desire: to cause the ruin of all who associated with him.

He knew that his rule would be over the instant he had served Amalric's purpose; he knew, too, that so long as he continued to oppress his native kingdom the Nemedian would suffer him to reign, for Amalric wished to crush Aquilonia into ultimate submission, to destroy its last shred of independence, and then at last to seize it himself, rebuild it after his own fashion with his vast wealth, and use its men and natural resources to wrest the crown of Nemedia from Tarascus. For the throne of an emperor was Amalric's ultimate ambition, and Valerius knew it. Valerius did not know whether Tarascus suspected this, but he knew that the king of Nemedia approved of his ruthless course. Tarascus hated Aquilonia, with a hate born of old wars. He desired only the destruction of the western kingdom.

And Valerius intended to ruin the country so utterly that not even Amalric's wealth could ever rebuild it. He hated the baron quite as much as he hated the Aquilonians, and hoped only to live to see the day when Aquilonia lay in utter ruin, and Tarascus and Amalric were locked in hopeless civil war that would as completely destroy Nemedia.

He believed that the conquest of the still defiant provinces of Gunderland and Poitain and the Bossonian marches would mark his end as king. He would then have served Amalric's purpose, and could be discarded. So he delayed the conquest of these provinces, confining his activities to objectless raids and forays, meeting Amalric's urges for action with all sorts of plausible objections and postponements.

His life was a series of feasts and wild debauches. He filled his palace with the fairest girls of the kingdom, willing or unwilling. He blasphemed the gods and sprawled drunken on the floor of the banquet hall wearing the golden crown, and staining his royal purple robes with the wine he spilled. In gusts of blood-lust he festooned the gallows in the market square with dangling corpses, glutted the axes of the headsmen and sent his Nemedian horsemen thundering through the land pillaging and burning. Driven to madness, the land was in a constant upheaval of frantic revolt, savagely suppressed. Valerius plundered and raped and looted and destroyed until even Amalric protested, warning him that he would beggar the kingdom beyond repair, not knowing that such was his fixed determination.

But while in both Aquilonia and Nemedia men talked of

the madness of the king, in Nemedia men talked much of Xaltotun, the masked one. Yet few saw him on the streets of Belverus. Men said he spent much time in the hills, in curious conclaves with surviving remnants of an old race: dark, silent folk who claimed descent from an ancient kingdom. Men whispered of drums beating far up in the dreaming hills, of fires glowing in the darkness, and strange chantings borne on the winds, chantings and rituals forgotten centuries ago except as meaningless formulas mumbled beside mountain hearths in villages whose inhabitants differed strangely from the people of the valleys.

The reason for these conclaves none knew, unless it was Orastes, who frequently accompanied the Pythonian, and on whose countenance a haggard shadow was growing.

But in the full flood of spring a sudden whisper passed over the sinking kingdom that woke the land to eager life. It came like a murmurous wind drifting up from the south, waking men sunk in the apathy of despair. Yet how it first came none could truly say. Some spoke of a strange, grim old woman who came down from the mountains with her hair flowing in the wind, and a great gray wolf following her like a dog. Others whispered of the priests of Asura who stole like furtive phantoms from Gunderland to the marches of Poitain, and to the forest villages of the Bossonians.

However the word came, revolt ran like a flame along the borders. Outlying Nemedian garrisons were stormed and put to the sword, foraging parties were cut to pieces; the west was up in arms, and there was a different air about the rising, a fierce resolution and inspired wrath rather than the frantic despair that had motivated the preceding revolts. It was not only the common people; barons were fortifying their castles and hurling defiance at the governors of the provinces. Bands of Bossonians were seen moving along the edges of the marches: stocky, resolute men in brigandines and steel caps, with longbows in their hands. From the inert stagnation of dissolution and ruin the realm was suddenly alive, vibrant and dangerous. So Amalric sent in haste for Tarascus, who came with an army.

In the royal palace in Tarantia, the two kings and Amalric discussed the rising. They had not sent for Xaltotun, immersed in his cryptic studies in the Nemedian hills. Not since that bloody day in the valley of the Valkia had they called upon him for aid of his magic, and he had drawn

163

apart, communing but little with them, apparently indifferent to their intrigues.

Nor had they sent for Orastes, but he came, and he was white as spume blown before the storm. He stood in the gold-domed chamber where the kings held conclave and they beheld in amazement his haggard stare, the fear they had never guessed the mind of Orastes could hold.

'You are weary, Orastes,' said Amalric. 'Sit upon this divan and I will have a slave fetch you wine. You have ridden hard—'

Orastes waved aside the invitation.

'I have killed three horses on the road from Belverus. I cannot drink wine, I cannot rest, until I have said what I have to say.'

He paced back and forth as if some inner fire would not let him stand motionless, and halting before his wondering companions:

'When we employed the Heart of Ahriman to bring a dead man back to life,' Orastes said abruptly, 'we did not weigh the consequences of tampering in the black dust of the past. The fault is mine, and the sin. We thought only of our ambitions, forgetting what ambitions this man might himself have. And we have loosed a demon upon the earth, a fiend inexplicable to common humanity. I have plumbed deep in evil, but there is a limit to which I, or any man of my race and age, can go. My ancestors were clean men, without any demoniacal taint; it is only I who have sunk into the pits, and I can sin only to the extent of my personal individuality. But behind Xaltotun lie a thousand centuries of black magic and diabolism, an ancient tradition of evil. He is beyond our conception not only because he is a wizard himself, but also because he is the son of a race of wizards.

'I have seen things that have blasted my soul. In the heart of the slumbering hills I have watched Xaltotun commune with the souls of the damned, and invoke the ancient demons of forgotten Acheron. I have seen the accursed descendants of that accursed empire worship him and hail him as their arch-priest. I have seen what he plots – and I tell you it is no less than the restoration of the ancient, black, grisly kingdom of Acheron!'

'What do you mean?' demanded Amalric. 'Acheron is dust. There are not enough survivals to make an empire. Not even Xaltotun can reshape the dust of three thousand years.'

'You know little of his black powers,' answered Orastes grimly. 'I have seen the very hills take on an alien and ancient aspect under the spell of his incantations. I have glimpsed, like shadows behind the realities, the dim shapes and outlines of valleys, forests, mountains and lakes that are not as they are today, but as they were in that dim yesterday – have even sensed, rather than glimpsed, the purple towers of forgotten Python shimmering like figures of mist in the dusk.

'And in the last conclave to which I accompanied him, understanding of his sorcery came to me at last, while the drums beat and the beast-like worshippers howled with their heads in the dust. I tell you he would restore Acheron by his magic, by the sorcery of a gigantic blood-sacrifice such as the world has never seen. He would enslave the world, and with a deluge of blood *wash away the present and restore the past!*'

'You are mad!' exclaimed Tarascus.

'Mad?' Orastes turned a haggard stare upon him. 'Can any man see what I have seen and remain wholly sane? Yet I speak the truth. He plots the return of Acheron, with its towers and wizards and kings and horrors, as it was in the long ago. The descendants of Acheron will serve him as a nucleus upon which to build, but it is the blood and the bodies of the people of the world today that will furnish the mortar and the stones for the rebuilding. I cannot tell you how. My own brain reels when I try to understand. *But I have seen!* Acheron will be Acheron again, and even the hills, the forests and the rivers will resume their ancient aspect. Why not? If I, with my tiny store of knowledge, could bring to life a man dead three thousand years, why cannot the greatest wizard of the world bring back to life a kingdom dead three thousand years? Out of the dust shall Acheron arise at his bidding.'

'How can we thwart him?' asked Tarascus, impressed.

'There is but one way,' answered Orastes. 'We must steal the Heart of Ahriman!'

'But I—' began Tarascus involuntarily, then closed his mouth quickly.

None had noticed him, and Orastes was continuing.

'It is a power that can be used against him. With it in my hands I might defy him. But how shall we steal it? He has it hidden in some secret place, from which not even a Zamorian thief might filch it. I cannot learn its hiding-place.

If he would only sleep again the sleep of the black lotus – but the last time he slept thus was after the battle of the Valkia, when he was weary because of the great magic he had performed, and—'

The door was locked and bolted, but it swung silently open and Xaltotun stood before them, calm, tranquil, stroking his patriarchal beard; but the lambent lights of Hell flickered in his eyes.

'I have taught you too much,' he said calmly, pointing a finger like an index of doom at Orastes. And before any could move, he had cast a handful of dust on the floor near the feet of the priest, who stood like a man turned to marble. It flamed, smoldered; a blue serpentine of smoke rose and swayed upward about Orastes in a slender spiral. And when it had risen above his shoulders it curled about his neck with a whipping suddenness like the stroke of a snake. Orastes' scream was choked to a gurgle. His hands flew to his neck, his eyes were distended, his tongue protruded. The smoke was like a blue rope about his neck; then it was faded and gone, and Orastes slumped to the floor a dead man.

Xaltotun smote his hands together and two men entered, men often observed accompanying him – small, repulsively dark, with red, oblique eyes and pointed, rat-like teeth. They did not speak. Lifting the corpse, they bore it away.

Dismissing the matter with a wave of his hand, Xaltotun seated himself at the ivory table about which sat the pale kings.

'Why are you in conclave?' he demanded.

'The Aquilonians have risen in the west,' answered Amalric, recovering from the grisly jolt the death of Orastes had given him. 'The fools believe that Conan is alive, and coming at the head of a Poitanian army to reclaim his kingdom. If he had reappeared immediately after Valkia, or if a rumor had been circulated that he lived, the central provinces would not have risen under him, they feared your powers so. But they have become so desperate under Valerius's misrule that they are ready to follow any man who can unite them against us, and prefer sudden death to torture and continual misery.

'Of course the tale has lingered stubbornly in the land that Conan was not really slain at Valkia, but not until recently have the masses accepted it. But Pallantides is back from exile in Ophir, swearing that the king was ill in his tent that day, and that a man-at-arms wore his harness, and a squire who but recently recovered from the stroke of a mace received at Valkia confirms his tale – or pretends to.

'An old woman with a pet wolf has wandered up and down the land, proclaiming that King Conan yet lives, and will return some day to reclaim the crown. And of late the cursed priests of Asura sing the same song. They claim that word has come to them by some mysterious means that Conan is returning to reconquer his domain. I cannot catch either her or them. This is, of course, a trick of Trocero's. My spies tell me there is indisputable evidence that the Poitanians are gathering to invade Aquilonia. I believe that Trocero will bring forward some pretender who he will claim is King Conan.'

Tarascus laughed, but there was no conviction in his laughter. He surreptitiously felt of a scar beneath his jupon, and remembered ravens that cawed on the trail of a fugitive; remembered the body of his squire, Arideus, brought back from the border mountains horribly mangled, by a great gray wolf, his terrified soldiers said. But he also remembered a red jewel stolen from a golden chest while a wizard slept, and he said nothing.

And Valerius remembered a dying nobleman who gasped out a tale of fear, and he remembered four Khitans who disappeared into the mazes of the south and never returned. But he held his tongue, for hatred and suspicion of his allies ate at him like a worm, and he desired nothing so much as to see both rebels and Nemedians go down locked in the death grip.

But Amalric exclaimed: 'It is absurd to dream that Conan lives!'

For answer Xaltotun cast a roll of parchment on the table. Amalric caught it up, glared at it. From his lips burst a furious, incoherent cry. He read:

> To Xaltotun, grand fakir of Nemedia: Dog of Acheron, I am returning to my kingdom, and I mean to hang your hide on a bramble.
>
> CONAN.

'A forgery!' exclaimed Amalric.

Xaltotun shook his head.

'It is genuine. I have compared it with the signature on the royal documents on record in the libraries of the court. None could imitate that bold scrawl.'

'Then if Conan lives,' muttered Amalric, 'this uprising will not be like the others, for he is the only man living who can unite the Aquilonians. But,' he protested, 'this is not like Conan. Why should he put us on our guard with his boasting? One would think that he would strike without warning, after the fashion of the barbarians.'

'We are already warned,' pointed out Xaltotun. 'Our spies have told us of preparations for war in Poitain. He could not cross the mountains without our knowledge; so he send me his defiance in characteristic manner.'

'Why to you?' demanded Valerius. 'Why not to me, or to Tarascus?'

Xaltotun turned his inscrutable gaze upon the king.

'Conan is wiser than you,' he said at last. 'He already knows what you kings have yet to learn – that it is not Tarascus, nor Valerius, no, nor Amalric, but Xaltotun who is the real master of the western nations.'

They did not reply; they sat staring at him, assailed by a numbing realization of the truth of his assertion.

'There is no road for me but the imperial highway,' said Xaltotun. 'But first we must crush Conan. I do not know how he escaped me at Belverus, for knowledge of what happened while I lay in the slumber of the black lotus is denied me. But he is in the south, gathering an army. It is his last, desperate blow, made possible only by the desperation of the people who have suffered under Valerius. Let them rise; I hold them all in the palm of my hand. We will wait until he moves against us, and then we will crush him for once and for all.

'Then we shall crush Poitain and Gunderland and the stupid Bossonians. After them Ophir, Argos, Zingara, Koth – all the nations of the world we shall weld into one vast empire. You shall rule as my satraps, and as my captains shall be greater than kings are now. I am unconquerable, for the Heart of Ahriman is hidden where no man can ever wield it against me again.'

Tarascus averted his gaze, lest Xaltotun read his thoughts. He knew the wizard had not looked into the golden chest with its carven serpents that had seemed to sleep, since he laid the heart therein. Strange as it seemed, Xaltotun did not know that the Heart had been stolen; the strange jewel was beyond or outside the ring of his dark wisdom; his uncanny talents did not warn him that the chest was empty. Tarascus did not believe that Xaltotun knew the full extent of Orastes'

168

revelations, for the Pythonian had not mentioned the restoration of Acheron, but only the building of a new, earthly empire. Tarascus did not believe that Xaltotun was yet quite sure of his power; if they needed his aid in their ambitions, no less he needed theirs. Magic depended, to a certain extent after all, on sword strokes and lance thrusts. The king read meaning in Amalric's furtive glance; let the wizard use his arts to help them defeat their most dangerous enemy. Time enough then to turn against him. There might yet be a way to cheat this dark power they had raised.

21 – DRUMS OF PERIL

CONFIRMATION OF THE WAR came when the army of Poitain, ten thousand strong, marched through the southern passes with waving banners and shimmer of steel. And at their head, the spies swore, rode a giant figure in black armor, with the royal lion of Aquilonia worked in gold upon the breast of his rich silken surcoat. Conan lived! The king lived! There was no doubt of it in men's minds now, whether friend or foe.

With the news of the invasion from the south there also came word, brought by hard-riding couriers, that a host of Gundermen was moving southward, reinforced by the barons of the northwest and the northern Bossonians. Tarascus marched with thirty-one thousand men to Galparan, on the river Shirki, which the Gundermen must cross to strike at the towns still held by the Nemedians. The Shirki was a swift, turbulent river rushing southwestward through rocky gorges and canyons, and there were few places where an army could cross at that time of the year, when the stream was almost bank-full with the melting of the snows. All the country east of the Shirki was in the hands of the Nemedians, and it was logical to assume that the Gundermen would attempt to cross either at Galparan, or at Tanasul, which lay to the south of Galparan. Reinforcements were daily expected from Nemedia, until word came that the king of Ophir was making hostile demonstrations on Nemedia's southern border, and to spare any more troops would be to expose Nemedia to the risk of an invasion from the south.

Amalric and Valerius moved out from Tarantia with twenty-five thousand men, leaving as large a garrison as they dared to discourage revolts in the cities during their absence. They wished to meet and crush Conan before he could be joined by the rebellious forces of the kingdom.

The king and his Poitanians had crossed the mountains, but there had been no actual clash of arms, no attack on towns or fortresses. Conan had appeared and disappeared. Apparently he had turned westward through the wild, thinly settled hill country, and entered the Bossonian marches, gathering recruits as he went. Amalric and Valerius with their host, Nemedians, Aquilonian renegades, and ferocious mercenaries, moved through the land in baffled wrath, looking for a foe which did not appear.

Amalric found it impossible to obtain more than vague general tidings about Conan's movements. Scouting-parties had a way of riding out and never returning, and it was not uncommon to find a spy crucified to an oak. The countryside was up and striking as peasants and country-folk strike – savagely, murderously, and secretly. All that Amalric knew certainly was that a large force of Gundermen and northern Bossonians was somewhere to the north of him, beyond the Shirki, and that Conan with a smaller force of Poitanians and southern Bossonians was somewhere to the southwest of him.

He began to grow fearful that if he and Valerius advanced farther into the wild country, Conan might elude them entirely, march around them and invade the central provinces behind them. Amalric fell back from the Shirki valley and camped in a plain a day's ride from Tanasul. There he waited. Tarascus maintained his position at Galparan, for he feared that Conan's maneuvers were intended to draw him southward, and so let the Gundermen into the kingdom at the northern crossing.

To Amalric's camp came Xaltotun in his chariot drawn by the uncanny horses that never tired, and he entered Amalric's tent where the baron conferred with Valerius over a map spread on an ivory camp table.

This map Xaltotun crumpled and flung aside.

'What your scouts cannot learn for you,' quoth he, 'my spies tell me, though their information is strangely blurred and imperfect, as if unseen forces were working against me. 'Conan is advancing along the Shirki river with ten thousand Poitanians, three thousand southern Bossonians, and barons of the west and south with their retainers to the number of five thousand. An army of thirty thousand Gundermen and northern Bossonians is pushing southward to join him. They have established contact by means of secret communications used by the cursed priests of Asura, who seem to be opposing me, and whom I will feed to a serpent when the battle is over – I swear it by Set!

'Both armies are headed for the crossing at Tanasul, but I do not believe that the Gundermen will cross the river. I believe that Conan will cross, instead, and join them.'

'Why should Conan cross the river?' demanded Amalric.

'Because it is to his advantage to delay the battle. The longer he waits, the stronger he will become, the more precarious our position. The hills on the other side of the river swarm with people passionately loyal to his cause – broken men, refugees, fugitives from Valerius's cruelty. From all over the kingdom men are hurrying to join his army, singly and by companies. Daily, parties from our armies are ambushed and cut to pieces by the country-folk. Revolt grows in the central provinces, and will soon burst into open rebellion. The garrisons we left there are not sufficient, and we can hope for no reinforcements from Nemedia for the time being. I see the hand of Pallantides in this brawling on the Ophirean frontier. He has kin in Ophir.

'If we do not catch and crush Conan quickly the provinces will be a blaze of revolt behind us. We shall have to fall back to Tarantia to defend what we have taken; and we may have to fight our way through a country in rebellion, with Conan's whole force at our heels, and then stand siege in the city itself, with enemies within as well as without. No, we cannot wait. We must crush Conan before his army grows too great, before the central provinces rise. With his head hanging above the gate at Tarantia you will see how quickly the rebellion will fall apart.'

'Why do you not put a spell on his army to slay them all?' asked Valerius, half in mockery.

Xaltotun stared at the Aquilonian as if he read the full extent of the mocking madness that lurked in those wayward eyes.

'Do not worry,' he said at last. 'My arts shall crush Conan finally like a lizard under the heel. But even sorcery is aided by pikes and swords.'

'If he crosses the river and takes up his position in the Goralian hills he may be hard to dislodge,' said Amalric.

'But if we catch him in the valley on this side of the river we can wipe him out. How far is Conan from Tanasul?'

'At the rate he is marching he should reach the crossing sometime tomorrow night. His men are rugged and he is pushing them hard. He should arrive there at least a day before the Gundermen.'

'Good!' Amalric smote the table with his clenched fist. 'I can reach Tanasul before he can. I'll send a rider to Tarascus, bidding him follow me to Tanasul. By the time he arrives I will have cut Conan off from the crossing and destroyed him. Then our combined force can cross the river and deal with the Gundermen.'

Xaltotun shook his head impatiently.

'A good enough plan if you were dealing with anyone but Conan. But your twenty-five thousand men are not enough to destroy his eighteen thousand before the Gundermen come up. They will fight with the desperation of wounded panthers. And suppose the Gundermen come up while the hosts are locked in battle? You will be caught between two fires and destroyed before Tarascus can arrive. He will reach Tanasul too late to aid you.'

'What, then?' demanded Amalric.

'Move with your whole strength against Conan,' answered the man from Acheron. 'Send a rider bidding Tarascus join us here. We will await his coming. Then we will march together to Tanasul.'

'But while we wait,' protested Amalric, 'Conan will cross the river and join the Gundermen.'

'Conan will not cross the river,' answered Xaltotun.

Amalric's head jerked up and he stared into the cryptic dark eyes.

'What do you mean?'

'Suppose there were torrential rains far to the north, at the head of the Shirki? Suppose the river came down in such flood as to render the crossing at Tanasul impassable? Could we not then bring up our entire force at our leisure, catch Conan on this side of the river and crush him, and then, when the flood subsided, which I think it would do the next day, could we not cross the river and destroy the Gundermen? Thus we could use our full strength against each of these smaller forces in turn.'

Valerius laughed as he always laughed at the prospect of the ruin of either friend or foe, and drew a restless hand jerkily through his unruly yellow locks. Amalric stared at the man from Acheron with mingled fear and admiration.

'If we caught Conan in Shirki valley with the hill ridges to his right and the river in flood to his left,' he admitted, 'with our whole force we could annihilate him. Do you think – are you sure – do you believe such rains will fall?'

'I go to my tent,' answered Xaltotun, rising. 'Necromancy is not accomplished by the waving of a wand. Send a rider to Tarascus. And let none approach my tent.'

That last command was unnecessary. No man in that host could have been bribed to approach that mysterious black silk pavilion, the door-flaps of which were always closely drawn. None but Xaltotun ever entered it, yet voices were often heard issuing from it; its walls billowed sometimes without a wind, and weird music came from it. Sometimes, deep in midnight, its silken walls were lit red by flames flickering within, limning misshapen silhouettes that passed to and fro.

Lying in his own tent that night, Amalric heard the steady rumble of a drum in Xaltotun's tent; through the darkness it boomed steadily, and occasionally the Nemedian could have sworn that a deep, croaking voice mingled with the pulse of the drum. And he shuddered, for he knew that voice was not the voice of Xaltotun. The drum rustled and muttered on like deep thunder, heard afar off, and before dawn Amalric, glancing from his tent, caught the red flicker of lightning afar on the northern horizon. In all parts of the sky the great stars blazed whitely. But the distant lightning flickered incessantly, like the crimson glint of firelight on a tiny, turning blade.

At sunset of the next day Tarascus came up with his host, dusty and weary from hard marching, the footmen straggling hours behind the horsemen. They camped in the plain near Amalric's camp, and at dawn the combined army moved westward.

Ahead of him roved a swarm of scouts, and Amalric waited impatiently for them to return and tell of the Poitanians trapped beside a furious flood. But when the scouts met the column it was with the news that Conan had crossed the river!

'What?' exclaimed Amalric. 'Did he cross before the flood?'

'There was no flood,' answered the scouts, puzzled. 'Late

173

last night he came up to Tanasul and flung his army across.'

'No flood?' exclaimed Xaltotun, taken aback for the first time in Amalric's knowledge. 'Impossible! There were mighty rains upon the headwaters of the Shirki last night and the night before that!'

'That may be, your lordship,' answered the scout. 'It is true the water was muddy, and the people of Tanasul said that the river rose perhaps a foot yesterday; but that was not enough to prevent Conan's crossing.'

Xaltotun's sorcery had failed! The thought hammered in Amalric's brain. His horror of this strange man out of the past had grown steadily since that night in Belverus when he had seen a brown, shriveled mummy swell and grow into a living man. And the death of Orastes had changed lurking horror into active fear. In the heart was a grisly conviction that the man – or devil – was invincible. Yet now he had undeniable proof of his failure.

Yet even the greatest of necromancers might fail occasionally, thought the baron. At any rate, he dared not oppose the man from Acheron – yet. Orastes was dead, writhing in Mitra only knew what nameless hell, and Amalric knew his sword would scarcely prevail where the black wisdom of the renegade priest had failed. What grisly abomination Xaltotun plotted lay in the unpredictable future. Conan and his host were a present menace against which Xaltotun's wizardry might well be needed before the play was all played.

They came to Tanasul, a small fortified village at the spot where a reef of rocks made a natural bridge across the river, passable always except in times of greatest flood. Scouts brought in the news that Conan had taken up his position in the Goralian hills, which began to rise a few miles beyond the river. And just before sundown the Gundermen had arrived in his camp.

Amalric looked at Xaltotun, inscrutable and alien in the light of the flaring torches. Night had fallen.

'What now? Your magic has failed. Conan confronts us with an army nearly as strong as our own, and he has the advantage of position. We have a choice of two evils: to camp here and await his attack, or to fall back toward Tarantia and await reinforcements.'

'We are ruined if we wait,' answered Xaltotun. 'Cross the river and camp on the plain. We will attack at dawn.'

'But his position is too strong!' exclaimed Amalric.

'Fool!' A gust of passion broke the veneer of the wizard's calm. 'Have you forgotten Valkia? Because some obscure elemental principle prevented the flood do you deem me helpless? I had intended that your spears should exterminate our enemies; but do not fear: it is my arts shall crush their host. Conan is in a trap. He will never see another sun set. Cross the river!'

They crossed by the flare of torches. The hoofs of the horses clinked on the rocky bridge, splashed through the shallows. The glint of the torches on shields and breastplates was reflected redly in the black water. The rock bridge was broad on which they crossed, but even so it was past midnight before the host was camped in the plain beyond. Above them they could see fires winking redly in the distance. Conan had turned at bay in the Goralian hills, which had more than once before served as the last stand of an Aquilonian king.

Amalric left his pavilion and strode restlessly through the camp. A weird glow flickered in Xaltotun's tent, and from time to time a demoniacal cry slashed the silence, and there was a low sinister muttering of a drum that rustled rather than rumbled.

Amalric, his instincts whetted by the night and the circumstances, felt that Xaltotun was opposed by more than physical force. Doubts of the wizard's power assailed him. He glanced at the fires high above him, and his face set in grim lines. He and his army were deep in the midst of a hostile country. Up there among those hills lurked thousands of wolfish figures out of whose hearts and souls all emotion and hope had been scourged except a frenzied hate for their conquerors, a mad lust for vengeance. Defeat meant annihilation, retreat through a land swarming with blood-mad enemies. And on the morrow he must hurl his host against the grimmest fighter in the western nations, and his desperate horde. If Xaltotun failed them now—

Half a dozen men-at-arms strode out of the shadows. The firelight glinted on their breastplates and helmet crests. Among them they half led, half dragged, a gaunt figure in tattered rags.

Saluting, they spoke: 'My lord, this man came to the outposts and said he desired word with King Valerius. He is an Aquilonian.'

He looked more like a wolf – a wolf the traps had scarred. Old sores that only fetters make showed on his wrists and ankles. A great brand, the mark of hot iron, disfigured his face. His eyes glared through the tangle of his matted hair as he half crouched before the baron.

'Who are you, you filthy dog?' demanded the Nemedian.

'Call me Tiberias,' answered the man, and his teeth clicked in an involuntary spasm. 'I have come to tell you how to trap Conan.'

'A traitor, eh?' rumbled the baron.

'Men say you have gold,' mouthed the man, shivering under his rags. 'Give some to me! Give me gold and I will show you how to defeat the king!' His eyes glazed widely, his outstretched, upturned hands were spread like quivering claws.

Amalric shrugged his shoulders in distaste. But no tool was too base for his use.

'If you speak the truth you shall have more gold than you can carry,' he said. 'If you are a liar and a spy I will have you crucified head-down. Bring him along.'

In the tent of Valerius, the baron pointed to the man who crouched shivering before them, huddling his rags about him.

'He says he knows a way to aid us on the morrow. We will need aid, if Xaltotun's plan is no better than it has proved so far. Speak on, dog.'

The man's body writhed in his strange convulsions. Words came in a stumbling rush:

'Conan camps at the head of the Valley of Lions. It is shaped like a fan, with steep hills on either side. If you attack him tomorrow you will have to march straight up the valley. You cannot climb the hills on either side. But if King Valerius will deign to accept my service, I will guide him through the hills and show him how he can come upon King Conan from behind. But if it is to be done at all, we must start soon. It is many hours' riding, for one must go miles to the west, then miles to the north, then turn eastward and so come into the Valley of Lions from behind, as the Gundermen came.'

Amalric hesitated, tugging his chin. In these chaotic times it was not rare to find men willing to sell their souls for a few gold pieces.

'If you lead me astray you will die,' said Valerius. 'You are aware of that, are you not?'

The man shivered, but his wide eyes did not waver.

'If I betray you, slay me!'

'Conan will not dare divide his force,' mused Amalric. 'He will need all his men to repel our attack. He cannot spare any to lay ambushes in the hills. Besides, this fellow knows his hide depends on his leading you as he promised. Would a dog like him sacrifice himself? Nonsense! No, Valerius, I believe the man is honest.'

'Or a greater thief than most, for he would sell his liberator,' laughed Valerius. 'Very well. I will follow the dog. How many men can you spare me?'

'Five thousand should be enough,' answered Amàlric. 'A surprise attack on their rear will throw them into confusion, and that will be enough. I shall expect your attack about noon.'

'You will know when I strike,' answered Valerius.

As Amalric returned to his pavilion he noted with gratification that Xaltotun was still in his tent, to judge from the blood-freezing cries that shuddered forth into the night air from time to time. When presently he heard the clink of steel and the jingle of bridles in the outer darkness, he smiled grimly. Valerius had about served his purpose. The baron knew that Conan was like a wounded lion that rends and tears even in his death-throes. When Valerius struck from the rear, the desperate strokes of the Cimmerian might well wipe his rival out of existence before he himself succumbed. So much the better. Amalric felt he could well dispense with Valerius, once he had paved the way for a Nemedian victory.

The five thousand horsemen who accompanied Valerius were hard-bitten Aquilonian renegades for the most part. In the still starlight they moved out of the sleeping camp, following the westward trend of the great black masses that rose against the stars ahead of them. Valerius rode at their head, and beside him rode Tiberias, a leather thong about his wrist gripped by a man-at-arms who rode on the other side of him. Others kept close behind with drawn swords.

'Play us false and you die instantly,' Valerius pointed out. 'I do not know every sheep-path in these hills, but I know enough about the general configuration of the country to know the directions we must take to come in behind the Valley of Lions. See that you do not lead us astray.'

The man ducked his head and his teeth chattered as he volubly assured his captor of his loyalty, staring up stupidly at the banner that floated over him, the golden serpent of the old dynasty.

Skirting the extremities of the hills that blocked the Valley of Lions, they swung wide to the west. An hour's ride and they turned north, forging through wild and rugged hills, following dim trails and tortuous paths. Sunrise found them some miles northwest of Conan's position, and here the guide turned eastward and led them through a maze of labyrinths and crags. Valerius nodded, judging their position by various peaks thrusting up above the others. He had kept his bearings in a general way, and he knew they were still headed in the right direction.

But now, without warning, a gray fleecy mass came billowing down from the north, veiling the slopes, spreading out through the valleys. It blotted out the sun; the world became a blind gray void in which visibility was limited to a matter of yards. Advance became a stumbling groping muddle. Valerius cursed. He could no longer see the peaks that had served him as guide-posts. He must depend wholly upon the traitorous guide. The golden serpent drooped in the windless air.

Presently Tiberias seemed himself confused; he halted, stared about uncertainly.

'Are you lost, dog?' demanded Valerius harshly.

'Listen!'

Somewhere ahead of them a faint vibration began, the rhythmic rumble of a drum.

'Conan's drums!' exclaimed the Aquilonian.

'If we are close enough to hear the drum,' said Valerius, 'why do we not hear the shouts and the clang of arms? Surely battle has joined.'

'The gorges and the winds play strange tricks,' answered Tiberias, his teeth chattering with the ague that is frequently the lot of men who have spent much time in damp underground dungeons. 'Listen!'

Faintly to their ears came a low muffled roar.

'They are fighting down in the valley!' cried Tiberias. 'The drum is beating on the heights. Let us hasten!'

He rode straight on toward the sound of the distant drum as one who knows his ground at last. Valerius followed, cursing the fog. Then it occurred to him that it would mask his advance. Conan could not see him coming. He would be at the Cimmerian's back before the noonday sun dispelled the mists.

Just now he could not tell what lay on either hand, whether cliffs, thickets or gorges. The drum throbbed unceasingly, growing louder as they advanced, but they heard no more of the battle. Valerius had no idea toward what

178

point of the compass they were headed. He started as he saw gray rock walls looming through the smoky drifts on either hand, and realized that they were riding through a narrow defile. But the guide showed no sign of nervousness, and Valerius hove a sigh of relief when the walls widened out and became invisible in the fog. They were through the defile; if an ambush had been planned, it would have been made in that pass.

But now Tiberias halted again. The drum was rumbling louder, and Valerius could not determine from what direction the sound was coming. Now it seemed ahead of him, now behind, now on one hand or the other. Valerius glared about him impatiently, sitting on his war-horse with wisps of mist curling about him and the moisture gleaming on his armor. Behind him the long lines of steel-clad riders faded away and away like phantoms into the mist.

'Why do you tarry, dog?' he demanded.

The man seemed to be listening to the ghostly drum. Slowly he straightened in his saddle, turned his head and faced Valerius, and the smile on his lips was terrible to see.

'The fog is thinning, Valerius,' he said in a new voice, pointing a bony finger. 'Look!'

The drum was silent. The fog was fading away. First the crests of cliffs came in sight above the gray clouds, tall and spectral. Lower and lower crawled the mists, shrinking, fading. Valerius started up in his stirrups with a cry that the horsemen echoed behind him. On all sides of them the cliffs towered. They were not in a wide, open valley as he had supposed. They were in a blind gorge walled by sheer cliffs hundreds of feet high. The only entrance or exit was that narrow defile through which they had ridden.

'Dog!' Valerius struck Tiberias full in the mouth with his clenched mailed hand. 'What devil's trick is this?'

Tiberias spat out a mouthful of blood and shook with fearful laughter.

'A trick that shall rid the world of a beast! Look, dog!'

Again Valerius cried out, more in fury than in fear.

The defile was blocked by a wild and terrible band of men who stood silent as images – ragged, shock-headed men with spears in their hands – hundreds of them. And up on the cliffs appeared other faces – thousands of faces – wild, gaunt, ferocious faces, marked by fire and steel and starvation.

'A trick of Conan's!' raged Valerius.

'Conan knows nothing of it,' laughed Tiberias. 'It was the

plot of broken men, of men you ruined and turned to beasts. Amalric was right. Conan has not divided his army. We are the rabble who followed him, the wolves who skulked in these hills, the homeless men, the hopeless men. This was our plan, and the priests of Asura aided us with the mist. Look at them, Valerius! Each bears the mark of your hand, on his body or on his heart!

'Look at me! You do not know me, do you, what of this scar your hangman burned upon me? Once you knew me. Once I was lord of Amilius, the man whose sons you murdered, whose daughter your mercenaries ravished and slew. You said I would not sacrifice myself to trap you? Almighty gods, if I had a thousand lives I would give them all to buy your doom!

'And I have bought it! Look on the men you broke, dead men who once played the king! Their hour has come! This gorge is your tomb. Try to climb the cliffs: they are steep, they are high. Try to fight your way back through the defile: spears will block your path, boulders will crush you from above! Dog! I will be waiting for you in Hell!'

Throwing back his head he laughed until the rocks rang. Valerius leaned from his saddle and slashed down with his great sword, severing shoulder-bone and breast. Tiberias sank to the earth, still laughing ghastlily through a gurgle of gushing blood.

The drums had begun again, encircling the gorge with guttural thunder; boulders came crashing down; above the screams of dying men shrilled the arrows in blinding clouds from the cliffs.

22 – THE ROAD TO ACHERON

DAWN was just whitening the east when Amalric drew up his hosts in the mouth of the Valley of Lions. This valley was flanked by low, rolling, but steep hills, and the floor pitched upward in a series of irregular natural terraces. On the uppermost of these terraces Conan's army held its position, awaiting the attack. The host that had joined him, marching down from Gunderland, had not been composed exclusively of spearmen. With them had come seven thousand Bossonian archers, and four thousand barons and their retainers of the north and west, swelling the ranks of his cavalry.

The pikemen were drawn up in a compact wedge-shaped formation at the narrow head of the valley. There were nineteen thousand of them, mostly Gundermen, though some four thousand were Aquilonians of the other provinces. They were flanked on either hand by five thousand Bossonian archers. Behind the ranks of the pikemen the knights sat their steeds motionless, lances raised: ten thousand knights of Poitain, nine thousand Aquilonians, barons and their retainers.

It was a strong position. His flanks could not be turned, for that would mean climbing the steep, wooded hills in the teeth of arrows and swords of the Bossonians. His camp lay directly behind him, in a narrow, steep-walled valley which was indeed merely a continuation of the Valley of Lions, pitching up at a higher level. He did not fear a surprise from the rear, because the hills behind him were full of refugees and broken men whose loyalty to him was beyond question.

But if his position was hard to shake, it was equally hard to escape from. It was a trap as well as a fortress for the defenders, a desperate last stand of men who did not expect to survive unless they were victorious. The only line of retreat possible was through the narrow valley at their rear.

Xaltotun mounted a hill on the left side of the valley, near the wide mouth. This hill rose higher than the others, and was known as the King's Altar, for a reason long forgotten. Only Xaltotun knew, and his memory dated back three thousand years.

He was not alone. His two familiars, silent, hairy, furtive and dark, were with him, and they bore a young Aquilonian girl, bound hand and foot. They laid her on an ancient stone, which was curiously like an altar, and which crowned the summit of the hill. For long centuries it had stood there, worn by the elements until many doubted that it was anything but a curiously shapen natural rock. But what it was, and why it stood there, Xaltotun remembered from of old. The familiars went away, with their bent backs like silent gnomes, and Xaltotun stood alone beside the stone altar, his dark beard blown in the wind, overlooking the valley.

He could see clear back to the winding Shirki, and up into the hills beyond the head of the valley. He could see the gleaming wedge of steel drawn up at the head of the terraces, and burganets of the archers glinting among the rocks and bushes, the silent knights motionless on their steeds, their pennons flowing above their helmets, their lances rising in a bristling thicket.

Looking in the other direction he could see the long serried lines of the Nemedians moving in ranks of shining steel into the mouth of the valley. Behind them the gay pavilions of the lords and knights and the drab tents of the common soldiers stretched back almost to the river.

Like a river of molten steel the Nemedian host flowed into the valley, the great scarlet dragon rippling over it. First marched the bowmen, in even ranks, arbalests half raised, bolts nocked, fingers on triggers. After them came the pikemen, and behind them the real strength of the army – the mounted knights, their banners unfurled to the wind, their lances lifted, walking their great steeds forward as if they rode to a banquet.

And higher up on the slopes the smaller Aquilonian host stood grimly silent.

There were thirty thousand Nemedian knights and, as in most Hyborian nations, it was the chivalry which was the sword of the army. The footmen were used only to clear the way for a charge of the armored knights. There were twenty-one thousand of these, pikemen and archers.

The bowmen began loosing as they advanced, without breaking ranks, launching their quarrels with a whir and tang. But the bolts fell short or rattled harmlessly from the overlapping shields of the Gundermen. And before the arbalesters could come within killing range, the arching shafts of the Bossonians were wreaking havoc in their ranks.

A little of this, a futile attempt at exchanging fire, and the Nemedian bowmen began falling back in disorder. Their armor was light, their weapons no match for the Bossonian longbows. The western archers were sheltered by bushes and rocks. Moreover, the Nemedian footmen lacked something of the morale of the horsemen, knowing as they did that they were being used merely to clear the way for the knights.

The crossbowmen fell back, and between their opening lines the pikemen advanced. These were largely mercenaries, and their masters had no compunction about sacrificing them. They were intended to mask the advance of the knights until the latter were within smiting distance. So while the arbalesters plied their bolts from either flank at long range, the pikemen marched into the teeth of the blast from above, and behind them the knights came on.

When the pikemen began to falter beneath the savage hail of death that whistled down the slopes among them, a trumpet blew, their companies divided to right and left, and through them the mailed knights thundered.

They ran full into a cloud of stinging death. The cloth-yard shafts found every crevice in their armor and the housings of the steeds. Horses scrambling up the grassy terraces reared and plunged backward, bearing their riders with them. Steel-clad forms littered the slopes. The charge wavered and ebbed back.

Back down in the valley Amalric re-formed his ranks. Tarascus was fighting with drawn sword under the scarlet dragon, but it was the baron of Tor who commanded that day. Amalric swore as he glanced at the forest of lance-tips visible above and beyond the head-pieces of the Gundermen. He had hoped his retirement would draw the knights out in a charge down the slopes after him, to be raked from either flank by his bowmen and swamped by the numbers of his horsemen. But they had not moved. Camp-servants brought skins of water from the river. Knights doffed their helmets and drenched their sweating heads. The wounded on the slopes screamed vainly for water. In the upper valley, springs supplied the defenders. They did not thirst that long, hot spring day.

On the King's Altar, beside the ancient, carven stone, Xaltotun watched the steel tide ebb and flow. On came the knights, with waving plumes and dipping lances. Through a whistling cloud of arrows they plowed to break like a thundering wave on the bristling wall of spears and shields. Axes rose and fell above the plumed helmets, spears thrust upward, bringing down horses and riders. The pride of the Gundermen was no less fierce than that of the knights. They were not spear-fodder, to be sacrificed for the glory of better men. They were the finest infantry in the world, with a tradition that made their morale unshakable. The kings of Aquilonia had long learned the worth of unbreakable infantry. They held their formation unshaken; over their gleaming ranks flowed the great lion banner, and at the tip of the wedge a giant figure in black armor roared and smote like a hurricane, with a dripping ax that split steel and bone alike.

The Nemedians fought as gallantly as their traditions of

high courage demanded. But they could not break the iron wedge, and from the wooded knolls on either hand arrows raked their close-packed ranks mercilessly. Their own bowmen were useless, their pikemen unable to climb the heights and come to grips with the Bossonians. Slowly, stubbornly, sullenly, the grim knights fell back, counting their empty saddles. Above them the Gundermen made no outcry of triumph. They closed their ranks, locking up the gaps made by the fallen. Sweat ran into their eyes from under their steel caps. They gripped their spears and waited, their fierce hearts swelling with pride that a king should fight on foot with them. Behind them the Aquilonian knights had not moved. They sat their steeds, grimly immobile.

A knight spurred a sweating horse up the hill called the King's Altar, and glared at Xaltotun with bitter eyes.

'Amalric bids me say that it is time to use your magic, wizard,' he said. 'We are dying like flies down there in the valley. We cannot break their ranks.'

Xaltotun seemed to expand, to grow tall and awesome and terrible.

'Return to Amalric,' he said. 'Tell him to re-form his ranks for a charge, but to await my signal. Before that signal is given he will see a sight that he will remember until he lies dying!'

The knight saluted as if compelled against his will, and thundered down the hill at breakneck pace.

Xaltotun stood beside the dark altar-stone and stared across the valley, at the dead and wounded men on the terraces, at the grim, blood-stained band at the head of the slopes, at the dusty, steel-clad ranks re-forming in the vale below. He glanced up at the sky, and he glanced down at the slim white figure on the dark stone. And lifting a dagger inlaid with archaic hieroglyphs, he intoned an immemorial invocation:

'Set, god of darkness, scaly lord of the shadows, by the blood of a virgin and the sevenfold symbol I call to your sons below the black earth! Children of the deeps, below the red earth, under the black earth, awaken and shake your awful manes! Let the hills rock and the stones topple upon my enemies! Let the sky grow dark above them, the earth unstable beneath their feet! Let a wind from the deep black earth curl up beneath their feet, and blacken and shrivel them—'

He halted short, dagger lifted. In the tense silence the roar of the hosts rose beneath him, borne on the wind.

On the other side of the altar stood a man in a black hooded robe, whose coif shadowed pale delicate features and dark eyes calm and meditative.

'Dog of Asura!' whispered Xaltotun, and his voice was like the hiss of an angered serpent. 'Are you mad, that you seek your doom? Ho, Baal! Chiron!'

'Call again, dog of Acheron!' said the other, and laughed. 'Summon them loudly. They will not hear, unless your shouts reverberate in Hell.'

From a thicket on the edge of the crest came a somber old woman in peasant garb, her hair flowing over her shoulders, a great gray wolf following at her heels.

'Witch, priest, and wolf,' muttered Xaltotun grimly, and laughed. 'Fools, to pit your charlatan's mummery against my arts! With a wave of my hand I brush you from my path!'

'Your arts are straws in the wind, dog of Python,' answered the Asurian. 'Have you wondered why the Shirki did not come down in flood and trap Conan on the other bank? When I saw the lightning in the night I guessed your plan, and my spells dispersed the clouds you had summoned before they could empty their torrents. You did not even know that your rain-making wizardy had failed.'

'You lie!' cried Xaltotun, but the confidence in his voice was shaken. 'I have felt the impact of a powerful sorcery against mine – but no man on earth could undo the rain-magic, once made, unless he possessed the very heart of sorcery.'

'But the flood you plotted did not come to pass,' answered the priest. 'Look at your allies in the valley, Pythonian! You have led them to the slaughter! They are caught in the fangs of the trap, and you cannot aid them. Look!'

He pointed. Out of the narrow gorge of the upper valley, behind the Poitanians, a horseman came flying, whirling something about his head that flashed in the sun. Recklessly he hurtled down the slopes, through the ranks of the Gundermen, who sent up a deep-throated roar and clashed their spears and shields like thunder in the hills. On the terraces between the hosts the sweat-soaked horse reared and plunged, and his wild rider yelled and brandished the thing in his hands like one demented. It was the torn remnant of

185

a scarlet banner, and the sun struck dazzlingly on the golden scales of a serpent that writhed thereon.

'Valerius is dead!' cried Hadrathus ringingly. 'A fog and a drum lured him to his doom! I gathered that fog, dog of Python, and I dispersed it! I, with my magic which is greater than your magic!'

'What matters it?' roared Xaltotun, a terrible sight, his eyes blazing, his features convulsed. 'Valerius was a fool. I do not need him. I can crush Conan without human aid!'

'Why have you delayed?' mocked Hadrathus. 'Why have you allowed so many of your allies to fall pierced by arrows and spitted on spears?'

'Because blood aids great sorcery!' thundered Xaltotun, in a voice that made the rocks quiver. A lurid nimbus played about his awful head. 'Because no wizard wastes his strength thoughtlessly. Because I would conserve my powers for the great days to be, rather than employ them in a hill-country brawl. But now, by Set, I shall loose them to the uttermost! Watch, dog of Asura, false priest of an outworn god, and see a sight that shall blast your reason for ever-more!'

Hadrathus threw back his head and laughed, and hell was in his laughter.

'Look, black devil of Python!'

His hand came from under his robe holding something that flamed and burned in the sun, changing the light to a pulsing golden glow in which the flesh of Xaltotun looked like the flesh of a corpse.

Xaltotun cried out as if he had been stabbed.

'The Heart! The Heart of Ahriman!'

'Aye! The one power that is greater than your power!'

Xaltotun seemed to shrivel, to grow old. Suddenly his beard was shot with snow, his locks flecked with gray.

'The Heart!' he mumbled. 'You stole it! Dog! Thief!'

'Not I! It had been on a long journey far to the south-ward. But now it is in my hands, and your black arts cannot stand against it. As it resurrected you, so shall it hurl you back into the night whence it drew you. You shall go down the dark road to Acheron, which is the road of silence and the night. The dark empire, unreborn, shall remain a legend and a black memory. Conan shall reign again. And the Heart of Ahriman shall go back into the cavern below the temple of Mitra, to burn as a symbol of the power of Aquilonia for a thousand years!'

186

Xaltotun screamed inhumanly and rushed around the altar, dagger lifted; but from somewhere – out of the sky, perhaps, or the great jewel that blazed in the hand of Hadrathus – shot a jetting beam of blinding blue light. Full against the breast of Xaltotun it flashed, and the hills re-echoed the concussion. The wizard of Acheron went down as though struck by a thunderbolt, and before he touched the ground he was fearfully altered. Beside the altar-stone lay no fresh-slain corpse, but a shriveled mummy, a brown, dry, unrecognizable carcass sprawling among moldering swathings.

Somberly old Zelata looked down.

'He was not a living man,' she said. 'The Heart lent him him a false aspect of life, that deceived even himself. I never saw him as other than a mummy.'

Hadrathus bent to unbind the swooning girl on the altar, when from among the trees appeared a strange apparition – Xaltotun's chariot drawn by the weird horses. Silently they advanced to the altar and halted, with the chariot wheel almost touching the brown withered thing on the grass. Hadrathus lifted the body of the wizard and placed it in the chariot. And without hesitation the uncanny steeds turned and moved off southward, down the hill. And Hadrathus and Zelata and the gray wolf watched them go – down the long road to Acheron which is beyond the ken of men.

Down in the valley, Amalric had stiffened in his saddle when he saw that wild horseman curvetting and caracoling on the slopes while he brandished that blood-stained serpent-banner. Then some instinct jerked his head about, toward the hill known as the King's Altar. And his lips parted. Every man in the valley saw it – an arching shaft of dazzling light that towered up from the summit of the hill, showering golden fire. High above the hosts it burst in a blinding blaze that momentarily paled the sun.

'That's not Xaltotun's signal!' roared the baron.

'No!' shouted Tarascus. 'It's a signal to the Aquilonians! Look!'

Above them the immobile ranks were moving at last, and a deep-throated roar thundered across the vale.

'Xaltotun has failed us!' bellowed Amalric furiously. 'Valerius has failed us! We have been led into a trap! Mitra's curse on Xaltotun who led us here! Sound the retreat!'

'*Too late!*' yelled Tarascus. '*Look!*'

Up on the slopes the forest of lances dipped, leveled. The ranks of the Gundermen rolled back to right and left like a parting curtain. And with a thunder like the rising roar of a hurricane, the knights of Aquilonia crashed down the slopes.

The impetus of that charge was irrestible. Bolts driven by the demoralized arbalesters glanced from their shelds, their bent helmets. Their plumes and pennons streaming out behind them, their lances lowered, they swept over the wavering lines of pikemen and roared down the slopes like a wave.

Amalric yelled an order to charge, and the Nemedians with desperate courage spurred their horses at the slopes. They still outnumbered the attackers.

But they were weary men on tired horses, charging uphill. The onrushing knights had not struck a blow that day. Their horses were fresh. They were coming downhill and they came like a thunderbolt. And like a thunderbolt they smote the struggling ranks of the Nemedians – smote them, split them apart, ripped them asunder, and dashed the remnants headlong down the slopes.

After them on foot came the Gundermen, blood-mad, and the Bossonians were swarming down the hills, loosing as they ran at every foe that still moved.

Down the slopes washed the tide of battle, the dazed Nemedians swept on the crest of the wave. Their archers had thrown down their arbalests and were fleeing. Such pikemen as had survived the blasting charge of the knights were cut to pieces by the ruthless Gundermen.

In a wild confusion the battle swept through the wide mouth of the valley and into the plain beyond. All over the plain swarmed the warriors, fleeing and pursuing, broken into single combat and clumps of smiting, hacking knights on rearing, wheeling horses. But the Nemedians were smashed, broken, unable to re-form or make a stand. By the hundred they broke away, spurring for the river. Many reached it, rushed across and rode eastward. The countryside was up behind them; the people hunted them like wolves. Few ever reached Tarantia.

The final break did not come until the fall of Amalric. The baron, striving in vain to rally his men, rode straight at the clump of knights that followed the giant in black armor whose surcoat bore the royal lion, and over whose head floated the golden lion banner with the scarlet leopard of Poitain beside it. A tall warrior in gleaming armor couched his lance and charged to meet the lord of Tor. They met like a thunderclap. The Nemedian's lance, striking his foe's helmet, snapped bolts and rivets and tore off the casque, revealing the features of Pallantides. But the Aquilonian's lance-head crashed through shield and breast-plate to transfix the baron's heart.

A roar went up as Amalric was hurled from his saddle, snapping the lance that impaled him, and the Nemedians gave way as a barrier bursts under the surging impact of a tidal wave. They rode for the river in a blind stampede that swept the plain like a whirlwind. The hour of the Dragon had passed.

Tarascus did not flee. Amalric was dead, the color-bearer slain, and the royal Nemedian banner trampled in the blood and dust. Most of his knights were fleeing and the Aquilonians were riding them down; Tarascus knew the day was lost, but with a handful of faithful followers he raged through the mêlée, conscious of but one desire – to meet Conan, the Cimmerian. And at last he met him.

Formations had been destroyed utterly, close-knit bands broken asunder and swept apart. The crest of Trocero gleamed in one part of the plain, those of Prospero and Pallantides in others. Conan was alone. The housetroops of Tarascus had fallen one by one. The two kings met man to man.

Even as they rode at each other, the horse of Tarascus sobbed and sank under him. Conan leaped from his own steed and ran at him, as the king of Nemedia disengaged himself and rose. Steel flashed blindingly in the sun, clashed loudly, and blue sparks flew; then a clang of armor as Tarascus measured his full length on the earth beneath a thunderous stroke of Conan's broadsword.

The Cimmerian placed a mail-shod foot on his enemy's breast, and lifted his sword. His helmet was gone; he shook back his black mane and his blue eyes blazed with their old fire.

'Do you yield?'

'Will you give me quarter?' demanded the Nemedian.

'Aye. Better than you'd have given me, you dog. Life for you and all your men who throw down their arms. Though I ought to split your head for an infernal thief,' the Cimmerian added.

Tarascus twisted his neck and glared over the plain. The

remnants of the Nemedian host were flying across the stone bridge with swarms of victorious Aquilonians at their heels, smiting with the fury of glutted vengeance. Bossonians and Gundermen were swarming through the camp of their enemies, tearing the tents to pieces in search of plunder, seizing prisoners, ripping open the baggage and upsetting the wagons.

Tarascus cursed fervently, and then shrugged his shoulders, as well as he could, under the circumstances.

'Very well. I have no choice. What are your demands?'

'Surrender to me all your present holdings in Aquilonia. Order your garrisons to march out of the castles and towns they hold, without their arms, and get your infernal armies out of Aquilonia as quickly as possible. In addition you shall return all Aquilonians sold as slaves, and pay an indemntiy to be designated later, when the damage your occupation of the country has caused has been properly estimated. You will remain as hostage until these terms have been carried out.'

'Very well,' surrendered Tarascus. 'I will surrender all the castles and towns now held by my garrisons without resistance, and all the other things shall be done. What ransom for my body?'

Conan laughed and removed his foot from his foe's steel-clad breast, grasped his shoulder and heaved him to his feet. He started to speak, then turned to see Hadrathus approaching him. The priest was as calm and self-possessed as ever, picking his way between rows of dead men and horses.

Conan wiped the sweat-smeared dust from his face with a blood-stained hand. He had fought all through the day, first on foot with the pikemen, then in the saddle, leading the charge. His surcoat was gone, his armor splashed with blood and battered with strokes of sword, mace and ax. He loomed gigantically against a background of blood and slaughter, like some grim pagan hero of mythology.

'Well done, Hadrathus!' quoth he gustily. 'By Crom, I am glad to see your signal! My knights were almost mad with impatience and eating their hearts out to be at sword-strokes. I could not have held them much longer. What of the wizard?'

'He has gone down the dim road to Acheron,' answered Hadrathus. 'And I – I am for Tarantia. My work is done here, and I have a task to perform at the temple of Mitra. All our work is done here. On this field we have saved

Aquilonia – and more than Aquilonia. Your ride to your capital will be a triumphal procession through a kingdom mad with joy. All Aquilonia will be cheering the return of their king. And so, until we meet again in the great royal hall – farewell!'

Conan stood silently watching the priest as he went. From various parts of the field knights were hurrying toward him. He saw Pallantides, Trocero, Prospero, Servius Galannus, their armor splashed with crimson. The thunder of battle was giving way to a roar of triumph and acclaim. All eyes, hot with strife and shining with exultation, were turned toward the great black figure of the king; mailed arms brandished red-stained swords. A confused torrent of sound rose, deep and thunderous as the sea-surf: '*Hail, Conan, king of Aquilonia!*'

Tarascus spoke.

'You have not yet named my ransom.'

Conan laughed and slapped his sword home in its scabbard. He flexed his mighty arms, and ran his blood-stained fingers through his thick black locks, as if feeling there his re-won crown.

'There is a girl in your seraglio named Zenobia.'

'Why, yes, so there is.'

'Very well.' The king smiled as at an exceedingly pleasant memory. 'She shall be your ransom, and naught else. I will come to Belverus for her as I promised. She was a slave in Nemedia, but I will make her queen of Aquilonia!'

A SELECTION OF BESTSELLERS FROM SPHERE

FICTION

CALIFORNIA DREAMERS	Norman Bogner	£1.75 ☐
HEART OF WAR	John Masters	£1.95 ☐
TUNNEL WAR	Joe Poyer	£1.50 ☐
LOVING	Danielle Steel	£1.50 ☐
REVELATIONS	Phyllis Naylor	£1.50 ☐

FILM & TV TIE-INS

THE FUNHOUSE	Owen West	£1.25 ☐
THE EMPIRE STRIKES BACK	Donald F. Glut	£1.00 ☐
BUCK ROGERS IN THE 25TH CENTURY	Addison E. Steele	95p ☐
LLOYD GEORGE	David Benedictus	£1.25 ☐

NON-FICTION

MARY	Patricia Collins	£1.50 ☐
EAGLE DAY	Richard Collier	£4.75 ☐
THE CLASSIFIED MAN	Susanna M. Hoffman	£1.50 ☐
WILL	G. Gordon Liddy	£1.75 ☐
MY LIFE AND GAME	Bjorn Borg	£1.25 ☐

All Sphere Books are available at your local bookshop or newsagent, or can be ordered direct from the publisher. Just tick the titles you want and fill in the form below.

Name _____

Address _____

_____

Write to Sphere Books, Cash Sales Department, P.O. Box 11, Falmouth, Cornwall TR10 9EN

Please enclose a cheque or postal order to the value of the cover price plus:

UK: 40p for the first book, 18p for the second book and 13p for each additional book ordered to a maximum charge of £1.49.

OVERSEAS: 60p for the first book plus 18p per copy for each additional book.

BFPO & EIRE: 40p for the first book, 18p for the second book then 13p per copy for the next 7 books, thereafter 7p per book.

Sphere Books reserve the right to show new retail prices on covers which may differ from those previously advertised in the text or elsewhere, and to increase postal rates in accordance with the PO.